A GOOD PLAN

REAGAN KEETER

Summithill Press
Marietta, Georgia

FIRST EDITION

Printed in the United States of America

ISBN 978-1-7343945-5-9
ISBN 978-1-7343945-4-2 (ebook)

GET AN EXCLUSIVE COPY OF *THE LAYOVER*

Connor Callahan has been through a lot. More than anyone should. It has left him with an overdeveloped sense of justice. Perhaps that is why when he sees a man discreetly tag a stranger's suitcase with a black magic marker, he sets out to discover what is going on. It's a decision that will thrust Connor into a conflict far more dangerous than he could have imagined, and when it's over he will know one thing for sure: You're not always safer on the ground.

Details can be found at the end of this book.

CHAPTER 1

DYLAN SAT AT a table in the corner of Cafe de Flore, a small, French-style eatery right in the heart of Midtown Atlanta. The food was served on small plates and cost too much. It was all very chic. And *very* crowded.

Dylan's cell phone was sitting face-up on the table. She tapped the screen, noted the time. Aleshia was late. That wasn't like her. Dylan told herself not to worry. Aleshia would have called if anything was wrong.

They'd been friends for two years now, and Dylan imagined Aleshia was the kind of girl she would be friends with all her life. She had a lot of spunk, a little sass. Dylan liked that, perhaps because they had those things in common.

She took a sip from her coffee and looked toward the door.

Dylan had met Aleshia while working at this very cafe. It was the first job she had gotten after moving down here, and she had needed the money.

Aleshia, however, was just killing time while she figured out what she wanted to do with her life. She was the daughter of Andrew Thompson, a world-renowned impressionist who'd been covered by all the major publications many times over and still—even after his death—had a standing exhibit at the National Gallery of Art in Washington, DC.

In other words, he was loaded.

It had not always been that way. When Maddie—his first

daughter—was born, Andrew was an art teacher at Middleton High School. In those days, he and his wife could barely afford one child. Had he not become a national sensation, they would likely never have had a second.

But he did (albeit fifteen years later), and as one of two heirs, now Aleshia was loaded, too.

It was because of Maddie that Dylan was meeting her here today. Maddie had disappeared a month ago. Aleshia put in a missing person report with the police but that had gone nowhere, so Dylan told her she would see what she could find out.

This wouldn't be the first missing person Dylan had helped locate, she'd said. What she didn't mention was that when she had done it before, she hadn't done it alone. She had help from her friends Connor and Olin. Having turned up nothing on Maddie so far, however, she wished she could call on them again.

But Dylan had moved to Atlanta after graduating college because she was tired of the cold, and New York was just too far away.

Dylan tried to call Aleshia to see where she was. The phone rang three times, then rolled over to voicemail. She didn't bother to leave a message. Instead, she gave it another thirty minutes, paid her check, and headed for the door.

If Aleshia wasn't here by now, she wasn't coming.

Dylan was on edge all the way to Aleshia's house.

Two months before Maddie had gone missing, someone tried to mug her in a parking lot outside the Ink Well.

The Ink Well was an art studio in the suburbs. It had a small gallery in the front and a large, open room where Sofia, who owned the studio, taught classes on weekends. Maddie was one of her students.

Dylan knew about the attack because Aleshia had told her, and she knew the details because Sofia had filled them in.

As the story went, Maddie was halfway to her car when a masked man came out of nowhere and attacked her. He was all over her, grabbing her arms, her purse. She'd screamed and fought back and eventually managed to work her pepper spray out of her bag. She'd fired the pepper spray at her attacker, and then he started screaming as well. He backed away, and an old Ford rolled up beside them. The attacker fumbled his way into the front passenger seat, and the driver took off.

At the time, the attack seemed like nothing more than a robbery gone wrong. After Maddie went missing, though, it took on new dimensions. Was the attacker really after *her*, not her purse? If so, why? Had he come back? Tried again?

According to the police, they reviewed the footage from the parking lot, but it was a dead end. The attacker could have been anyone. They couldn't clearly see the driver, and the car had exited the lot in a way that never revealed the license plate.

And now Dylan had another question: *Had Aleshia been taken, too?*

Dylan told herself she was worrying for nothing.

She pulled up to a modest house in a quiet Dunwoody neighborhood. People who'd known Aleshia's father would have been surprised to find her living here. They would have expected something with more flair, more drama. Dylan, however, thought the gray-and-white bungalow suited Aleshia perfectly. It offered plenty of space, didn't draw a lot of attention. After spending her childhood in the public eye, the last thing Aleshia wanted was more attention.

Dylan noticed Aleshia's BMW in the driveway. She made her way up the stone steps to the front door and knocked. When no one answered, she tried calling Aleshia again. Like before, the call went to voicemail. She stepped off the porch, moved along the side of the house, and squeezed between the shrubbery so she could get close to the window. She had to hold her hands over her eyes like a visor, blocking out the sun, to see anything. Even then, the blinds obscured most of her view.

Oh, God, she thought, once she could make out what she was looking at. This was bad. She should have called Connor, after all.

She pulled her cell phone out of her pocket and dialed a number.

CHAPTER 2

THE TWO-BEDROOM apartment in Manhattan was tight. It was also almost exactly as far from Connor's office as it was from Olin's, which had a lot to do with why they had selected it as opposed to the more spacious options they'd seen that were farther from the city.

Each bedroom was barely big enough for a bed and a nightstand, so Connor and Olin had agreed Connor could set up a small desk in the living room. It was at that desk that Connor was sitting now.

When Connor was in college, he had imagined himself getting a job at Google or Facebook. Any prestigious firm, really, would have been fine. When it came to computers, he certainly had the skill for it. But life hadn't shaken out that way. Instead, he was refactoring code for a small shop called TexRaid in the data analytics space.

Connor had tried on more than one occasion to explain to Olin the specifics of what the firm did. Olin, whose degree was in finance and who (perhaps inevitably) had taken a job as an accountant at another small company, didn't get it. Neither did most people outside of the tech space, Connor had come to realize. So, these days, he simply stuck with calling it "data analytics," which was usually enough to avoid any follow-up questions.

All that was fine with Connor, since he, too, found the work boring.

In college, Connor had entertained himself by hacking into strangers' websites and disrupting their service. Not just anybody's site, mind you. Just those he determined were promoting violence, encouraging cult-like behavior, or disseminating lies he considered harmful for society. He felt a rush when he was doing that, driven by the idea that he was one of the good guys fighting back the evils of the world.

How could the day-to-day grind of any job compare with that?

It was the question Connor asked himself whenever he felt like quitting, followed by: *Where else would I go?* It wasn't as if another firm, even a Google or a Facebook, would be any different.

So, on some nights—those like tonight, when that longing for more meaningful work overtook him—he would fire up his laptop and hunt down the same kinds of websites he had in college.

Olin never asked what he was doing at the computer. Connor suspected he didn't want to know. He also never asked Connor if he would like to watch a basketball game—which was what Olin, who was sitting on the sofa with the TV on, was doing tonight. Connor had no interest in sports.

They shared the occasional conversation, acknowledging each other without talking about either's specific interest. That's probably how the whole night would have gone had Connor's cell phone not rung.

The caller ID read "Dylan Naese."

Dylan had entered Connor's life through the same tragic events that brought Olin into it, and even though Connor did not live with her, he felt his bond with her was just as close.

He looked at the time. It was after ten p.m. Too late for her to be calling. But she was also a night owl. He picked up the phone and crossed the apartment to his bedroom to get away from the TV.

"What's up?"

"Can you—" She stopped short, sounded like she was choking up.

"Connor, I've got a problem. Can you come to Atlanta?"

He felt the hairs on his arms stand up as his mind raced through all the horrible things that might have happened to her. "What's going on, Dylan? Are you okay?"

"I'm fine. You know, as fine as I can be. Considering . . ."

"Considering what?"

"I have a friend whose sister went missing about a month ago."

That was bad enough, but Connor could tell Dylan wasn't done. He held his breath, waited.

"Now she's gone, too."

This all reminded Connor too much of what he had been through before. He could feel himself getting lightheaded. He sat down on the edge of his bed. "Are you sure? How long ago did you find out your friend was missing?"

"This morning."

"Well, maybe she's—"

"She hasn't been answering her phone all day. She's not texting me back. She's not at home. Something's wrong."

Okay, that didn't sound good. "You've gone to the police, right?"

"They went by her house to do a wellness check. Since she wasn't there, that was a big waste of time. And when I told them I wanted to file a missing person report, they told me I had to wait twenty-four hours. Can you come—help me figure out what happened to her? I can't sit around and just wait for the police. They still haven't found her sister, and, well, I'm worried."

Connor nodded to himself. *Yes, of course, I'll come*, he thought, as his gaze shifted to the window and the night sky beyond it. Somewhere in the back of his mind, he could feel himself already plotting the trip. "I'll get a flight out in the morning. File a missing person report as soon as you can. At least it will put her on their radar."

"Okay, I will. Thank you."

"I'll call you as soon as I land." Connor hung up. He hurried back into the living room. "Olin."

"One second," Olin said, leaning forward, watching a player in a white jersey bounce the basketball as he prepared for a free throw.

Connor moved in front of the TV.

"What are you doing?"

"That was Dylan. She needs our help."

The look of annoyance on Olin's face immediately transformed into concern. "What do you mean?"

Connor relayed the story Dylan had told him. "I'm flying out in the morning. Are you coming?"

"What about work?"

"Seriously? Tell them you're sick. Who cares? It's Dylan. Just come up with something."

Olin licked his lips. A twitch turned into a nod. "Yeah. I mean— yeah, you're right. I'll come up with something."

Connor then went to his computer to search for plane tickets. The earliest flight he could find that had room for him and Olin departed at four o'clock tomorrow afternoon. It would have to do. He had no idea how long they would be gone, so he made reservations for only one way.

CHAPTER 3

CONNOR SQUEEZED ENOUGH clothes for a week into a carry-on and tried to get some sleep. It didn't come easily. He tossed and turned. He would force his eyes closed, and they would pop back open.

He kept thinking back to his parents' abduction: the man driving up onto the lawn, attacking Connor's parents in their home, and loading them into the back of his van.

For a long time, he had thought about that horrible event every day. Although time had dulled the sharpest edges of the memory, the months that followed that event had changed him forever.

Now, here he was again—facing a mystery that he knew would take him places he didn't want to go and force him to see things he didn't want to see. If he could, he would turn his back on it. Let the police solve it. Every missing person couldn't be his problem.

But Dylan had asked . . .

He got out of bed and went to the kitchen to make some chamomile tea. That would usually help him sleep, calm his dreams. He wouldn't be any good tomorrow if he didn't get some sleep.

There was a half wall that separated the kitchen from the living room and three bar stools on this side of it. Olin was sitting on one of them in a pair of plaid pajama pants, nursing a beer.

"Can't sleep either, huh?" Connor asked.

Olin spun around, startled. He must not have heard Connor open his bedroom door. He immediately calmed down once he saw who it was. "No, I guess not."

Connor filled a kettle with water from the sink and put it on the stove. "You're thinking about . . ." He let the question hang in the air. It was easier for them both if they didn't speak directly about the events that had bound them together.

Olin shrugged.

"It's not going to be like that," Connor said.

"How do you know?"

Connor didn't. But dwelling on how things might go wrong wasn't going to help either of them. Wasn't that the whole reason he'd come into the kitchen to make tea? To clear his head? To push out the bad thoughts? To get some rest? Sometimes the best you can do is tell yourself, "This time it will be better." Tonight was one of those times.

Olin's gaze shifted to the Budweiser in front of him. He picked at the corner of the label with one fingernail. He took a deep breath, a sip of his beer. Connor wasn't sure Olin got his point until he said, "You're right. Things are going to be fine." Then he directed the conversation toward the new *Avengers* movie, and Connor changed gears right along with him.

He was happy to pretend for a while that tonight was like any other.

When he finally went to bed—groggy from the tea and his mind calmed from the conversation—he was able to get the sleep he knew he needed.

His last thought before he nodded off was, *This time it will be better.*

CHAPTER 4

CONNOR AND OLIN stepped off the escalator in the Atlanta airport near the baggage carousels and saw Dylan standing in the waiting area.

Connor hadn't been face-to-face with her since she'd come up to New York to visit them six months ago. She'd looked well. Atlanta agreed with her, he had said.

Today, he felt like he was standing in front of a different woman. Dylan had her hair pulled back into a ponytail, which probably drew more attention than she wanted to her bloodshot eyes. She looked tired. Weak. Her flannel shirt was wrinkled and stained. When they hugged, she collapsed into Connor.

"It's going to be okay," he said, with more confidence than he felt.

Her head was pressed to his chest. He felt her nod.

She hugged Olin next. When she let go, she wiped her eyes with the heel of her hand. "You probably want to go to a hotel first, right? Get settled?"

Connor and Olin looked at each other. "No," Connor said. "We can do that later. Take us to Aleshia's house."

"Why there?"

"Do you have a better place to start?" When Dylan didn't answer, he added, "I'd like to see what we're dealing with."

Dylan led Connor and Olin to an old white Volvo in the parking deck. The interior was a mess. Fast-food wrappers littered the floor. A makeup bag was poking out of the center console. Hairbands and bobby pins were everywhere.

Olin made a face as he pushed the fast-food wrappers aside and climbed into the back seat. Connor pretended not to notice.

Dylan drove them to a small house in the suburbs. She parked along the curb.

"This is it?" Olin asked, gesturing toward the house.

"Yes."

Connor saw a BMW in the driveway. "There's a car here."

"That's Aleshia's. It was here yesterday, also."

"All right," Connor said. "Here we go." He got out first and headed straight for the front porch. Dylan and Olin fell in behind him. He pounded on the door.

"What are you doing?" Dylan said. "I told you—she's not here."

"I know. But before we start looking in her windows, I just want to be sure no one else is either."

When no one answered the door, Connor squeezed through the shrubs along the side of the house, exactly like Dylan had done the day before. Since it was just after seven o'clock, the sun had already set, meaning he did not need to try to block it out like she had.

The darkness, however, presented its own complications, and getting closer to the window hadn't improved his visibility.

Connor pulled his cell phone out of his pocket. He clicked the flashlight app, hoping it would help. It didn't. Not much, anyway. No matter how he angled it, the blinds blocked out most of the light.

He sighed. "We've already lost a day." Then, to Dylan: "Were you able to put in a missing person report on Aleshia finally?"

"Yeah, but—"

"I know," Connor said, as he slid back between the shrubs. "At least it's done." He stepped onto the porch, looked at the front door. "The police probably aren't coming back here anytime soon."

"So, what do you want to do?" Olin asked.

Connor looked at him. "I think you know what we have to do."

Olin groaned.

"What?" Dylan asked.

Connor tried the doorknob. The door was locked. Then he shined his light on the ground around the porch to see if he could find one of those fake rocks people sometimes hid a key in. He had one outside his house growing up, so maybe he would find one here, too. When he didn't, he gestured for Dylan and Olin to follow him. "Come on." He walked around the gray-and-white bungalow to the backyard.

He tried to open the first set of windows. They wouldn't budge. Neither would those on the other side of the back door, or the back door itself. The house was locked up tight.

"We're *not* breaking in," Olin said, glancing at the surrounding houses.

"No, I guess we're not," Connor said, disappointed.

"What do you want to get inside for?" Dylan asked. "I already know she's not there."

"I wanted to see what we could find out. It doesn't sound like the police are going to go in there looking for clues anytime soon, and right now, I can't think of anything better we could do to find out what happened to her."

Dylan considered that. "Hold on." She scurried away.

Olin got a worried look on his face. Connor suspected they both knew what she was about to do.

Dylan returned less than a minute later with a pair of bobby pins she'd no doubt found on the floor of her car. "I can get us into the house," she said, as she twisted the bobby pins into place and then wiggled them into the lock on the back door.

Dylan had learned a lot of unusual skills when she was going through her "spy phase" as a teenager. Picking locks was one of them. It had come in handy for Connor before, and he was glad to see she had kept it up.

"We shouldn't be doing this," Olin said.

"Aleshia's my best friend. She'd want me to."

"What if the alarm's set?" There were ADT signs by both the front and back doors, so there was no question Aleshia had one.

"It's fine. Even if it is, I know the code."

Dylan continued to apply pressure to the cylinder until it rotated as far as it would go. Then she slid the bobby pins back into the pocket of her jeans and turned the knob. The door opened.

Connor followed Dylan inside. He heard Olin—who, no doubt, was still unhappy about what they were doing—step in behind him.

The living room featured modest furniture and a warm feel. A sofa was positioned along one wall and a TV stand was pressed up against the wall opposite. There was barely enough space between them for the rustic coffee table that occupied it. Most of the art looked uninspired— kind of like what you might expect to find in a hotel room.

Most of it.

Among the small, store-bought paintings that hung in a mosaic above the sofa, there was one that gave Connor chills. The frame hung from a rope. The woman in it was wearing a blue dress and sitting in a cafe. The left side of her face seemed to be melting off.

Connor could tell this was an original.

"That's one of Maddie's," Dylan said. "The one to the left of it is their father's."

Connor shifted his attention to the painting beside it and realized what he had mistakenly assumed was one of many generic prints was actually another original. The watercolor of two men walking along a cobblestone street was so meticulously detailed that the rain gathering in puddles by their feet looked almost real.

"You'd never guess how much that thing is worth," Dylan said.

Connor had no doubt that was true. He didn't know much about art.

He turned his attention back to the room. Clothes were strewn about. Loose hangers littered the floor. Books and magazines were stacked up in an unorderly heap on the coffee table. The place was a mess, but not the kind that would point to foul play.

Dylan seemed to know what he was thinking. "There's more," she said, and led Connor and Olin toward the dining room. From its position in the house, Connor could tell this was the room he was trying to see into from outside.

Dylan turned on the light.

The chair closest to the window was pulled back from the large ebony table that filled the space. The place was set with a plate, a fork, and a glass of milk. On the plate was a half-eaten omelet. There was an assortment of makeup on the table around it—lipstick, foundation, eyeliner—and a freestanding mirror to apply it. Two other chairs were askew, with more clothes hanging over them.

"That's what I saw yesterday," Dylan said. "That's how I knew something was wrong. Aleshia might not be good about her clothes, but she would never leave food out like that. And she certainly wouldn't go anywhere without her purse."

Connor noticed the Louis Vuitton bag hanging over the back of another chair. He picked it up, started rifling through its contents.

"What are you doing?" Olin asked.

Connor didn't answer him directly. "Dylan, do you know the code for Aleshia's cell phone?" Since she knew the code for the alarm, it seemed reasonable to assume she might know this one, also.

"Yeah. I saw her enter it once." She repeated the word "one" six times in a row. "I teased her about the simplicity of it for a while. She said that was the whole point. You only get a few tries to enter the passcode for an iPhone before it locks up for good, so who's going to waste a guess on something so obvious?"

In most cases, a password like that would be a terrible idea. But there was a certain logic to Aleshia's reasoning, Connor thought.

When he couldn't find the phone by touch, he dumped the contents of the purse onto the table. More makeup, hand wipes, iPhone earbuds, keys. No phone.

Even if you wanted to argue that she might have left in a hurry—that this *one* time she had left without her purse—the door had been locked. She couldn't have done that without taking her keys.

Unless . . .

He circled around to the foyer to check the front door. The latch on the knob had been turned, securing it in place, but the deadbolt was unlocked. However, he cautioned himself, anybody could have turned that latch before exiting the house. Including a kidnapper. And if someone really wanted to hide an abduction, they just might have.

"All right, let's see what we can find," Connor said.

Olin looked around like he was lost. "What are we looking for?"

"Anything. If you see something suspicious—or even weird, I guess—just let the rest of us know."

"Gotcha." Olin made his way back toward the living room. He might not have wanted to break in, but now that he was here, at least he was willing to help search the place. Connor wasn't surprised. They had broken into a house once before. Olin had been just as reluctant then to cross the threshold. And then, like now, he became a team player once they were inside.

Since there was nothing of interest in the purse and the dining room contained only the table, Connor went into the kitchen. It was the next closest room. He intended to search all of them, so he might as well start there.

Dylan followed him.

Before they could begin their search, though, Olin popped his head in. "Should we be wearing gloves for this?"

Connor shrugged. "She's Aleshia's friend," he said, referring to Dylan. "If the police ever bother looking for prints, they shouldn't be surprised to find hers. And we're Dylan's friends, so . . ." He trailed off, looked from Olin to Dylan and back, then disappeared down the hall. When he returned, he was carrying three towels. "Still, probably better to be safe." He handed one towel to Olin as he passed and tossed another to Dylan, who was on the opposite side of the kitchen. "Wipe down everything you touch."

Then, to avoid (as he called it) "compromising the scene," he returned to the dining room, swept the contents of Aleshia's purse back into her bag, and hung the bag back over the chair. After carefully wiping the bag down, he did one last visual inspection of the room to make sure everything looked like it had when they'd entered. "Done," he said when he came back to the kitchen.

While Olin searched the living room, Connor and Dylan scoured the cupboards and the pantry. Connor spoke only once before they were finished, and that was when he saw Dylan clearing plates off a shelf and moving on without putting them back.

"What are you doing?" he asked her. "We have to leave everything like it was when we found it."

Dylan gave him a look but followed his instructions.

The house consisted entirely of one bathroom, two bedrooms (one of which had been converted into a home gym), a living room, a dining room, and the narrow kitchen. There was no basement, and the only way to get to the attic was through a set of pull-down stairs, making it less than ideal for any sort of storage.

After Olin finished searching the living room, he went up there, anyway, just to be sure. As Connor suspected, he found nothing. Not even a box of Christmas decorations.

"If we're going to find anything here at all, it's got to be in the bedroom," he said when Olin came back down.

Dylan nodded. "I think you're right. How about you two check that out while I give the bathroom a once-over?"

With nothing more than an elliptical machine, a yoga mat, and some free weights, there was no reason to spend any time on the gym.

The three friends moved down the hall together. Connor and Olin broke off at the bedroom. Connor checked the nightstands and Olin the dresser, both diligently using the towels to wipe down everything they touched.

The bed was unmade, which made it easy to tell which side Aleshia slept on. In that nightstand, Connor found a Chapstick, earplugs, and a dog-eared copy of James Patterson's *Honeymoon*. The other one—no surprise—was empty.

He turned around. "Nothing. What about you?"

Olin was on the third drawer from the top. "Nothing here, either. Not yet, anyway."

Dylan had finished searching the bathroom and was now standing in the doorway. "Did you check the closet?"

Connor did. It was also a bust.

He was just about to give up when a flicker of light on the bed caught his attention. A hard piece of plastic glinted in the light from the overhead lamp. Although only the corner of the object was visible, he knew what it was right away. He pushed the blankets aside to reveal a laptop. "Hey, guys."

Connor sat down on the bed with the computer in his lap and pressed the power button. The computer came to life. Olin and Dylan moved in close so they could see what he was doing.

When the computer finished booting up, it presented them with a login screen.

Connor glanced at Dylan. "Do you know the password?"

"No, not to this."

Connor took a deep breath. He knew from experience people kept all sorts of secrets on their personal computers. They had to find a way to get in. However, that could take some time.

He shut down the laptop to preserve the battery and closed it. He tucked it under one arm as he got to his feet. "Let's take it back to the hotel. We'll work on it there."

"What about leaving things like they were?" Dylan said.

"I think we can make an exception for this."

CHAPTER 5

WHILE CONNOR HAD made reservations for their flight, Olin found a hotel: The Grand Hyatt in Buckhead. He'd cleared it with Connor, then booked a suite. He also made a point of paying for it in advance. This came as no surprise to Connor. Olin had inherited a lot of money, and whenever a big expense came their way, he insisted on taking care of it.

On their way there, Connor asked Dylan to stop by Target so he could pick up an external hard drive. He'd found an article online about a heist in Chicago a few years back where a hacker broke into someone's computer using just such a device. The details of the article were sketchy, but he knew more than enough about how computers worked to understand the contours of the scheme. While he was there, he also grabbed three pairs of gloves in case they decided they needed to break into anyone else's house.

The suite was even bigger than Connor expected. He and Olin each had their own bedrooms. They dropped off their luggage and joined Dylan at the small dining table in the living room.

Connor placed the laptop and the external hard drive on the table. While he was at Target, he'd also bought a universal power cable. He wanted to make sure the laptop wouldn't run out of juice before they were finished with it. He plugged the power cable into the computer and said, "This is going to take a couple of hours. You two should find something to do to entertain yourselves. Dylan, if you need to go . . ."

She waved him off. "Are you kidding? I'm staying here until we get into that thing."

Olin looked at Dylan. "Is there anyone else you and I could talk to while we wait? What about Aleshia's parents?"

"Her father died of cancer a few years ago. Her mother went in her sleep not long after that. Something with her heart. I think it was probably grief. Either way, all Aleshia has left is her sister Maddie, and, as you know, she's missing too. Even if she wasn't, she's fifteen years older than Aleshia, so I don't think they have much in common. And she's kind of a recluse on top of that. They don't see each other very often. Which only makes this whole thing stranger, doesn't it?"

Olin didn't respond, and Connor understood why. There was nothing to say. First a woman goes missing. Then her sister disappears. They have no other family, so there would be no one to pay a ransom if that had been the goal. And even though their father had been famous, Aleshia and Maddie lived quiet lives out of the public eye, minimizing the number of enemies they might have. With Maddie a recluse and her relationship with her sister limited, the number of *shared* enemies would have to be nearly zero.

In other words, the question answered itself. Yes, the situation was strange. Yes, the fact that Maddie was a recluse made it stranger. However, none of that mattered until they had a lead.

Olin looked at his phone. "There's a basketball game on," he said to Dylan. "Kentucky versus Auburn."

Dylan looked from Olin to Connor.

"Really," Connor said. "There's nothing you can do right now. I'll let you know once I'm in."

Olin and Dylan moved to the sofa and Olin turned on the TV.

Connor hardly noticed when they put the game on. He was in the zone.

First, Connor used his own laptop to download a recent version of the Windows operating system. He installed it onto the external hard drive and booted his computer from that drive to make sure it worked. When it did, he switched laptops and booted Aleshia's computer from the external drive using the same technique.

He browsed through recent files and folders, looking for anything that stood out. She didn't have a lot on the machine. Several dozen pictures. A spreadsheet for bills. And an assortment of miscellaneous files. Nothing that would explain her disappearance.

He opened her browser to check the history. She was a frequent user of Facebook and Twitter, so he started there first. She hadn't posted anything in the last two days—from here or her phone. There were no intimidating messages, no suspicious activity of any kind, actually.

That was a bust.

Next on the list: CupidsCorner.com.

It sounded like a dating site to Connor, which, it turned out, it was.

Connor started with her profile. She had uploaded a nice closeup of her face as her primary photo and filled out every question in exhaustive detail.

She liked beaches more than mountains, thought small towns had a lot of charm, ran three miles every day. She liked to travel and wanted a partner who would go with her.

There was no indication from the profile she had a job, which fit with what Connor had already learned from Dylan. Instead, she seemed to do a lot of volunteer work at Helping Hand, an agency that delivered meals to the poor and elderly.

"Did you know Aleshia was on a dating site?" Connor asked.

Dylan leaned forward on the sofa, turned to face him. "You're in?"

"Yes."

"You were supposed to let me know." She got up and came over to the table.

Olin turned off the game and followed her.

"Did you know?" Connor asked again.

"Yeah. I even helped her set up her profile."

That made sense, Connor thought. Dylan never half-assed anything. If she was going to fill out a profile on a dating site, she would answer every question in detail, exactly like Aleshia had.

Connor browsed through her recent messages. There were several from a guy named Tyler921. According to the messages, Tyler was a trainer at Power Fitness who also liked to travel.

"Did you know Aleshia had a date with a guy named Tyler the night before she disappeared?"

Dylan's eyes grew wide. "Let me see that." She turned the laptop toward her, read their exchange. "It doesn't say where they went."

"Aleshia gave him her phone number," Connor said, directing Dylan to that part of their conversation. "They probably worked that out on the call."

Dylan clicked on Tyler921's screen name. She was redirected to Tyler's profile. Like Aleshia's, the profile included a large photo with several smaller ones underneath it. In the primary picture, Tyler stood facing the camera. He was visible from the waist up and wearing a tight shirt that made it clear he wasn't lying when he called himself a trainer. He had a square face that worked for him and a sharp jaw line. His hands rested on his hips. One corner of his mouth was turned up in a half-smile that made him seem both serious and approachable.

The pictures underneath suggested he lived an active life—sailing, running, playing tennis. Connor had no doubt he did all of those things. Although he doubted they comprised as much of his life as the pictures might have you believe.

"Did you talk to Aleshia the day she went missing?" Connor asked.

Dylan shook her head. "No. We'd made plans to meet at the cafe the day before."

"So as far as you know, Tyler may have been the last person to see her."

Her face dropped. "She should have told me she was meeting him."

"At least we know where he works," Olin said.

"We'll go by Power Fitness first thing in the morning," Connor said.

"What if he's not there?"

"Then we'll track him down."

Connor finished perusing the messages on the dating site. As far as he could see, Aleshia hadn't met with anybody else.

CHAPTER 6

JAKE AVARNATTI ENJOYED his morning run. Especially in winter. The beach along Lake Lanier was quiet at this hour, and he often made the run without seeing another soul. Dressed in gray sweats and Nike tennis shoes, he would park in the public lot, then tread his way through the sand down and back. Twenty minutes in all. Enough to work up a sweat and loosen up the muscles that used to ache from too many hours at the computer.

Today, however, he didn't even get a quarter of a mile down the beach before he saw somebody stretched out along the edge of the water. With the sun just over the horizon and facing him, he couldn't make out any details at first.

Once he could, he realized the woman wasn't on the edge of the water—she was in it. And she was fully dressed. Nothing fancy. Just jeans and a tee shirt. But it was too cold to be dressed like that, and even if she liked the cold, that wasn't what you would wear if you were going into the water.

Perhaps she wandered down here drunk, Jake thought. There was a hotel not far away. Even a neighborhood within walking distance. That made the most sense, he decided. He figured he'd better check on her.

Jake jogged up to the woman. Once he was close enough to see her in detail, the scene changed from merely unusual to alarming. The woman had blood smeared across her forehead and her shirt.

Jake dropped to his knees, instinctively pulled her farther onto the sand, shook her shoulders. "Ma'am. Ma'am, are you okay?"

No response. He leaned in close to check for breathing, heard none, and then realized how cold she really was. That wasn't just from the water.

With his heart pounding faster than it ever did when he ran, Jake pulled back. He fumbled to get his phone out of his pocket, dialed 911. "I need to report . . . Well, I don't know. A body, I guess." He didn't want to say "murder." He didn't want to imagine a killer dumping a body along his running route. Even though he knew there was nothing else it could be.

There was a halting jerkiness to his voice as he answered the operator's questions. When she was done, she asked him to stay where he was, and he said he would. Once he got off the phone, he stepped far enough away from the body that he could no longer see the blood on the woman's forehead.

Although he tried to keep his attention on the road, his gaze kept shifting back to the woman. There was a part of him that felt like he had to watch her, to make sure she was still there when the police arrived. It was absurd. Even as alarmed as he was, he could think straight enough to be sure of that. But it didn't stop him from looking.

There was also a part of him that worried the killer was still out here, that simply by being close to the body he would become the next victim. Which was also probably absurd (although somewhat less so).

Road. Body. Road. Body.

What the hell was taking the police so long?

CHAPTER 7

ALEX SHAW PARKED behind a line of black-and-whites. He grabbed his Styrofoam cup of Dunkin' Donuts coffee and stepped out of the car. Uniformed officers had swarmed the scene first. They'd stuck posts in the sand around the body, run crime scene tape around them, and gathered preliminary information from Jake.

Alex saw his partner, Howie Muller, standing with his arms crossed over his chest, watching the CSI team work. He waved. Howie waved back. Then Alex trudged through the sand to where his partner was standing.

"I gather he's the one who found the body," he said, nodding toward a man in gray sweats some twenty feet away.

"Yeah. Jake Avarnatti. He told the responding officers he comes down here to run almost every day." Howie rolled his head. His spine cracked. "We'll need to verify that."

That's a given, Alex thought. You never took a person at their word, especially not a person who reported a body. Most of the time they were exactly who they said they were. Every once in a while, they were something more.

"CSI found anything?"

"Not yet. Not sure they will, either. Maybe once the ME gets a look at the body, but here . . ." He frowned.

"This was just a dumping ground, huh?"

"That's what it looks like to me. They're combing through the sand to see if the killer might have dropped something. I don't have high hopes." Howie shifted his attention to Alex. "You look tired."

Alex had been up late last night helping his thirteen-year-old son with a school project. It was one of those three-panel corkboard things that he hated doing as a kid and still hated doing as an adult. The subject: volcanoes.

It wouldn't have been so bad if his son had come to him about it when the project had been assigned. But true to form, Dexter had waited until the last minute to say anything.

If it weren't for the coffee, he'd probably fall asleep right where he was standing. "I'll be fine. You talk to Mr. Avarnatti yet?"

"You're better at that stuff than me."

Alex patted his partner on the shoulder and then made his way over to Jake. The man was pacing in small, nervous circles. "Mr. Avarnatti?"

Jake turned. "Yeah?"

"I'm Detective Shaw. You want to fill me in on what happened?"

Jake licked his lips. "Yeah. Sure, okay. Well, I was—um—I was running this way." He pointed north.

Alex noticed a tremor in his hand. That wasn't unusual. Most people were pretty shaken up when they found a body. Especially those who were innocent.

"I saw this woman lying on the beach," Jake continued. "I couldn't tell much about her at first. Thought she might have wandered down from the Marriott up there and passed out or something. Anyway, I went over to see if she needed some help, and, well . . ." He shivered. "You saw her. I think a part of me knew she was dead right away. But I couldn't help myself. I dragged her out of the water, gave her a good shake to see if I could wake her up. You can't imagine how much I wanted to be wrong. When she didn't open her eyes, I checked to see if she was breathing, and that's when I knew it was too late."

Alex wished Jake hadn't touched the victim. Everything he could gather from the man's body language told him Jake wasn't the killer, but this was going to make ruling him out more difficult. Even worse, it might allow the real killer's lawyer to raise enough doubt with a jury to get him off.

Still, what was done was done. There was no reason to chastise Jake for it. Alex just needed to get the man's story and move on. "How often do you come down here?"

"Every day."

"Every day?"

"Almost every day," Jake said, correcting himself. Another sign of an honest man. "There's a parking lot that way. I leave my car there, then jog up and down the water."

"You got anybody who can verify your routine?"

"My wife."

Alex pulled a small notepad and pen out of his jacket pocket. "What's her name?"

"Adri—"

"Hey, Alex!" It was Howie. "Come over here." He was standing with somebody from the CSI team.

Alex slipped the notepad and pen back into his pocket. "I'll be right back."

"Looks like I was wrong," Howie said, once Alex returned.

"What are you talking about?"

"Show him."

The CSI agent held up a plastic baggie. Alex recognized it as an evidence bag. Inside, there was a small silver ring. "Is that an earring?"

"Looks like a nose ring to me," Howie said.

The CSI agent agreed.

"Could that have come off our victim?" Alex asked.

"I don't think so. I had a close look at our vic before you got here. Didn't see any holes in her nose. Plus, the guys found it way over there." Howie nodded toward the road, as if to suggest the ring had been found farther up the beach.

Alex was also sure it wasn't Jake's. He had no visible piercings and didn't seem like the type to get one in his nose. So whose was it?

CHAPTER 8

CONNOR CONTINUED TO explore the laptop after Dylan left. He checked for deleted files and downloads, anywhere someone might stash documents they had forgotten about. By the time he was done, it was clear the dating site had provided them their only lead.

He and Olin met Dylan in the lobby of the hotel the next morning and she drove them to Power Fitness. The gym anchored a dying shopping mall. Half a dozen stores had "For Rent" signs taped to the windows. Most of the parking lot was empty.

They walked through the doors and were met by an expansive fitness center, far larger than it looked from the outside, with high ceilings and mirrors along the back wall that made it look even bigger. Beyond the front desk were a variety of weight-lifting machines. To the right, a designated area for aerobic equipment: bikes, treadmills, ellipticals. Along the back wall, free weights.

At a glance, Connor estimated there were more than forty people working out at that moment. As big as it was, the place still looked empty.

A young woman in fitness attire was filling out paperwork at the front desk. She looked up, smiled. "Welcome to Power Fitness." She reached out a hand. "Membership cards, please?"

"We're not members," Connor said.

"Oh, I see." She regrouped. "That's great. I'd be happy to have somebody show you around, answer all your questions. You really can't do any better than this place. You're going to like it here."

"We're not—"

"It's no trouble. I promise. That's what we're here for."

Dylan rolled her eyes. "Chill."

The woman jerked her head back with surprise.

Connor hadn't seen Dylan talk to anybody like that in a while. He thought she might have grown out of it. Apparently, she was still just as fiery as she used to be. "We're not here to become members. We need to talk to Tyler about something. Is he around?"

When Connor had estimated the number of people inside, he had also looked at each of them with the hope of spotting the man they were here to see. So far, no luck.

"He's in back."

"Can you get him for us?"

The woman hesitated, and Connor hoped she wasn't going to ask who they were since it would have been a hard question to answer. Their names would have meant nothing to Tyler, and invoking Aleshia's might lead to trouble if he was their suspect. Fortunately, she picked up a walkie-talkie without further comment and told Tyler he had guests in the lobby.

Tyler appeared from a door near the back of the gym a moment later. He was wearing the same tight shirt he'd been wearing in his profile picture. A small white towel was slung over one shoulder. He had an easy swagger about him, smiled and waved at some of the members as he passed by.

Connor instantly disliked him.

When Tyler reached the front of the gym, he walked right up to

Connor, Olin, and Dylan, and addressed the three of them at once. "What's up?"

It seemed like an odd way to introduce yourself to a group of strangers, Connor thought. But perhaps, as a trainer, he was used to getting referrals. This probably wasn't the first time someone he didn't know had stopped in to see him.

"We wanted to talk to you about Aleshia," Connor said.

A flash of emotion too quick to interpret crossed Tyler's face. He glanced at the woman behind the front desk. "Sure." Then he nodded toward the front door, stepped outside.

Connor got the impression he wanted to talk privately and followed. Olin and Dylan stayed right behind him.

"What's this about?" Tyler said to Connor. "Is she your girlfriend or something?"

"No."

Tyler looked at Olin. "Yours?"

"No."

"She's my friend," Dylan said.

"Okay. Why are you here?"

"You had a date with her a couple of nights ago, right?" Connor asked.

"Shhhh." He gestured for Connor to keep his voice down. "Don't talk so loud." He glanced back at the woman behind the desk, and Connor finally understood the flash of emotion he'd seen on Tyler's face earlier. He was dating the receptionist.

Connor felt a crack form in his theory that this man might be responsible for Aleshia's disappearance.

"Calm down," Dylan said.

"Can you tell us about it?" Connor said.

"I took her to Mariano's. It's this little Italian place I know."

"Does she know about your date?" Dylan asked, referring to the woman behind the desk.

"Carla and I are having problems. I was exploring my options. What are you doing here, anyway? It was *one* date. Did Aleshia send you to talk to me?"

And with that, the theory crumbled entirely. Connor could tell the question had been genuine. Tyler didn't know Aleshia was missing. However, he still might know something about what happened to her, even if he didn't *know* he knew it. He might have seen something when he picked her up or dropped her off, might have heard something. With nothing else to go on, Connor would need to play this out to see what he could learn.

"Why would she send us to talk to you?" he asked.

"I said I'd call her, and I didn't. So, is that why you're here?"

"She's not crazy," Dylan said.

"How would I know?"

"Why didn't you call her?" Olin asked.

Tyler shrugged. "I wasn't sure she was over her ex."

"What made you think that?"

"All night she kept getting these text messages. Like, every ten minutes her phone would buzz. Eventually, she put it on silent. That seemed a little . . ." He made a face, and Connor got the point.

"How do you know it was her ex?"

"She wouldn't have told you that," Dylan added.

"She didn't. At some point, she got up to go to the bathroom, and I looked at her phone. She had three new messages from some guy named James. They read: 'Call me back,' 'This is important,' 'I need to talk to you.' Who else would be sending her messages like that?"

"Did anything else about the date strike you as unusual?"

Tyler didn't seem to understand what Connor was driving at.

"For example, when you picked her up, did you notice anyone hanging around her house who looked suspicious? Anything like that?"

"I didn't pick her up. I met her at the restaurant."

Connor should have figured that. They'd met online. It was their first date. Aleshia might have given Tyler her phone number, but she wouldn't have given him her address.

Tyler rubbed his hands over his exposed arms to warm them up. "Are we done here?" When no one answered, he added, "I'm not sure what you guys are after, but you can let Aleshia know I won't be calling her again. Especially not after this. You're all a little crazy, aren't you?" Then he hurried back inside.

"Do you know James?" Connor asked Dylan on the way back to the car.

"Sure. Aleshia dated him for six months or so. We all hung out a bunch of times."

"Why did they break up?" Olin asked.

"She said he was clingy."

It sounds like he still is, Connor thought. "Do you know where he lives?"

"You're thinking we got our very own Dateline Special on our hands?"

"I don't know. We should see what he has to say."

CHAPTER 9

JAMES LIVED IN a six-story apartment building in Buckhead, a ritzy area known for its nightlife. A variety of shops occupied the ground floor. Dylan used the callbox by the lobby doors to announce herself, and James buzzed her in.

She had given no indication Connor and Olin were with her. Connor suspected that was not by accident. If she really was worried James might be their "very own Dateline Special," she might also be worried how he would respond if she said she was bringing two strangers up to see him. They took the elevator to the top floor, and Dylan led them to a unit at the far end of the hall.

James greeted Dylan with a yawn and a "Hello" that Connor could barely understand. He was a bartender at an upscale establishment called Brick's, Dylan had told Connor and Olin on their way over. As such, Connor wasn't surprised he was just waking up.

When James realized Dylan wasn't alone, he cinched his robe a little tighter. "Who's this?"

"Some friends," Dylan said. "Can we come in?"

He ran a hand through his hair while he thought about the request, then stepped aside.

The living room looked to Connor liked it had been furnished by Ikea, with a do-it-yourself coffee table and TV stand. A round glass table with four chairs occupied the small dining room to the left.

James closed the door and entered the kitchen. Since the layout of the apartment made it visible from both rooms, no one else moved. "Coffee?"

"No," Connor said. "Thanks."

Dylan held out a hand to indicate the same thing.

"It's been a while," James said, as he poured a mug for himself.

"Too long," Dylan responded.

James moved to the sofa and took a seat. "Why are you here?"

Dylan sat down on the sofa next to him. "I wanted to talk to you about Aleshia."

Connor could have taken that as an invitation to move to the La-Z-Boy nearby, but he stayed by the door. He got the impression James didn't have much interest in talking to him or Olin and thought it best not to draw attention to himself. Olin, who also remained where he was, must have picked up on the same thing.

"You sent her some messages the other night," Dylan continued. "You're still not over her, are you?"

"It's hard. I miss her, sure. But that's not what those messages were about."

"What were they about, then?"

James took a sip from his coffee. Then, for the first time since Connor and Olin had entered the apartment, he shot them each a look. "I'd rather tell Aleshia."

Connor got an uneasy feeling. Was James playing coy because he and Olin were strangers? Or was there something more going on here?

"She's missing," Dylan said. "We're trying to—"

"What?" James said, leaning forward. "She's missing?"

"Yes."

He shook his head. "She can't be missing."

"We're trying to find out what happened to her."

James took a second to process the news. "And you think I had something to do with it?"

"I'm not saying that."

"You are. That's why you're asking about the text messages."

Dylan turned to Connor with an expression that said *Help me*, and Connor took a step forward. The time for standing on the sidelines was over. "We're worried about her. That's all."

"You don't think I am?" His voice rose. "You come here accusing me of Aleshia's disappearance—"

"We didn't do that," Olin said.

"You didn't come right out and tell me she was missing, either." James stood up. "Who are you two, anyway? Are you like private investigators or something?"

"We're just concerned friends," Connor said.

"You think I sent those messages because I was trying to get back with her, right?"

"What would you think?" Dylan asked, also on her feet now and moving backward toward Connor.

James watched her go. When he spoke again, he still sounded angry, but at least he wasn't yelling anymore. "I sent those messages because I saw her sister. I thought she would want to know."

Connor needed a second to process what James had just told them. It seemed like they all did.

"You saw Maddie?" Dylan asked.

"At the Southern Trust on Lexington."

"Why didn't you put that in the message?"

"Because it seemed like the kind of thing you tell someone in person. Or at least over the phone. I wanted to be there for her in case she didn't believe me. I didn't want her to think I was playing some sort of mean trick or something." He slumped back into the sofa. "But now Aleshia's missing. One shows up and the other disappears." He shook his head. "What do you think that means?"

Nobody answered.

"Did you speak to Maddie?" Connor finally asked.

"No. I tried. She was talking to one of those personal bankers. A skinny, young woman with blonde hair. I called her name to get her attention. When she saw me, she took off running. It was very strange."

Connor shifted his weight from one foot to the other. "What about the banker? Did you talk to her after Maddie left?"

"Why would I?"

Connor shrugged.

"Are you sure it was her?" Dylan asked.

"Absolutely. She used to come into Brick's all the time. She'd get a tea, then sit at a table by the window and read. Aleshia came in to talk to her once and that was how I met her. After that, Maddie and I also became friendly. We never talked a lot. She kind of keeps to herself, you know? In fact, except for Aleshia and this guy she'd meet there sometimes, I don't remember seeing her with anyone. Either way, we talked enough. I know what she looks like."

CHAPTER 10

WHEN CONNOR, OLIN, and Dylan left James's apartment, they promised to let him know if they found out anything. Nobody spoke again until they boarded the elevator.

"Do you think he's telling the truth?" Dylan asked.

"I don't know," Connor said.

Olin pressed the button for the lobby. "If it's true, it's one strange story." He bit his lip, then added, "You don't think this is some sort of plan, do you?"

"What do you mean?" Connor asked.

"Like maybe Aleshia took off *because* James spotted Maddie? That maybe Aleshia knew where Maddie was the whole time?"

The elevator doors opened. A young couple was waiting on the other side, and the three friends fell silent again. Once they were outside, Dylan said, "That doesn't make sense. Why would Aleshia want me to look for her if she knew where Maddie was?"

"Maybe she didn't think you'd find her," Olin said.

Dylan slapped his arm.

"Hey! I'm just saying—it's possible."

"So, she left home without her purse or her keys?"

Olin climbed into the backseat without answering.

"That seems like a stretch," Connor said as he, too, got in.

"It's more than a stretch," Dylan responded. "It's impossible."

Connor closed his door. "Either way, I think we should go by the bank and see what we can find out."

"Agreed," Dylan said, as she started the car.

CHAPTER 11

SOUTHERN TRUST WAS one of those rare old banks with high ceilings and massive columns in the lobby. Connor's footsteps squeaked and echoed as he crossed the polished tile floor. Once he was ten feet in, he stopped and looked around.

There were four active teller windows, all with lines, and two personal bankers in offices along the outer wall. One of the personal bankers was a man. The other was a woman who matched James's description. On a plaque beside her door was the name "Skylar Hall." Unfortunately, she wasn't alone. Another woman was sitting on the opposite side of her desk.

Connor went over to the sign-in form and wrote down his name, then took a seat in one of four leather chairs to wait. He sent a text to Dylan: *She's talking to someone. I have to wait.*

Olin and Dylan were in the car outside. There had been no place to park nearby, so they had parked in a loading zone. Dylan had said she would stay with the car in case anyone asked her to move. And Olin had stayed because he thought two men coming in to ask questions might alarm the banker. "Best to handle this one-on-one," he had said.

Dylan responded to Connor's text with a thumbs up. He put the phone back in his pocket.

His mind wandered, eventually landing on a child's rhyming game. Looking at the chair across from him, he launched into the rhyme.

Chair-chair-bo-bear. Banana-fana-fo-fair, me-my-mo-mare. Chaaair!

He continued to kill time by repeating that same rhyme with other items he saw—*Pen-pen-bo-ben, banana-fana-fo-fen, me-my-mo-men. Peeen!*—eventually landing on his own name and then Skylar's.

The man who was in the second office came out, looked at the sign-in form, and called Connor's name.

Connor had worried this might happen. He snapped back into the moment. "I'm waiting to speak to Ms. Hall."

The man glanced at his coworker's office. "She might be a while. Come on in."

"I'd rather wait," Connor said firmly and hoped the man didn't press him for more details about his visit.

Fortunately, his only response was to put up his hands in a "suit yourself" gesture before retreating to his office.

That could have gone worse, Connor thought. Perhaps it hadn't gone quite as well as he assumed it had though, since the man kept looking over his computer at Connor.

Ten minutes later, the woman left Skylar's office and Skylar called Connor in. From here, he was out of the man's direct line of sight.

"What can I do for you?" Skylar asked.

Connor took a seat in one of the guest chairs. He realized he could see Dylan's Volvo through the window behind her. "This might seem unusual."

Skylar's smile faltered, and Connor decided he'd better get straight to the point. He didn't want the banker's imagination running away with her.

"I want to ask you about someone named Maddie Thompson."

That didn't seem to put Skylar any more at ease, but at least she didn't ask who Maddie was, which must mean she knew the woman.

"Who are you?"

"Connor Callahan."

"Why are you here asking about Ms. Thompson?"

"A guy told us he saw her here."

The banker leaned forward, placed her elbows on her desk. "No. Why are *you* asking about her?" She sounded like she was getting annoyed. "Are you a PI?"

This was the second time Connor had been asked that question today. He hadn't thought much about it when James asked. Maybe he should lean into that assumption. It would probably get him further than simply saying he was a friend.

Then again, a PI likely carried some form of ID. If Skylar asked to see it, that would be the end of the conversation. Best to play this straight.

"No. Just a friend."

"Okay, back to my original question: Why are you asking about her?"

"She's missing. We're worried about her," Connor said.

"How do you know she's missing?"

The question felt so invasive Connor wondered if he had misunderstood. "What do you mean?"

"Is she answering her phone? Have you been by her house? Maybe she ghosted you. People do that, you know."

"That's not what happened here."

"Well, be that as it may, we take our customers' privacy seriously. I'm not sure how much help I can be."

"I'm not asking for you to tell me her balance. I'm just asking if you've seen her."

Skylar relaxed back into her seat. She sighed. "When did your friend say this happened?"

"A few days ago."

"They are mistaken. I haven't seen Ms. Thompson in over a month."

Skylar answered the question without hesitation. That could only mean one thing: James was lying. Why? Was he involved in Aleshia's disappearance, after all?

It seemed like a stupid thing to lie about. He must have suspected they would follow up with the bank after talking to him. Then again, if it was a lie he had made up on the spot (which it probably was), he would not have had time to think through the ramifications of it.

Outside the window, Connor saw a cop car pull up behind Dylan's Volvo. He put on his lights and stepped out.

Since there wasn't anything else to ask, Connor figured he'd better wrap this up. He got to his feet. "I'm sorry for wasting your time."

"It's fine. I'm sorry I can't be of more help."

At the door, Connor turned around. There were pens and a stack of sticky notes on Skylar's desk. He grabbed one of each and wrote down his name and phone number. "If she stops by, would you let me know?"

Skylar didn't answer.

"Think about it."

Then Connor noticed the cop was now on the way back to his car, carrying something in one hand. It had to be Dylan's license.

He was going to give her a ticket.

Connor hurried outside, caught up with the cop just before he got back into his vehicle. "Officer!"

The cop froze. His head snapped up. His shoulders straightened. It was the posture of a man ready for trouble.

Connor had taken him by surprise, he realized. That probably wasn't a good idea. He, too, stopped where he was. "Please don't write Dylan a ticket. This is my fault. I told her to park here. I just needed to run into the bank for a second, and I didn't think it would be a big deal."

"There's a paid lot two blocks over."

"I know. We should have parked there. We will next time, I promise."

The cop still looked uneasy. "You have an ID on you?"

Connor pulled his license out of his pocket and handed it over.

The cop studied it. "New York, huh?"

"Yes, sir."

"Look, we don't park wherever we want down here."

"I understand. It was a mistake. We don't do it in New York, either."

The cop stacked Connor's license on top of Dylan's and cupped them in one hand. "Go on back to the vehicle. I'll be over in a minute."

Connor did as he was told.

"I'm sorry," he said to Dylan, once he got in.

"It's not your fault. What did you find out?"

"Nothing."

"The woman was there, though, right?" Olin asked. "Why else would you have been gone so long?"

"She was there. She says she hasn't seen Maddie since before she went missing."

"You think James was lying?"

Connor glanced in the side mirror. The cop was sitting in his car, doing whatever cops did once they took your license. "It seems like it. But if he was, why was he lying?"

Olin shifted onto the hump between the seats to give himself a better view of Connor and Dylan. "I think—no matter what happened—we should assume that if we find one sister, we'll be closer to finding the other."

"So, what now?" Dylan asked.

"I don't know," Connor said.

The cop returned and handed both licenses to Dylan. Then he passed her a slip of yellow paper. "I'm just writing you a warning today. Next time, park where you're supposed to."

Dylan thanked the cop, and he returned to his car.

She sighed with relief.

"We should go by Maddie's house," Olin said.

"We already know she's not there," Dylan said, as she passed Connor's license back to him.

"Are you suggesting we break-in?" Connor asked.

"No, I'm not suggesting that. I think we should just go have a look and, you know, see what we see."

Connor didn't think they'd see anything unless they had a look around inside like they did at Aleshia's. He figured Olin must know that. But Olin also wasn't big on breaking the law, even for a good cause, so maybe this was his way of easing into the idea.

It wasn't a bad idea. If these disappearances were connected, looking for either one of them was the same as looking for both.

"What the hell?" Connor said. "I think it makes sense."

Dylan pulled out without comment. She didn't seem to care where they went right then. She was just happy to get away from the cop.

CHAPTER 12

IN COMPARISON TO Aleshia's house, Maddie's was a mansion. It had three stories, plus a basement, and because it sat atop a steep hill, all four floors were visible from the street. It had a stucco face. Flower boxes hung outside the uppermost windows.

Connor and Olin were in awe. Dylan, less so. "Aleshia told me about it," she said. "Aleshia didn't need so much space because she liked to be out on the town. Maddie . . . I guess spending so much time alone like she did, she wanted as much room to roam around as possible."

Dylan parked at the top of the driveway. She got out of the car, straightening her back and stretching her arms up to the sky. "The only thing I don't like about Atlanta is you have to drive everywhere."

Connor followed a brick path to a set of stairs that, in turn, led to a small patio. He knocked on the front door.

"I told you she's not here," Dylan called from the driveway.

The comment was similar to the one she'd made at Aleshia's, and he answered it in an equally similar way. "It doesn't mean nobody else is." Dylan's car was the only one in the driveway, but Maddie had a garage. Anybody with a garage door opener could come and go without drawing attention.

Olin was still standing in the driveway with Dylan.

"All right, we're here now," she said to him. "What are you hoping to find out?"

He was still staring up at the house. "I had no idea it would be *so big*. I thought my house was big growing up. This . . . this is huge."

She snapped her fingers in front of his face. "Olin. Focus."

He looked from the house to her. "Right. Um . . . I don't know."

Connor knocked twice more, each time louder than the last, just to be certain they were alone, before calling Dylan over. "Can you get us past that?" he asked, pointing to the lock.

It was a digital model with a keyhole as well as a touchpad.

"That I can't do," Dylan responded. "You know how some car keys have a chip in them to make the car harder to steal?"

Connor nodded.

"This works basically the same way. Unless the device detects the presence of the chip, the pins in the tumbler will remain locked in place. There's no picking it."

That was disappointing. But every house had its weak point. Every house could be broken into if you took the time to find it. Just like every computer could be cracked. Nothing was impenetrable.

Connor descended the stairs to the brick path, stood back, and studied all four floors of the house. There were a lot of windows to secure. Was it possible Maddie had left one of them unlocked?

The obvious ones to try were those on the basement level. He waded through pine-straw, and an assortment of plants he couldn't name, to the nearest one.

"Don't do that," Olin said from the driveway.

"That's a bad idea," Dylan agreed.

Connor turned around. "Why?"

Dylan gestured to the neighborhood.

Of course. Connor had been so focused on the task at hand, he had forgotten about the neighborhood he was in. There were only two houses that had a direct view of Maddie's, and the odds were thin that anybody was looking out of those windows at that moment, but they were no doubt already suspicious of Connor and his friends if they were. Should Connor try to open a window, that same stranger would be on the phone with 911 in a heartbeat.

There was also another concern Olin rightly pointed out at the same time. "What if she has an alarm?"

Connor returned to the brick path and followed it back to the driveway. He circled up with Olin and Dylan. "So, what do we do?"

"You really want to get inside, don't you?" Olin asked.

Connor responded by saying what he'd thought in the car. "You didn't actually suggest we come here intending to limit our investigation to the outside of the house?"

Olin didn't answer, which was as good as admitting Connor was right. Olin wasn't ready to give up his role as the group's moral compass, but he seemed to be inching closer to the idea that there was a degree of gray between the black and white of right and wrong.

Was it objectively wrong to break into Maddie's house? *Yes.* Was it wrong to do it when your reason for doing so was to find out what had happened to her and her sister? *Maybe not.*

"All right, so as far as the alarm goes, I'll tell you what I told you in New York," Connor said, referring to the one time they'd had to break into a house there. "If an alarm goes off, we'll run like hell. At least this time it doesn't look like we'll have to worry about getting shot."

"When did you have to break into a house in New York?" Dylan asked.

Connor figured it was better not to answer that question. Even between friends, some things are best kept secret. "Let's just figure out how we're going to get inside." His next comment was directed back at

Olin. "Dylan can't get us past the lock on the front door. It's one of those electronic ones. I'm guessing the lock on the back door would be the same."

"Probably," Olin agreed.

"Which means all we have left are the windows."

"Maybe not," Dylan said thoughtfully.

"What do you mean?" Connor asked.

"Did you bring the gloves?"

Dylan was referring to the gloves Connor had bought at Target yesterday. He pulled a pair out of a jacket pocket and handed them over.

"Wait here," Dylan said, as she slipped them on.

CHAPTER 13

SKYLAR TURNED OFF her computer and got ready to go home. The bank had been cutting back on her hours as they tried to move more and more services online. After Connor left, she had considered throwing the sticky note with his number on it in the trash but decided to put it in her desk drawer instead. And now that she was going home, she decided to put it in her purse instead of leaving it at the office.

Skylar lived with her parents in a small ranch house. The neighborhood was not particularly unsafe. That said, it probably wouldn't be a good idea to go wandering around by yourself at night, either.

She saw her stepdad's pickup and her mom's old Hyundai in the driveway. There was also a third car parked along the curb. A black Escalade. She had come to recognize that car as trouble. Skylar double-timed it into the house.

Three men in suits were standing in the living room, blocking her stepdad's path to the front door. They looked like middle management.

Her mother was standing in the kitchen doorway, nervously holding onto the doorframe. Leon, her stepdad, had his hands held out in front of him. "I promise, Sam. Everything's moving right along. This stuff just takes time."

Leon had borrowed a shit ton of money from Sam Crawford. The intention was to open a restaurant, he had claimed. Sam would be one of two investors.

After getting the money, Leon signed the lease on a space and hired the cheapest architectural firm he could find to draw up some plans, but that was as close as he ever got to actually launching The Greenway Diner.

In truth, he had only done even that much to buy some time. Leon never intended on opening the restaurant. The money was for a different purpose entirely. But things hadn't gone according to plan, and now the money was almost gone.

"I have been by the building. It still looks exactly like it did."

"The permits were delayed, that's all," Leon said.

Sam licked his lips. "And the other investor you told me about. Where is he? I said I want to meet him."

"I told you—he doesn't live in town."

"Then call him!"

Skylar could practically see the cheap wood paneling shake as Sam's voice echoed around the room. She didn't think she'd made a sound, but maybe she had because Sam turned around to look at her.

"Come on in. Join the party."

Skylar slid past Sam and hurried over to her mother. When she had seen Sam's Escalade, she thought she might be able to do . . . *something*. She had no idea what that something might be. Now that she was inside, she realized how helpless she was. How helpless they all were. Leon had met Sam at a bar some time ago—Skylar couldn't remember which one. She didn't know much about him other than that he had a lot of money, some shady connections, and didn't react well when people made trouble for him.

"Pick up your phone and call your other investor. It's long past time I know who I'm in bed with. Maybe he can explain to me what's going on, because I must be missing something. I don't see how the permits could be taking this long."

Leon pointed to the coffee table. "My phone's over there."

"Then go get it."

Leon went the long way around the sofa, so he didn't have to get too close to Sam or his goons. He grabbed his phone, retreated to his previous position, and dialed a number.

"Put it on speaker."

Leon did.

The phone rang until it rolled over to voicemail. The default message—a female voice, clearly generated by a computer—notified the caller no one was available. Leon hung up before it repeated back to him the number he had dialed.

Skylar knew that was not by chance. Her purse, slung over her shoulder and tucked under one arm, had vibrated when Leon had clicked SEND. She knew he had called her for two reasons. First, because she didn't have her voicemail set up, and second, because there were no other investors.

Sam's face twisted with annoyance. The men beside him remained as still as statues. "You'd better not be screwing with me."

"I'm not. It just takes time. Have you ever opened a restaurant before?"

Skylar knew the answer to that question because Leon had told her Sam had never opened a restaurant. It was the main reason Leon selected that sort of establishment over any other. He also liked the idea that opening such a business no doubt meant jumping through a whole bunch of hoops, each of which could translate into delays.

"No."

"If it was easy, everyone would do it. Please be patient."

Sam considered the request. "If you don't get these permits sorted out soon, things are going to get a lot worse."

"I understand."

That didn't seem to be enough for Sam. His hands balled into fists. His face turned red. Then he pointed at Leon. "I'm not kidding. Get these permits sorted out." Then, before turning to leave, he added, "And get me on the phone with your other investor, you got it?"

"I do."

Sam stormed out without further comment and the two men with him followed.

Skylar had seen these conversations escalate over the months. She was relieved Sam hadn't turned violent yet. She also knew it was only a matter of time until he did.

She went to the door to watch him leave. "What the hell did I get in business with this asshole for?" she heard him say as he climbed back into his car.

She closed the door and turned back around to face her stepdad.

He took the Mets cap off his head, ran his hand through his hair, and slid it back on. "We're going to have to figure this thing out," he said.

"If you hadn't screwed up, everything would be fine," Skylar's mom replied.

That couldn't be truer, Skylar thought. He had screwed up. In a big way. When Leon had drawn up this plan, it had included five simple steps. The first three depended on him, and only the first one— borrowing the money from Sam—had gone as it should have.

Skylar wished she could go back in time and put a stop to the whole thing. It was too late for that, though. The wheels were in motion. All they could do now was hold on.

Leon went to the fridge, grabbed a Pabst Blue Ribbon, and popped it open. He took a long drink from the beer, then closed the fridge and returned to the living room. He neither looked at nor spoke to his wife on the way in or out of the kitchen.

Skylar knew why, too. It wasn't because he was angry with her for what she'd said. It was because she was fragile.

When she was under too much stress for too long, she would start sleepwalking and stop eating. The last time it had happened was when she was working as a cashier at QuikTrip. Leon and Skylar had worried, but they hadn't made her quit until Leon found the bottles of Xanax she had hidden at the back of the pantry, all prescribed by different doctors and covering the same period of time.

Skylar suspected if she and Leon didn't find a way to right the ship soon, her mom would slide back into that self-destructive behavior.

Then she thought about Connor's visit to the bank earlier. Could he be their way out of this mess?

CHAPTER 14

THE BACK OF Maddie's property was fenced, and the gate had a padlock on it. That wasn't going to stop Dylan. She grabbed the top of the fence, pulled up, and hoisted herself over.

"Where are you going?" Olin asked.

"Trust me," she said when she landed.

Maddie's backyard was as wild as her front, but it was not untamed. Dylan could tell from looking at it this was a cultivated wilderness. The bushes and trees were trimmed so they didn't grow out of control. Pine bark and grass met at meandering, predictable lines. White stones of varying sizes were discreetly organized in patterns that were pleasing to the eye. This carefully crafted illusion of Mother Nature roaming free was all very Zen, Dylan thought.

She hurried along the side of the house without bothering to check the windows.

She had learned a lot about Maddie since she started looking for her. One of those things was that Maddie had a dog. A Golden Retriever that, Aleshia said, would sooner lick you to death than bite you.

Dylan already knew the dog had gone missing along with his owner. She wasn't sure what to make of that, but a dog often meant a doggy door. And a Golden Retriever meant a big doggy door.

Dylan found what she was looking for next to the back door. She kicked her foot through it to make sure it hadn't been sealed from the other side.

I can fit through that, she thought.

She had to contort her body to do it, first getting one arm through and then the other. The doggy door led into a kitchen. She looked around for an alarm panel before going any farther and found it on the opposite wall. A glowing red light on it indicated that it was armed. But it also hadn't gone off yet, so maybe there were no motion detectors. Sometimes people with big dogs didn't install them since they figured they wouldn't be able to use them anyway.

Dylan decided to keep going. If the alarm sounded, she could hightail it out the back door and they could be gone long before the police got here.

Getting her hips through was the hardest part. She could feel the doggy door scraping hard against them. She was glad she was wearing jeans.

Once she was inside, she stood up, brushed her hands together. Her heart was pounding. She looked again at the little red light on the alarm. So far so good. She decided to take a trip into the formal living room to her right. If she hadn't set off the alarm by then, she was probably all right.

She charged into the living room, bracing for the sudden, blaring sound of the alarm system. When it never came, she decided she must have been right about the motion detectors and refocused her mind on the next challenge: getting Connor and Olin inside. Neither of them was small enough to get through the doggy door and opening the front or back doors wasn't an option. She examined the windows to see if they had sensors on them. They did, which meant those were out, too.

She pulled out her phone, called Connor. "I'm in."

"Great. How did you do it?"

"I went through the doggy door. You're not going to fit. I'm trying to find another way for you and Olin." She moved from one room to the next, looking for inspiration to strike. Despite the conservative façade, the interior was modern in the extreme. Dylan felt almost as if she had entered one house and ended up in another. There was a lot of black and white, a lot of drama. It was the kind of place Dylan, herself, might have lived in, if she could afford it.

That penchant for drama might be the writer in her, she thought.

When she was younger, Dylan had a website where she posted all sorts of stories. Mostly things about werewolves and vampires and the like. As she aged, however, her taste had changed. These days, she tried writing about detectives and spies. The stories always felt flat. She figured it was because she had no experience in these areas. (Not that she had experience with werewolves or vampires.) That was part of the reason she'd offered to help Aleshia find her sister. At best, it would have been a win all around: she'd have found Maddie, gotten the life experience she wanted. Besides that, the whole idea of doing a little detective work was, frankly, kind of cool.

"I assume you can't just go open the front door, right?"

"The alarm is set."

"All right. Well, if there's no other way in, I suppose that's okay. We can stay out here and keep an eye on the street."

"No way," Dylan said. If it had been just Olin out there, that would have been fine. But Connor had a way of seeing things she might miss. He needed to be a part of the search. "Getting in is the hard part. There's always more than one way out. Give me some time." She hung up before Connor could protest any further.

She was standing in the family room now. The fireplace on the far wall was wrapped in black tile. On each side of it was one of Maddie's original paintings. Like the painting in Aleshia's house, both frames appeared handmade and had been hung with rope. One was of a man who seemed to be turning to sand and blowing away. The other was of two children who were joined by a single long arm.

She looked up. Here, the room went all the way to the roof. She knew this not only because of the cavernous space above her, but because there was a skylight in the ceiling. It was the sun coming through that skylight that had drawn her eye up, to begin with.

Bingo.

Maybe.

Some skylights could be opened. She needed to find out if this was one of them.

Dylan scoured the room. She suspected if there was a way to open the skylight, she would find it in a predictable place. The most predictable place she could think of would be with the light switches, so she checked them out first.

When she didn't find anything that would do the job, she turned her attention to the room itself. *There has to be a way*, she thought. More a wish than a statement of fact.

Then she saw it. There was a series of remote controls laid out in a row on a marble and oak coffee table with multiple levels and unexpected angles. Those for the wall-mounted TV and assorted accessories were easy to spot, which also made the one standout easy to spot. She grabbed it, aimed it up, took a beat.

It seemed unlikely Maddie would wire the skylight up to the alarm system, but it wasn't impossible.

This was just like going through the doggy door, Dylan told herself. The only way to find out if she would set off the alarm was to press the button.

She took a breath.

Click.

Dylan expected if the skylight did anything at all it would rotate toward the sky on a hinge. Instead, it slid into the ceiling, which was a far more elegant implementation than she had anticipated.

If that was going to trigger the alarm, it should have gone off already. But she waited for fifteen or twenty seconds anyway, ready to bolt for the door. Nothing happened.

Dylan called Connor back. "We're halfway there. Maddie has a skylight."

"So?"

"It opens. You get yourself on top of the house. I'm going to see if I can find a ladder or something."

"How am I supposed to do that?"

"I don't know. Figure it out."

CHAPTER 15

DYLAN HAD ALREADY done the hard part, Connor told himself. He and Olin could find a way onto the roof. It would just take some ingenuity.

He looked up the side of the house. The garage was attached in such a way that it was only a single story high. Its roof appeared to slope gently away from the main structure, which would make it easy enough to stand on if they could get up there.

"Dylan found a skylight," he told Olin.

"Okay."

"She asked us to get on the roof."

"We're going through the skylight?" Olin looked doubtful.

"That seems to be the plan."

Olin shook his head. Connor could tell he did not like this idea one bit.

"Let's take it a step at a time. For now, let's find our way onto the roof. We can always come back down the way we go up."

"Why doesn't she search the house on her own?"

"She wants me in there, so I'm going. You can stay out here if that's what you prefer."

Olin considered that. "Fine. How are we going to do this?"

That was the million-dollar question. Dylan was inside looking for a ladder. Connor wished there was also one out here he could use to get them on top of the garage. He could even imagine a scenario where, if all went well, they could pull the ladder up behind them and use it to get them all the way to the roof of the house.

However, when he thought more about it, he decided balancing the ladder on the roof over the garage could be tricky business. That was assuming they could find a ladder.

Connor took several steps back so he could get a better look at the house. The corners had been designed such that they had large, evenly spaced blocks that ran from the ground to the roof, as if each wall had been snapped into place. He had an idea.

"Give me a boost."

"What are you thinking?"

Connor gestured for Olin to hurry up. "Come on, come on."

Olin cupped his hands together, and Connor stepped into them, jumped. At the same time, Olin lifted, propelling him even higher. Connor grabbed hold of the roof of the garage. He pulled and scratched and scrambled his way onto it, finally throwing one leg up and then rolling away from the edge.

"And how am I supposed to get up there?" Olin said.

Before Connor made his way onto the roof, he thought he would be able to reach down and help pull Olin up. That now seemed impossible. Even if Olin could jump high enough to grab his hand, Connor wouldn't have the leverage he would need. "It's probably best to have a lookout, anyway. You can let us know if anyone's coming."

Olin looked toward the street, and then back at Connor. He nodded. "You're right."

Connor knew Olin wouldn't put up a fuss. And it really was for the best, anyway, he decided. He moved toward the corner farthest from the street. Beyond the backyard, Connor could see only untamed wilderness. Any prying eyes they might need to worry about from the house across the street would not be a problem back there.

He estimated the distance from the corner of the house to the second-story window ledge. He grabbed hold of one of the blocks that ran up the side of the house. They did not extend as far from the wall as they appeared to from the driveway. He could barely get his fingertips onto the lip.

He would only get one shot at this, he realized. If he didn't swing wide enough to get a foot onto the window ledge, he would likely fall to the ground and break something. He felt himself go a little lightheaded as he looked down at a group of white rocks that seemed to be strategically positioned at this corner of the house to stop an intruder from trying just such a move.

If he landed wrong, he might break *multiple* things, he thought.

He wiped his hands on his jeans to make sure they were as dry as they could be. He grabbed the tip of the block again. Then, without any more thought, he swung, got a foot onto the windowsill, pushed up, grabbed hold of the gutter.

"Be careful," Olin said.

The flower box snapped and broke away. The gutter started to give. Connor reached farther. And then, somehow, he was on the roof. It all happened so fast. He remembered clawing, pushing, pulling, twisting, turning . . .

Lying on the roof, he took several deep breaths and turned his head so he could take one last look at the ground.

This plan was a lot riskier than it had seemed when he first dreamed it up. Thank God he wasn't dead. Dylan had better have found a ladder because he sure as hell wasn't coming back down this way.

With his arms held out beside him and leaning forward to help himself balance, he made his way along the roof in search of the skylight. He'd barely gone ten feet before he decided he'd better call Dylan to see if she could guide him to it. "Where am I going? Front of the house? Back of the house? Which side?"

"Back of the house."

That's good. At least it was close.

"There's a fireplace here. Do you see the chimney?"

"Yes."

"Go toward that. You should be able to see the skylight once you get to the chimney."

Dylan was right—he could. He peered through the skylight and saw a living room far beneath him. Ground level. He had imagined there was only a single story between the skylight and the floor, but it was more like two. Maybe three.

"Dylan?"

She stepped into view, craning her neck up at him.

"What were you thinking sending me up here? Did you really think you'd find a ladder tall enough for me to climb down?"

"There's recessed lighting in the ceiling. There's got to be a way to change the bulbs when they go out."

"Did you find one?"

"No."

Connor lay down and stuck his head through the opening so he could get a look at the lighting. "Those are LEDs. They last ten years. Maddie probably hasn't even had to replace them yet."

Dylan smiled sheepishly. "Sorry."

"So how am I supposed to get down?"

"I'm not sure you're going to like it. Is Olin with you?"

"No. He stayed out front. What's your plan?"

"I found Maddie's studio."

"And?"

Dylan disappeared from Connor's view without a word. When she returned, she was carrying a rope. "Do you remember the painting you saw at Aleshia's house? Maddie's painting? She's got a couple here, too. She uses these sort of rope-hangers on all of her frames. She's got a whole bunch of it in her studio. I thought you might be able to find something up there you could attach it to and then you could use it to climb down."

Dylan was right—Connor didn't like that plan. However, it was better than staying up here. He looked around. The only thing he saw that might work was the chimney. "Toss it up."

Dylan did, and Connor tried to catch one end of it. The rope fell back to the floor in a heap. They repeated the process half a dozen times before Connor managed to grab hold. Then he carefully maneuvered his way back along the roof to the chimney. As wide as it was, he had to circle the whole thing to get the rope around it. He tied a double knot and another one on top of that. He wanted to be absolutely certain it wasn't going to come loose.

Connor stood a few feet back from the chimney and pulled the rope as hard as he could. As far as he could tell, this would work. He wrapped the rope around one hand to work as a sort of safety and lowered himself through the skylight.

"You can do this," Dylan said.

Connor's muscles were already tired from the climb onto the roof. He could feel his forearms starting to burn. He went slowly, refusing to look down and telling himself the entire time he was "almost there."

When he felt his feet touch the floor, he could hardly believe it. He let go of the rope.

"Nice job," Dylan said.

"We're not doing this again," Connor said, panting.

"Come on. Let's see what we can find."

Dylan started moving, and Connor, after taking a moment to catch his breath and slip on a pair of gloves, as well, went after her. Together, they searched all four floors. Unlike at Aleshia's, there wasn't even a plate out of place. Nor, as far as they could see, was there a laptop.

At first, Connor was starting to think he had gone to all the trouble of getting in here for nothing. Then, in the master bathroom, it was what he didn't see that got his attention. "Dylan?"

"I already looked in there," she said from the bedroom. Connor could hear her going through the drawers.

"Did you happen to notice Maddie's toothbrush was missing?"

Dylan stopped her search, entered the bathroom. "Are you sure?"

"Look." He pointed to an empty granite toothbrush holder. "Unless she was using her finger to brush her teeth, then I'd say yes."

"You think . . . ?"

"Exactly. The way this house is locked up tight. No laptop. No toothbrush. No dog. Maddie disappeared by choice."

"But Aleshia didn't, so what does that mean?"

"Let's not get ahead of ourselves. We *assumed* Aleshia didn't disappear by choice. We don't actually *know* anything." Connor thought for a moment. "Aleshia said she put in a police report, right?"

"Yeah."

"I think we should stop by the station and see what we can find out."

"I'm not sure if they'll tell us anything."

"Maybe not. But they might tell us if a report was even filed."

CHAPTER 16

SKYLAR'S MOM WENT down the hall to her bedroom and closed the door. She and Leon had not spoken to each other since Sam left. Skylar watched her go. It was best to let her be by herself in times like this. If she didn't come out of the room in an hour or two, Skylar would go check on her.

She sat down on the sofa next to Leon. He was watching *Lethal Weapon* on TBS and drinking his beer. If she had walked into the house now, she would never have known Sam had been here.

"What do you think he's going to do if you can't get him the money soon?"

Leon shrugged.

Skylar understood why he was sitting there, zoning out in front of the TV. There wasn't anything else he could do. Their plan had gone to hell, so what choice did he have?

She dug around in her purse until she found the slip of paper with Connor's name and number on it.

Skylar's family had only one computer. It was an old desktop that sat on a table along the back wall near the kitchen. An ever-growing stack of mail was piled up beside it. Bills and junk mail, mostly, from companies like Georgia Power, AT&T, Russell's Tree Repair, and Just Fences. There were stacks of coupon booklets for local fast-food restaurants and loose flyers for a whole manner of things. Most of it had been there for a while, and all of it would likely be there for a while still.

None of them used the computer much.

Skylar went over to it and fired it up. Although she could browse the internet from her phone, she thought a good old-fashioned web search was better done on a computer, if only for the size of the monitor.

She started her search with Maddie's Facebook account, which in turn led her to Aleshia's. Skylar already knew Maddie was missing. Everyone at the bank did. When you had that much money, the staff at Southern Trust would go out of their way to make sure you were happy. But she hadn't imagined there would be a friend out there doing his own PI work. What else might she learn about Maddie if she were to look?

The only answer she would get from Facebook came pretty far down on Aleshia's page. The post promised a reward for any information about her sister. According to the date on it, it had been posted only days after Maddie had disappeared and shared a dozen times since.

Skylar wished she had seen that sooner. But there was no changing the past.

Either way, if Connor was looking for Maddie because of the reward, she needed to know whether he had a chance of finding her. She browsed through Maddie's friends list hoping to see a picture of Connor. When she didn't, she moved on to Aleshia's friends list.

The problem she faced was the shares. Connor could be a friend of a friend. Skylar might never find his picture this way. She might have better luck putting his name and phone number in Google, although even that felt like a long shot.

Suddenly, she stopped scrolling. *Was that . . . ?*

After Connor had rushed out of her office, Skylar had seen him talking to a cop through the window behind her desk. She had gathered he was with the woman who had parked her Volvo in the loading zone out front. Baker Street was known for its heavy police presence, which meant the woman's encounter with a cop was almost inevitable.

That wasn't what mattered now, though. What mattered now was what the woman looked like. The answer to that question was—she read the name beside the picture—Dylan Naese.

Skylar was not completely certain she was right when she had matched her memory to the picture, since she had only seen the driver from a distance and the woman had never gotten out of the car. But since it was also the best lead she had, she clicked the name to see where it would take her and scrolled through Dylan's friends list.

There he was. Connor Callahan.

"All right, Connor. What can we find out about you?" she mumbled.

Would she be wasting her time if she joined forces with him to look for Maddie?

Skylar expected the answer to that question would be one she would have to gauge using circumstantial evidence about Connor's life. She had no idea how wrong she would be. Page after page on Google presented her with news stories about a crime in New York he had helped solve. And not just him. That woman—Dylan Naese—had been a part of it also. So had a guy named Olin Wilson.

Skylar remembered seeing a third person in the back of the Volvo. Although she couldn't make out any details about that person at the time, common sense told her that must have been Olin.

If anybody was going to be able to find Maddie, it was them.

"I've got something over here you're going to want to see," she said.

Leon waved a hand over his shoulder. "Not now."

"No, really. Come here. This is important."

Leon sighed. He drained the last of his beer and came over. "What is it, Skylar?" He sounded weary.

Skylar pointed to the monitor. "Look."

"Yeah, so? Some guy in New York solved some crime. Good for him."

"There's a reward out for Maddie, and he's looking for her. I think this may be what we need to get us out of this mess."

Leon's focus sharpened. He leaned closer to get a better look at the screen. "I think you might be right."

CHAPTER 17

CONNOR AND DYLAN made their way to Maddie's front door.

"Once we open this, we'll have about a minute until the alarm goes off," Dylan said.

"I know."

It wasn't as if they had a choice. Dylan might be able to squeeze back through the doggy door, but every option Connor had would mean setting off the alarm. At least going out the front door would mean they wouldn't also have to jump a fence to get to the car.

Dylan turned the deadbolt and threw the door open. "Go!"

Connor was already running.

They knew they would get away long before any police showed up. What they hoped to avoid by being quick was the prying eyes Connor had imagined might be watching them when they'd arrived. The last thing they needed was somebody writing down Dylan's license plate number.

"Get in the car!" Connor shouted at Olin as he came around the brick path.

"What's going on?"

"I couldn't go back through the skylight. This was my only way out. The alarm will go off any second. Just get in."

Olin did as he was told, taking what had become his usual seat in back. Connor and Dylan hopped into the front seats at almost the same time. She backed up quickly, turned the wheel, and sped down the steep driveway, her rear bumper thumping and scraping against the cement as she pulled onto the road.

They weren't even twenty feet away from the property when they heard the alarm start to sound. That would be far enough as long as Dylan didn't draw attention to the Volvo with her driving.

"Slow down," Connor told her, as he stripped off his gloves and returned them to his coat pocket.

"What?"

He explained his reasoning. Dylan eased off the gas pedal, letting the car naturally slow to the speed limit. She removed her gloves, too, and put them in her purse. Then, once they were far enough away from the house that they couldn't hear the siren anymore, Connor asked Dylan if she knew where they were going, and she said she did.

"What's going on?" Olin asked.

"Maddie's toothbrush is missing. So is her dog. Which probably means she disappeared by choice." He turned around in his seat. "This is all just a theory right now. That's why we're going by the police station. I want to find out if Aleshia really did put in a missing person report for her sister."

"You're thinking she didn't?"

"Maybe."

"Like perhaps Aleshia already knew where her sister was?"

Connor shrugged.

"Just like I said back at James's apartment she might?"

This was not exactly the same. At James's, Olin had theorized Aleshia knew where Maddie was because James claimed to have spotted Maddie at the bank. Olin had also gone on to theorize that the two women had disappeared together. Connor was coming around to that idea, but he wasn't all the way there yet. A missing toothbrush was not evidence of a conspiracy.

Not even the missing dog could connect those dots.

But if no missing person report was filed? Now that would be the sort of thing that could really give Olin's theory a shot in the arm.

"You weren't right then, and you're not right now," Dylan said to Olin as the three of them pulled up to the police station. "I don't know what happened to Maddie—maybe she did run off. But someone took Aleshia; I'm sure of that."

The station was on the ground floor of a nondescript government building. When they walked through the front door, they were met by metal detectors. A police officer told them to empty their pockets into a series of blue baskets while another police officer stood nearby, ready for trouble. Connor and Olin had only their keys and wallets on them. Dylan was carrying a small purse.

The officer looked over the contents with little interest and waved them through the metal detectors. They collected their belongings, and then Dylan led Connor and Olin to an elevator and pressed the button to take them down.

The doors opened directly onto the station lobby. It was not as big as Connor expected it to be, considering the size of the building. Chairs lined the wall on both sides of the elevator. An American flag hung from a pole in one corner.

They approached the oversized desk in front of them.

"Excuse me," Connor said to the officer behind it.

The officer was busy with something on the computer. He held up a finger, telling Connor to wait. When he was done, he looked up. "What can I do for you?"

"We're here about a missing person."

"You want to file a report?" The officer's fingers were already back on the keyboard, ready to take down the specifics.

"No. This is about a report that was already filed. We just wanted to see if there was an update," Dylan said.

"What's the name?"

"Madeleine Thompson."

The officer typed something into his computer and read the screen for much longer than Connor would have expected. His brow furrowed. "Give me a minute," he said, and then disappeared through a door along the back wall.

"That was strange," Olin said.

"It seems like they might know something," Connor said.

Dylan nodded in agreement.

While they waited, Connor slid his hands into his pockets and turned to face the lobby. There were only four other people present.

A man and a woman—a couple, it looked like—were sitting in the farthest corner. The woman looked worried. Her mascara was smeared like she had been crying. The man had one arm wrapped around her shoulders to comfort her. From the way they were dressed, Connor would not have expected to see them in a place like this. They must be here for someone else. Perhaps their child, he theorized.

The other two individuals were both men and, it seemed to Connor, looked exactly like they belonged here. One had so many piercings, Connor wasn't sure how he'd got through the metal detectors. The other, in ragged and dirty clothes, might have been homeless.

The officer returned. "Are you family?"

"No," Connor said.

"We're just friends," Dylan added.

The officer frowned. "Sorry. I can't tell you anything about that case, then, I'm afraid."

"Please," Dylan said, leaning forward and grabbing the edge of the desk as she did so. "We're worried about her."

"Ma'am, please step back."

Dylan did as instructed.

"If you didn't file the report and you're not family, I can't help you."

Connor sighed, gestured to the elevator. "Come on."

Dylan grabbed his arm. "Wait." Back to the officer: "What about Aleshia Thompson? I filed that report yesterday. She's missing, too. Can you tell me anything about that?"

This time, the officer asked to see her license before pulling up the record. "No news there. These two women related?"

"They're sisters," Connor said.

The officer frowned. "I'll tell you what. I'll let the detectives working Madeleine's case know you came by. Maybe they'll be able to fill you in."

"Thanks," Connor said, already at the desk and once again writing his name and number on a slip of paper. "I'd appreciate that."

The officer looked questioningly at Dylan.

"That's fine," she said. "They can call that number."

The officer took the slip of paper. "Anything else I can do for you?"

Connor, Olin, and Dylan agreed there was not.

CHAPTER 18

DYLAN TURNED TO Connor once they were back on the elevator. "You know they already had my number," she said, and Connor immediately felt a little foolish for rushing in to give the officer his. Of course, the police already had Dylan's number. It would be associated with the case she had filed.

If he wasn't so eager for a break—something solid to move them forward—he probably would have realized the officer had been directing the offer to Dylan to begin with.

"Sorry."

"It's fine."

"At least that rules out the possibility that they're in this together," Dylan said.

"Maybe," Olin said.

"What do you mean 'maybe'? Clearly Aleshia filed a report when her sister went missing."

"We don't know that. We only know somebody filed a report. The officer said if we weren't family and if we didn't file the report, he couldn't give us any information. If anything, that suggests the person who filed the report *wasn't* Aleshia."

Dylan waved a hand dismissively in his direction. "*Pshh.*"

"What's that supposed to mean?"

"It means you're getting caught up in semantics."

The elevator doors opened. They stepped into the lobby.

Connor, who had been quietly parsing the conversation his own way, said, "Maybe we should go talk to Sofia."

Sofia was the woman who owned the Ink Well. That was the studio where Maddie had been taking art classes. She was the first person Dylan had talked to when she'd begun her search for Aleshia's sister. Sofia had told her—and she had told Connor—about the man who had attacked Maddie in the parking lot. Although Dylan admitted to wondering if there might be a connection between that and Maddie's disappearance after Aleshia, too, went missing, she had since reasoned her way back to her previous position: the man had been after Maddie's purse. It was a mugging gone wrong—nothing more. The incident had happened two months before Maddie disappeared, and unfortunately, that kind of thing happened from time to time in a city as big as Atlanta.

Connor had initially agreed with her assessment when she'd relayed the information. But the conversation with the officer had raised more questions than it had answered, and he felt like it might be worth talking to Sofia again. He could see a look of doubt on Dylan's face, so he elaborated. "Maybe she remembered something since you spoke to her that would help us see the incident in a different light. Maybe she even told the police what she remembered and that's why they have something to go on with Maddie's case."

Connor knew he was grasping at straws. Since Maddie seemed to have disappeared on her own, the odds that an old mugging had anything to do with it were slim, at best. Still, this wouldn't be the first time Connor had chased down an unlikely lead. If he had limited his search for his parents to only the most probable, he might never have found out what had happened to them. He certainly never would have met Dylan.

"Maybe," Dylan said.

Connor pushed open the doors that would lead them outside. "Then it's settled," he said, taking Dylan's maybe for a yes. "Let's go see Sofia."

CHAPTER 19

THE INK WELL was attached to one end of a strip mall anchored by a Kroger. In front of the grocery store, the parking lot was full. At the end where the Ink Well was located, not so much.

The place looked like a scaled-back gallery, with artwork hanging on every wall, a handful of small statues on pedestals, and a lot of unused floor space. Each piece had a small sign posted beside it with the title, the author's name, and a price.

There seemed to be no theme—stylistically or otherwise—that connected the art. It was a mishmash of modern and surrealism, abstract and art deco. There were even a few pieces of pop art thrown in, and a bin near the back with sealed prints you could buy for cheap.

"Hello?" Olin said to no one in particular.

A woman appeared from the doorway beside the bin. Her hair was pulled back in a scrunchie. She had splashes of paint in her hair and on her clothes. "You're late. Class has already started." She made a follow-me gesture and started back through the doorway. "Come on. I'll get you set up."

Dylan stepped forward. "Sofia. It's me."

The woman turned back around. "Oh, sweetie, I didn't see you there. I guess you're not here for the class, huh? Is this about Maddie? Do you have news?"

"No, not exactly. I mean—yes, it's about Maddie, but I don't have any news."

Sofia wiped her paint-stained hands on a paint-stained shirt. "Okay, what can I do for you?"

"I'm not sure if you're aware—Aleshia's missing now, too."

Sofia sighed. "That's terrible. No, I didn't." She paused for a second before she added, "You think they're connected?"

"There's a good chance," Olin said.

"I'm not sure how I can help. I've only seen Aleshia once or twice, and you already know everything I do about Maddie." Sofia directed the latter part of her statement to Dylan.

"So, you didn't talk to the police recently?" Connor said.

"No. Why?"

"We went by the station," Dylan said. "It kind of seemed like they might know something."

"They didn't tell you what?"

"No. That's why we're here," Connor said. "We wanted to see if her disappearance might have anything to do with the attack you witnessed a few months back, like maybe you remembered something and passed the information on to them."

Sofia's face changed. She looked down, subtly shook her head. "I'm sorry. I don't."

"Could you tell us what happened again, anyway? Maybe there's a detail or something in there that would help us. Something you didn't think too much about before. Maybe something even Dylan didn't think too much about the first time she heard it."

"Sure. Whatever I can do to help." Sofia took a step toward the stool near the register and leaned back so that she was half-sitting on it. "Maddie had stayed late that day, helping me clean up—arranging the chairs, folding up the easels, stuff like that."

"Was that unusual?" Connor asked.

"No. She usually stayed late to help me clean up. I think she liked the company. I don't know how much you know about Maddie—" She briefly shifted her attention to Dylan. "Well, you know. She didn't like crowds of people. I think helping me clean up was a sort of social activity for her."

"What did you talk about?"

"I don't remember. Nothing much. We never did. We probably talked about the weather or something like that. Nothing ever got deep. I think that's all she ever wanted from that time—a quiet moment where she could be with someone."

Connor thought about Maddie's artwork. It was so different from her father's. It seemed infused with a certain pain he couldn't quite put his finger on. Maybe loneliness. Like she wanted to connect with those around her but didn't know how. This story certainly seemed to support that theory. Then again, he wasn't a psychologist—or an artist. He was curious what Sofia's take on the theory might be.

"I don't know," she said. "I never thought about it. I've seen all sorts of paintings from all sorts of artists. Some of the happiest people I've met have done the darkest work and vice versa. I think it's hard to get inside a person's mind by looking at their artwork. But I'll tell you this. Now that you mention it, I do think there has been a shift in her paintings lately. It was subtle . . ." Sofia paused as she seemed to slide back into memory for a second. "I think the colors she was using lately were a little brighter." She shook her head. "I don't know. She did mention a guy a month or two before she disappeared, so perhaps you're right."

"Was she dating him?"

"I asked her the same question. She just kind of shrugged, so I didn't think too much about it. Like I said, she never got deep. But, between you and me, I think so."

A guy. It was probably nothing, Connor thought. But James had mentioned a guy, also. They should at least try to find out who he was, even if doing so amounted to no more than checking another box. "You don't know his name, do you?"

"I don't think Maddie ever mentioned it."

That was disappointing. He shifted back to the questions they were there to ask. "So, there was nothing unusual about that day."

"Not until she left the studio, no."

"Okay, so tell us about that."

"Well, I was over there." Sofia pointed to the bin of prints along the back wall. "A customer had called a few minutes earlier and asked me to set one aside. When I found what I was looking for and turned back around, Maddie was halfway to her car. I probably wouldn't have noticed if it wasn't for what happened next."

"The attack," Olin said.

"Right. There was a man. He was running straight for Maddie. That's what really caught my eye. I didn't know what to do. I could tell Maddie didn't see him because he was coming up from behind."

"Did you see what he looked like?" Connor asked.

"I don't remember. He was wearing a mask, that much I can tell you. Other than that . . . Jeans, maybe. A long-sleeved shirt of some sort. Nothing distinctive."

Connor remembered Dylan mentioning the mask. He was hoping by asking the question Sofia would be able to give them something more to work with. So much for that.

"Anyway, Maddie must have finally heard him coming because she turned around right before he reached her. The whole thing happened fast. It seemed to me like he might have been after her purse, but Maddie got her pepper spray out of her bag and fired it right into his eyes before he could get hold of it. He stumbled back, and then this truck rolled up."

"A truck?"

"Yeah. One of those F-150s, I think."

Connor also remembered Dylan mentioning a Ford. He had assumed she meant a car. "Okay, go on."

"That's all there is to tell. He got in the truck, and it sped off. The police never figured out who it was. I'm not sure they tried very hard. I don't blame them either. Nobody had been hurt, and there wasn't a lot to go on. There's a camera that overlooks that part of the lot, but the license plate wasn't visible."

There was chatter coming from the hall behind Sofia. It sounded as if her students were getting impatient.

"I have to get back to my class," Sofia said, rising from the stool. "I'm sorry I can't be of more help. Please let me know if you find anything out. I can't believe Aleshia is missing now, too."

"I will," Dylan said.

Then Sofia offered a half-hearted smile and returned through the doorway at the back of the gallery.

CHAPTER 20

CONNOR, DYLAN, AND Olin ate dinner in the hotel restaurant. It was Olin's treat.

Connor asked for a table far enough away from the other guests that they could talk without being overheard.

All three of them ordered overpriced burgers.

"I think my boss is starting to get suspicious," Olin said after the food came. "I got a voicemail from him earlier today asking if I would be in on Monday."

Connor wasn't sure how to respond. He thought his boss was getting suspicious, too. But neither of them needed their jobs—Olin could afford to be unemployed the rest of his life and Connor could easily find another one. What they were doing here was important. They needed to stay until they figured out what had happened to Maddie and Aleshia.

Fortunately, Dylan knew what to say. "You're not thinking about leaving, are you?" She looked first at Olin, then at Connor.

"No," Connor said.

Olin, a little less confidently, agreed. "I was just saying . . ."

Connor took a bite of his burger. "All right, let's think about what we know. Maddie was attacked outside of the Ink Well two months before she disappeared. Probably a purse snatching—"

"It could be like what happened in New York," Olin said.

"Maybe. Either way, they weren't successful. So, wherever Maddie went, it seems she went there by choice."

Olin nodded in agreement.

"Then, a few days ago, Aleshia disappears, also."

"She *didn't* go by choice," Dylan said.

Connor was still on the fence about whether that was true, so he let it pass. "Whatever happened to her, I think we can all agree, she left in a hurry."

"Then we've got the ex-boyfriend," Olin said.

"Right. He claims to have seen Maddie at the bank the same day Aleshia disappeared. Supposedly, that is why he was texting her that night. But the banker I talked to said Maddie hasn't been by in a long time."

"So why is he lying?" Dylan asked.

Connor waited until the server refilled their water glasses before responding. "We don't know that he is. He might be mistaken."

"At least we can be sure Aleshia didn't know where Maddie was, because she put in a police report."

Connor shrugged. "Maybe the guy Maddie was dating put in the report. Until we know for sure who filed it, we shouldn't make assumptions."

"Either way, we need to find out more about him," Olin said.

"Absolutely."

"So where does that leave us?" Dylan said. "It's almost like every time we think we're a step closer to figuring out what happened to them, it's contradicted by something else."

Connor felt his phone vibrate in his pocket. He pulled it out to see who it was. An Atlanta number showed on the screen. That had to be either the banker or someone from the Atlanta Police Department. "Hold on." He clicked to answer. "Hello?"

"Is this Connor?" It was a woman's voice.

"Yes."

"This is Skylar Hall. You came by Southern Trust earlier today to ask me about Ms. Thompson."

Connor felt his heart rate pick up. Had she learned something new? He mouthed the word "banker" at Olin and Dylan. "Yes," he said, trying to keep the excitement out of his voice. "I remember. What's up?"

"I think I might be able to help you find her. I've got information."

"Really? That would be great."

"Hold on. If I give it to you, I want you to promise we can do this together. I want to be part of the search."

That seemed odd. Why would she want to be part of the search?

Olin must have picked up on something because he stopped chewing and raised an eyebrow in Connor's direction.

Connor mouthed, "She wants to help us."

Olin didn't seem to understand.

"Sure. The more the merrier," he said into the phone.

"And I want to split the reward."

Now it made sense.

Connor didn't know there was a reward. He didn't care, either. Skylar could have the whole thing, as far as he was concerned. But before he said anything to that effect, he wanted to be sure a reward existed. He mouthed the word "reward" at Dylan and gave her a questioning look. He figured if there was one available, she would know about it.

Dylan nodded and pulled her phone out of her purse to type something.

"Okay," Connor said.

"Great. I looked you up online. If anybody can find Ms. Thompson, I believe it's you."

She paused, and Connor said "Thank you" just because he felt like he needed to say something.

Dylan turned her phone around so Connor could read the screen. She had typed: *Aleshia posted a reward online.*

Then Skylar explained the information she had was on her computer at Southern Trust. She could stop by the bank in the morning and get it.

"All right. What time should I expect your call?"

"No. Let's meet. Like I said, I want to help you find her."

Connor considered that. There wouldn't be much for Skylar to do after they spoke again in the morning. Perhaps she was worried that, if she wasn't present when they found Maddie, they would keep the reward for themselves.

He should probably tell Skylar that Aleshia was missing, too, and that getting the reward would mean finding both of them. And he would. Eventually. Right now, he didn't want to complicate the conversation. He needed the information Skylar could provide.

"What time?"

"Ten o'clock?"

"All right. I'm staying at the Grand Hyatt in Buckhead. How about you meet me here?"

"Swanky."

"Is that a yes?"

"I'll see you then." Skylar hung up.

Connor put his phone back on the table. "Why didn't you mention the reward?" he asked Dylan.

"Because we started this thing looking for Aleshia. Besides, it's been out there for a while, and it hasn't turned up anything. I pretty much forgot about it."

"Well, it turned up something now."

"Did I hear you right?" Olin asked. "Skylar is coming here in the morning?"

"She wants to be part of the search. Probably wants to make sure she's there to claim the reward when Maddie is found."

"Whatever," Dylan said.

Olin made a face.

"What?" Connor asked. "As far as I'm concerned, if all of Atlanta wants to help us in the search, that's okay with me."

"I've got a bad feeling about this."

"That's because you worry about everything," Dylan said.

"What does she say she has for us, anyway?" Olin asked.

Connor filled them in on the information Skylar had told him she could get and his plan for how to use it.

Dylan leaned back in her chair. "I take it she doesn't know Aleshia is missing, too."

"It doesn't seem like it."

Dylan responded to that with only a nod, and Olin did not seem to respond at all. As far as Connor could tell, they both seemed to have reached the same conclusion he had: They needed that information. If it got them to Maddie, it would almost certainly get them closer to Aleshia, anyway, which would also get Skylar closer to the reward. Everyone would win.

"We're stuck until tomorrow, then, I guess. Right?" Dylan said.

"Maybe not," Connor said. "When we're done here, let's go back up to the room and see what else we can find out about James." He was about to take another bite of his burger when he added, "While we're at it, let's see what we can dig up about Maddie, as well."

"I already did that," Dylan said.

"You looked into James?"

"No. Maddie."

"When?"

"As soon as I told Aleshia I would see if I could find her."

"Let's look again, anyway," Connor said. "Maybe there's something new we can find out. Like who that guy was Sofia and James told us about."

CHAPTER 21

BACK IN THEIR suite, they took a divide-and-conquer approach. Connor looked into James on his computer while Dylan looked into Maddie on Aleshia's. Olin sat back and watched them work. Dylan was better than Connor was at scouring the dark web, and since she had already been through public records, she started there. Connor went straight for the social media sites. When each had gone as far as they could with the name they had selected, they would switch.

Right away, Connor picked up on a disturbing trend. James seemed to have clicked the like button on every single one of Aleshia's Facebook posts. Then he navigated to James's profile and saw he still had himself marked as "in a relationship."

If that wasn't a bad sign, Connor wasn't sure what was.

He thought about how James had reacted when they had talked to him. James had gotten angry, defensive. While it had made him look innocent at the time, it occurred to Connor now that that might have been exactly what it was intended to do. This was, after all, a common tactic employed by the guilty when they were cornered.

It was too bad they hadn't found Aleshia's phone at her house. He wished he could see the messages James had sent.

Then he got an idea. Not about James. About Maddie. He should have thought to check this out yesterday when he'd first gone through

Aleshia's computer. "Does she have Outlook?" he asked Dylan.

Dylan moved the mouse, clicked a few times. "No."

"What's her email address?"

Dylan told him. The only part he cared about was the domain. Gmail. There was a chance he could hack into the account if he needed to. But this was Aleshia's personal computer. He probably wouldn't need to. "Go to Gmail. See if she's already logged in."

Dylan brought up a new browser window, and Connor slid his chair over so he could see the screen.

Olin, whose chair was already positioned to give him a view of Aleshia's monitor, leaned in. "What are you thinking?"

"Their disappearances are related, right? That much we all agree on. So maybe we can find an email to or from Maddie that will help us figure out how. If it was something big enough to cause all this, they must have talked about it one way or another."

Dylan scrolled through the inbox and then the sent emails. Since she didn't know Maddie's email address, she opened every message that she couldn't automatically rule out. When she was done, they still had nothing. Any exchange the two women might have had on the subject that had led to their current situation had not happened here.

"It was a good thought, anyway," Dylan said, and went back to her previous search.

Connor likewise went back to his. He could feel an idea niggling at the back of his brain. There was still something he could do, something he had missed.

If I could only see James's messages . . .

Then the idea pushed forward into conscious thought. He felt himself straighten up a little. A sudden, shallow breath. *Of course.* It was so obvious; he couldn't believe he hadn't thought of it before.

"What kind of phone did Aleshia have?"

"An iPhone. Why?"

Connor slid his chair back over, directed her to iCloud.

"You're thinking . . . ?"

"Exactly."

"What?" Olin asked.

Dylan needed no more instruction. She went straight to iCloud.com. "If she's not already logged in . . ." Dylan said, ignoring Olin's question.

"But if she is . . ." Connor responded.

"*What?*" Olin asked again.

The page loaded. As Connor and Dylan had hoped, Aleshia was already logged in. Dylan clicked the icon for "Find My iPhone."

According to the next screen that loaded, the phone was still on. It had last broadcast its location less than a minute ago.

"That's her," Olin said. "There she is. I can't believe this worked."

"Should we call the police?" Dylan said.

Olin turned to face her. "What for? We know where she is. Let's go find out why she disappeared."

Connor wasn't sure either idea was great. If Aleshia had been taken against her will, like Dylan suspected, calling the police was the right move. If she had run off, like Olin suspected, she probably didn't want to be found, and confronting her would have to be done carefully.

"I think we should go out there and assess the situation. Then we can decide how to handle it." He could tell Olin and Dylan both wanted to object. "Regardless of what you two think, we don't know what we're walking into, okay? I'm simply suggesting we get the lay of the land first."

"Fine."

Olin shrugged.

Connor pointed to the green dot on the map that represented Aleshia's phone. It was located along Highway 9, on top of a large gray mass that represented a building. "Do you know where that is?"

"Not exactly," Dylan said. "But we've got the cross street. We should be able to find it."

The cross street was Briarcliff Lane. It was a tiny strip of a road. Perhaps an apartment complex or a neighborhood, Connor thought. He put the street name into the map application on his phone. "It's thirty minutes away." Then he closed the screen on Aleshia's laptop, unplugged it from the power cable, and headed for the door with the machine under his arm. "Let's go."

"What are you taking that for?" Olin asked.

"She might not still be there when we arrive," Connor said. "If that's the case, we need to know where to go next."

CHAPTER 22

THEY FOLLOWED THE directions to Highway 9, a busy four-lane road with a wide median, and from there up to Briarcliff Lane.

Briarcliff Lane was neither a neighborhood nor an apartment complex. A metal gate closed it off to the public and a chain secured the gate in place. A sign next to it indicated the road led onto government property, the purpose of which seemed intentionally vague.

Dylan pulled to the side of the road. She put on her hazards, looked around. "Are you sure this is right?"

Most of the way up here, Highway 9 had been crowded with strip malls and restaurants. All sorts of businesses, really. For the last mile, that started to thin. And here, there was only one building close enough to Briarcliff Lane that it could be the gray mass Connor had seen on the map.

A warehouse. Lights off. Parking lot empty.

Sitting in the passenger seat, Connor lifted Aleshia's laptop off the floor and turned it on. After using his phone to connect it to the internet, he refreshed the screen. Find My iPhone reported the device was still in this area.

Dylan looked over at the warehouse. It was hard to see much in the dark. "They could have lights on in back."

"Let's go check it out," Connor said.

"All of us?" Olin asked.

That was what Connor was thinking, but now that he had heard Olin's question, he began to wonder if it was indeed the best plan. The more people who went up there, the greater the odds were of getting caught. "You're right. You guys stay here."

"Hold on," Dylan said.

"If I see something and think you guys should come up there, I'll call you." Then he got out of the car and started up the driveway.

This was not ideal, he thought uneasily. He would rather have made his way along the edge of the property and approached the building from the rear. But since buildings were few and far between here, he would have had to fight his way through the thick vegetation surrounding the parking lot to do so, and that would undoubtedly draw even more attention if somebody saw him.

At least this way, if someone intercepted him, he could say Dylan's car had broken down, that he was looking for help.

The gravel driveway crunched under his shoes. With every step, the warehouse seemed farther away than it did before. He kept his eyes glued to the only window he could see. If there was even a flicker of light beyond it, he wanted to know.

There had been no sign by the road identifying the business. Now that he was close enough to the warehouse to see beyond the shadows that engulfed it, he could tell there was none here, either.

Something was wrong. What business wouldn't take advantage of the free advertising that came with a brick-and-mortar location?

That answer came when Connor got close enough to the window to see the "For Rent" sign placed behind it. That sign did not make him feel any better. There was no debate about whether Aleshia's phone was here, and he couldn't imagine a reason in the world she would be hanging out in an empty warehouse by choice.

Lately, Connor had been on the fence about whether he agreed with Dylan's assessment that Aleshia was taken against her will. This development put him firmly back in her camp.

Connor gently tried the door to see if it was unlocked. Then he circled the building in search of another window. He found ten or so along the rear wall, all six feet or more in diameter. They were dark, as well.

Maybe Aleshia had been here at one time but was no longer, he thought. Maybe the only reason her phone was here was that she had left it behind.

He weighed his options. There did not seem to be any good ones. He wasn't going to call the police out to an empty warehouse. He also wasn't going to break a window and charge into a space so dark that— Aleshia or no Aleshia—it might be hiding all kinds of nasty secrets.

Well, there was no longer any reason to be discreet, he decided. If there was anybody inside, they would have a clear view of him. And, at this point, he'd been standing around the back of the building so long, they would no doubt be wondering what he was up to.

He pulled out his phone, turned on the flashlight app, and shined the light through the nearest window. The space was nearly empty. Half a dozen machines of indiscernible purpose were scattered across the floor, abandoned and covered in dust. A catwalk ran along three of the walls close to the ceiling. A pair of large bay doors had been built into the wall to his left and, no doubt, faced a loading dock.

Connor returned to the car and got in. "It's empty. Just some old, abandoned place. I have no idea what it was for. Manufacturing, I suppose."

"So, she's not here?" Dylan asked.

"It doesn't look like it."

Olin shifted forward in his seat. "But her phone . . ."

Connor shook his head. "I didn't see it. It has to be in there somewhere, but I'm not sure it matters. I don't see how we would get to it."

Then all three of them were quiet for a moment. Perhaps, like Connor, Olin and Dylan were trying to decide what to do next. Suddenly, Dylan turned in her seat to face him, practically bouncing as she did so. "What if it's not in the warehouse?"

"You've seen the computer. It has to be."

"What if it's outside?"

"Like around the building somewhere?"

"Or out here," she said, pointing toward the side of the road.

Connor looked out at the darkness stretching infinitely beyond the headlights. He had assumed the phone would have to be in the building the icon was closest to. Now that he thought about it, though, he couldn't remember seeing any footprints along the dusty floor—or any other disturbance, for that matter.

It didn't seem like anybody had been there in a long time.

So maybe Dylan was right. However, if the phone was out here, around the building or somewhere along this dark stretch of road, how were they going to find it? They could spend hours searching through the weeds alone. Even if they were right on top of it, they might miss it.

Connor had an idea. He lifted the laptop back onto his lap, waited for it to reconnect to the internet, and clicked on the green dot that represented Aleshia's phone. Then he clicked "Play Sound."

The feature was one Apple had built to help users find a lost device. Likely, the developers hadn't imagined anyone would be looking for said device along the side of a road, and certainly they hadn't imagined anyone would be looking for it intending to track down a missing person, but if there was ever a reason to use the feature, this was it.

He opened the door, listened, heard nothing.

He explained in brief to Dylan and Olin what he had done. "Let's spread out, see what we can find."

Each of them headed off in a different direction. Olin walked north along Highway 9 and Dylan went south. Connor went back up the driveway toward the warehouse.

He was halfway to the building when Dylan shouted, "I hear it! It's somewhere over here!"

Connor turned to see her moving slowly into the weeds along the side of the road. He and Olin hurried over to where she was, and now Connor could hear it, too. "It's that way," he said.

They pushed the weeds aside with every step so they could see the ground.

"Found it!" Olin said, as he reached down and grabbed Aleshia's phone.

At the same time, Connor heard his own phone ring. It was an Atlanta number, but not Skylar's. Or, at least, not the one she had called from before. He held up a finger to tell Dylan and Olin to quiet down and then answered.

"Mr. Callahan?" It was a male voice.

"Yes?"

"This is Detective Shaw. You were down at the station earlier asking about Ms. Thompson, correct?"

Connor wasn't sure if he meant Aleshia or Maddie. Either way, the answer was "Yes."

"Is Dylan Naese with you?"

Connor glanced at Dylan. "Yes."

What? she mouthed.

"Could you come back?" the detective said. "I'd like to have a word with you two."

"Now?"

"Yes, now."

CHAPTER 23

SEVERAL HOURS EARLIER, Detective Alex Shaw had arrived at the medical examiner's office. After he and his partner had done their due diligence to verify Jake Avarnatti's story, Howie had left for the day. Alex was on his own. That was okay with him. He was in no rush to go home. Dexter was staying with his ex-wife tonight, so the house would be quiet.

One might expect that, after a late night working on a last-minute school project about volcanoes, a quiet night at home would be exactly what he needed. But no matter how frustrating Dexter could be sometimes, Alex always missed him when he wasn't around.

The chief medical examiner was named Lucas Walsh. He was barely in his thirties. Too young for the job, some of the detectives complained. Especially when the evidence didn't go their way. But Alex knew he was good at what he did. He trusted the man.

Lucas was aware of all this. As such, he would prioritize Alex's cases whenever he could.

Alex pushed through a pair of double doors into a lab. The room had a chill to it he wasn't sure he would ever get used to. It smelled of formaldehyde. In the middle of the room, there was a body on a rolling metal gurney and covered with a sheet.

It was their Jane Doe.

Lucas was wearing a white lab coat and had his back to both the body and the doors. He seemed to be writing something down.

"Doctor."

Lucas turned around. Alex could see a folder filled with a small stack of paper behind him. "Good to see you, Alex."

"What have you got for me?"

Lucas pulled back the sheet, revealing the victim's head and shoulders. The blood had been cleaned off her forehead, exposing a small cut. "The victim suffered multiple blows to the head and torso, pre- and postmortem."

The latter had likely occurred when the killer was moving the body to Lake Lanier, Alex suspected.

"The cause of death appears to have been a single blow to the back of the skull. Based on where the body was found as well as indicators like rigor mortis and decomposition, I suspect she was killed in the last forty-eight to seventy-two hours."

"Any idea what the killer might have used?"

Lucas shook his head. "I can't help you there."

"How about a name?"

Lucas turned to the papers behind him. "DMV came back with a fingerprint match about an hour ago. Aleshia Thompson."

"Are you sure?"

"Yes."

Lucas then reviewed the rest of his findings. In all, it took about twenty minutes. When he was done, the takeaways were only those he had stated upon Alex's arrival: the victim had been killed by a blunt object, she had been dead for two to three days, and her name was Aleshia Thompson.

Alex knew the name because he and his partner had been assigned her sister's missing person case when it came in. He called Howie to report the news on his way back to his car.

Howie responded with one word: "Shit."

They both knew what he meant.

Alex originally planned to go straight home after he was done with the ME. Now, though, he felt an urgent need to get back to his desk. There was information in it he wanted to review again with fresh eyes.

He drove slowly as he tried to think through the implications of what he had just learned. Muscle memory guided him through turn after turn. A subconscious switch in his brain moved his foot to the brake at red lights and back to the gas when they turned green.

On most nights, that would have been fine. Because on most nights, a kid on a bicycle wouldn't have hopped off the curb right in front of him.

Alex slammed on the brakes, swerved left to avoid the kid, then right to avoid a stop sign (which he also hadn't seen until now). He braced for the sound of crunching metal, the screams of a child.

Thank God he heard neither.

When the car came to a stop, his head whipped around as he tried to assess the situation. The kid—not much older than Dexter—was still on his bike, pedaling quickly away and looking over his shoulder at Alex. There were no other cars around.

Alex took a deep breath. He wasn't just distracted. He was also exhausted. The coffee he'd been pounding all day was wearing off.

He cursed himself for not being more careful and decided to shelve his thoughts about the case until he got back to HQ. Then he backed up into his lane and straightened out the car. He paused at the stop sign, even though he was still alone. He wasn't taking any more chances. Not tonight.

When he got back to his desk, he found a slip of paper waiting for him. In one style of handwriting, it said, "Someone came by asking about Madeleine Thompson."

That part of the message was signed by the officer who had been working the front desk. Below it, in another handwriting, was the name "Connor" and a phone number.

Alex had a bad feeling.

First Aleshia had turned up dead. Now this.

It felt like too much of a coincidence. Alex didn't like coincidences.

He sat down at the computer and used one of the department's many internal tools to search for the phone number, which provided him with Connor's full name and address, as well as various links that could take him to common areas of interest, like the man's criminal history.

Other than a few traffic tickets in New York, Connor had none.

Wait, there was one thing—a note detailing a conversation an officer had had with Connor outside Southern Trust earlier today. He was with a Ms. Dylan Naese, who had illegally parked in a loading zone, the officer had noted. Connor had tried to take responsibility for Dylan's decision to park there, pleaded with the officer not to write her a ticket.

A link to the related record for Dylan confirmed he must have been successful since she left with just a warning.

Police officers regularly recorded their interactions with the public when they made arrests or issued citations. In itself, nothing about their exchange struck Alex as unusual. The part that got his attention was where it had happened.

Alex already knew Madeleine Thompson had bank accounts at Southern Trust, which added another touchpoint between Connor and the Thompson family in the last twenty-four hours. Where a single coincidence was enough to make one wonder, two was enough to start looking like circumstantial evidence.

He pulled out his cell phone and called Howie again. "I think you'd better come back in."

CHAPTER 24

CONNOR GOT THE impression there was only one right answer to the question Detective Shaw had asked. "We'll be right there." He hung up, looked at Olin and Dylan. All three of them were still standing in the weeds along the side of Highway 9.

"That was a detective from the Atlanta Police Department. He wants us to go back to the station. Something about Maddie or Aleshia."

"Great," Olin said. "Let's go."

"Hold on. I'm not so sure it's such a good idea for you to come with us. He only asked for Dylan and me. You should go back to the hotel. We'll come when we're finished."

"Why shouldn't I go with you?"

"Well, first of all, it's late. Why is he asking us to go down there at this hour? If this was just a routine update, why not tell me on the phone? Until we know what he wants, I think it would be best to keep you out of it."

"Why do you think he only asked for you two?"

"I don't know," Connor said. Then he pointed to Aleshia's phone. "But, second of all, now we've got that. Until we've had a chance to check it out ourselves, I don't want to get it anywhere near the station. If they find out we have it, they'll take it into evidence, and we'll never see what's on it."

"They wouldn't find out," Olin said.

Connor shrugged. "Let's err on the side of caution, okay?"

He didn't want to say that part of him also worried the detective might split them up, question them individually. Dylan was a good liar; she and Connor could agree on a story in advance, and he could trust she would stick to it. Olin was not.

What would happen if it came out they had been in Aleshia's house? Or Maddie's? What would happen if Olin slipped up and mentioned they had been on Aleshia's computer?

What if, somehow, the police already knew one or all of those things?

What if—and this could be the only reason Detective Shaw would be asking Connor and Dylan to meet at this time of night—the police thought they were involved?

"Fine," Olin said. "We'll do it your way."

Dylan handed the car keys over to Olin. He dropped her and Connor off at the police station and returned to the hotel.

Connor watched the Volvo until it was out of sight. He told himself everything would be fine. Then he and Dylan retraced their steps— through the metal detector, across the lobby, down the elevator—to the same desk they had stood at earlier today, asking about information on Aleshia and Maddie. A different officer was behind it.

Connor announced himself and said Detective Shaw had asked them to come by. A moment later, Detective Shaw was ushering them through a series of doors to a room somewhere deep in the building. The room was mostly empty. A table was pushed up to the wall with chairs on three sides. No two-way mirror, Connor noticed. But there was a camera mounted near the ceiling, which, he figured, was the modern-day equivalent.

Connor had been right to be concerned when the detective called them in. You don't put somebody in a room like this unless you want to question them.

The detective sat down in one chair and directed Connor to another—this one facing the camera. Dylan took the third.

The detective looked tired. TV-cop tired, Connor thought. Like this man was up night and day chasing down bad guys and drinking hard when he wasn't. Perhaps that was why he was toting around a Styrofoam cup of coffee.

The detective seemed to notice Connor looking at it. "Want some?"

"I'm fine."

Connor wondered who might be on the other side of that camera. Don't detectives usually work in pairs? Then again, who knew? He didn't have much experience with the police. The only other detective he had ever encountered was up in New York. She had seemed to be working on her own, so maybe this guy was, too. Maybe the only thing on the other side of that camera was a digital recorder so Detective Shaw could later parse their answers, looking for lies.

Connor could feel his thoughts spinning wildly. He tried to calm down. "What can we do for you, Detective?"

"Call me Alex. I wanted to talk to you about Ms. Thompson."

"You mean Maddie or Aleshia?" Dylan said.

That seemed to give the detective pause. He took a sip from his coffee, stared at Dylan for an uncomfortably long time. "Madeleine," he finally said.

"I take it you didn't call us down here just to give us the information we were asking about earlier," Connor said, trying to play it cool.

"About that. Why were you down here asking about her, anyway?"

"We were trying to find her."

"That's why you were at Southern Trust earlier today, also?"

A memory of Skylar sitting behind her desk flashed through Connor's mind. Had she called the police and told them he had been there asking about Maddie? No. That didn't make sense. Why would she tell Connor she would help him find Maddie and then call the police to report his visit? If she wanted to get any part of the reward Aleshia was offering, she needed him. Besides, that wouldn't explain why he had asked for Dylan as well.

Then Connor remembered the police officer he had encountered outside the bank. The one who had taken his ID and ultimately let Dylan off with a warning. That had to be how Alex knew they had been there, which begged the next series of questions: Why *had* he asked them to come in? Didn't Alex know Dylan was the one who had filed the missing person report for Aleshia? And if he did, why would it seem so strange to him that they were looking for Aleshia's sister?

Because it definitely seemed strange to him—that much was obvious.

"Yes, that's why we were at Southern Trust."

"You don't think that would be a job better left to the police?"

"No offense," Dylan said, "but Maddie has been missing for a month, and so far, you guys haven't turned up anything. And now Aleshia's missing, too."

"How do you know Aleshia's missing?"

Connor noticed the detective didn't ask who Aleshia was. Not when her name was first mentioned or now. Nor did he seem surprised by the news.

Dylan looked directly into the camera. "I'm the one who put in the missing person report. Duh."

"What's your relationship to the Thompson sisters?"

"I'm Aleshia's friend."

"How long have you known her?"

"Four years."

"How did you meet?"

"We worked together at Cafe de Flore. It's like a restaurant—"

"I know it. When was the last time you saw her?"

"A week ago."

"What day?"

"Sunday."

"What makes you think she's missing?"

Dylan huffed. "I was supposed to meet up with her a few days ago. She didn't show up, didn't answer my texts, and wasn't at her house when I went by. That's not like her. Something's wrong."

The detective marched through a list of questions about Dylan's relationship to Aleshia, asking them as fast as she could answer and ending with one he had asked already: "How did you meet?"

"I told you." Dylan sounded like she was getting impatient.

Alex took another slow sip from his coffee. Connor wasn't sure if he had repeated the question because he was tired or because he was testing the veracity of Dylan's story.

"How well do you know Madeleine?"

"I don't. Not really."

"But you thought it would be a good idea to go looking for her."

"We thought if we found one of them, we might find the other," Connor said.

"And you," Alex said, now turning his attention to Connor. "How do you know Madeleine and Aleshia?"

"I don't."

"You came down from New York to look for two women you don't know?"

"Dylan asked me to help her, so I'm here."

"Don't try to explain," Dylan said. "He wouldn't understand. I can tell by looking at him he doesn't have any friends."

Connor thought he saw annoyance on the detective's face.

Alex tapped his cup of coffee on the table as he looked from Connor to Dylan, then finished what was left in it. He glanced down at the empty cup. "I'm going to get a refill. I'll be back soon."

This time, Connor noticed, he did not ask either of them if they would like any. Once the detective left the room, he turned to Dylan. "Don't say stuff like that."

"Why not?"

"You're just going to antagonize him."

"This whole thing is ridiculous," Dylan said. "You know he thinks we're suspects or something. Why? Because we went by Southern Trust to ask about Maddie? Because we came by here?" She pointed to herself. "I'm the one who put in the missing report on Aleshia—why shouldn't I come ask about it?"

"I know. You're right. But you saw how the cop reacted when we were here earlier asking about Maddie. They know something. Maybe they think because we came here earlier, we're trying to find out what it is. Like how criminals will sometimes insert themselves into investigations to try to keep tabs on the police."

"That doesn't happen in real life."

"I bet it does once in a while."

"Fine. But even if it does, they can't go around treating every person who comes in asking about a case as a suspect."

"Look, I don't have all the answers. Can you keep your lip under control for now? It would be nice to get out of here without making things worse."

CHAPTER 25

ALEX WENT DOWN the hall to another small room with a stack of monitors along one wall, a coffee maker, and a table with chairs that matched those in the room he had just left. Howie was sitting in the one farthest from the door.

He stepped inside just in time to hear Connor's voice from the speaker: "Look, I don't have all the answers. Can you keep your lip under control for now? It would be nice to get out of here without making things worse."

"What was that about?" Alex said.

"Callahan's telling Naese to keep her mouth shut. He doesn't want her antagonizing you."

"That's it?"

"They talked a little about your questions, why you're talking to them. Stuff like that. You've seen it before."

Alex had, and knew better than to put much stock in the conversations people had when he was not in the room. Often it was simply "play-acting for the camera," as Howie called it.

Alex closed the door. "Did you know about the missing person report?"

"How would I know about that? I didn't even know who Dylan was until you called me."

"What do you think?"

"If she really put in a report . . ." His head teetered from side to side.

"Yeah, maybe. She also could have put it in to make herself look innocent. All we know is these two came out of nowhere looking for Maddie right after Aleshia turned up dead."

"Why don't you try using that? Tell them Aleshia's dead and see how they react."

Alex went over to the coffee maker and refilled his cup. "I'll think about it."

CHAPTER 26

ALEX CALLED CAFE de Flore and confirmed that, yes, Dylan and Aleshia had worked there at the same time. He looked up the missing person report she claimed to have filed and saw that it was in order, as well. Then, before he returned to the room, he stopped by to see his partner one more time. "How are they looking?"

"They're not saying much."

"Anything I can use?"

He shook his head.

Alex put Connor and Dylan through another thirty minutes of questions. He never split them up, Connor noticed. Never asked whether they had been at Aleshia's or Maddie's house. Then he dropped the bomb. "We found Aleshia's body this morning."

Connor, who was about to ask if they were almost finished, was stunned into silence.

"Are you sure?" Dylan said. "Couldn't it be . . ." She trailed off to nothing. Connor could see her struggling to come up with a theory that would explain away the news as a mistake.

"We're sure," Alex said before she could speak again.

Dylan's hands started to tremble. She clasped them together in her lap.

Alex sighed. "I'm sorry." It seemed like the first genuine thing he had said since they'd arrived.

"Where?" Dylan asked.

"Along Lake Lanier."

"What was she doing there?"

The detective didn't answer.

"Do you know what happened to her?"

"Not yet, but we will." Alex crossed back to the door and held it open. "Go home."

Connor let Dylan leave first. On his way out, Alex grabbed his arm. "Hey, where are you staying?"

"The Grand Hyatt. Why?"

"Are you planning on going back to New York soon?"

"I don't know."

"How about you stick around town for a while, all right?"

Connor nervously nodded, and Alex let go of his arm.

Alex had seen his share of con artists. There were plenty of people who could cry on cue. Was Dylan one of them? He wasn't sure. Either way, he had no reason to hold her or Connor any longer. When someone started to break down, real or not, it was best to call it quits. He could always take another crack at them later.

Like after the lab got back to him with DNA results from the nose ring.

Alex had looked closely at Connor and Dylan to see if he could see evidence of a piercing. He could not. But that didn't mean it wasn't there.

Dylan managed to hold herself together until she and Connor were outside. Then the trembling in her hands was joined by sniffles and, by the time Connor had finished ordering an Uber, tears.

He held her until the car came. "Everything's going to be all right," he said, which clearly wasn't true. Things were already well past that point.

"We have to find out what happened to her," Dylan said, her voice strained and halting. "Somebody has to pay for this."

"We will." Not just to make sure somebody paid for it either, Connor thought. To make sure the *right* person paid for it. Based on their conversation with Alex, that might not happen if they sat on the sidelines. (Connor refused to consider the possibility that, no matter how things played out, they might be the "someone" who paid for it.)

"And we need to find Maddie. If she's still alive, she might be in danger, too. Maybe that's even why she ran off."

CHAPTER 27

THE UBER DRIVER had 4.6 stars, according to the app. He had snacks and sodas for passengers in various places around the car, as well as a wide variety of magazines tucked into the pockets behind the front seats. *People, Cosmopolitan, Time, Vogue*. And *Highlights* for the kids.

He offered them all to Connor and Dylan when they got in the car via a spiel that sounded rehearsed. He even had a box of Kleenex, which, when he realized Dylan was crying, he passed back to her. However, he must not have had much experience with passengers who were so upset, because he seemed unsure about what to do next.

An uncertain "You're welcome" bled into a question about what music they would like.

When Connor said, "Just take us to the hotel," the driver did not speak again until they arrived.

"I don't want to go upstairs yet," Dylan said, once they were out of the car. "I don't want Olin to see me like this."

Connor put his arm around her. "He's here for you, just like I am."

"I don't even want *you* to see me like this." She gestured to Connor and then to herself and then to the Kleenex the driver had given her, which she proceeded to wipe under her nose.

Connor understood. Dylan came across as a tough, no-nonsense girl who didn't have a problem telling you what was on her mind. Connor knew that if he hadn't already been there, she would have found somewhere private to work through her emotions by herself.

"You want to go to the bar?" he asked. "We can sit there as long as you like."

"People will see me."

Connor remembered an outdoor dining area off the restaurant and metal benches along the exterior wall. Although it was open to the public, he suspected it was too cold outside for anyone to be there. "Come on," he said and led Dylan around the building.

He was right. Although people were eating indoors, they had the patio to themselves. They sat down on a bench.

"I can't believe she's gone," Dylan said.

"I know."

"I was sure we were going to find her in time."

"I know."

"Do you think Maddie's dead, too? Do you think it's just a matter of time until her body turns up?"

It was possible, Connor thought. He had worried about the same thing in New York years back when his parents were abducted. He told Dylan what he'd told himself then. "Don't think like that. All we know is Maddie's missing. It's like you said—we're going to find her. Let's stay focused on what we need to do."

Dylan nodded and cried some more. When the tissue was no longer usable, she wiped her eyes with her sleeve.

Connor could tell from the way Dylan was breathing she was trying to bring her emotions under control. Eventually, she did. "We need to go look at Aleshia's phone," she said. She sounded fragile, like the pain might overtake her again at any moment.

But Connor wasn't going to say as much. Sometimes the only way to move forward in life was to just keep going. He knew that firsthand.

They went back to the room, where they found Olin sitting at the table, staring at Aleshia's cell phone. He jumped out of his chair when they came in. "What's going on? What did the police want?"

"They just wanted to ask us some questions," Connor said.

"About what?"

Connor waved his hand dismissively. "It's not important."

"Did they ask about what we did at Aleshia's? Or Maddie's?"

"It didn't come up."

Olin had been moving closer to them with each question. When he was practically on top of them, Dylan slipped past him and went for the phone.

Olin turned in her direction. "What's wrong?"

He must have been able to tell she had been crying, Connor thought. Not that it was hard to figure out with her bloodshot eyes and the skin under her nose still raw.

"Aleshia's dead," Connor said.

"Oh my God."

"I don't want to talk about it." Dylan's voice sounded steadier than it had outside. She picked up Aleshia's phone. "Let's see what this thing has for us." She punched in Aleshia's code. "You'd better be worth it for all the trouble we went through to get you."

Connor felt the same way. He and Olin moved close enough to Dylan that they could see the screen over her shoulder.

Aleshia had nine new messages and twice as many missed calls from James.

Where are you?

Why don't you pick up?

Don't ignore me. This is important.

I'm worried about you. Your friends seem to think you're missing. Call me back as soon as you get this.

Seriously. I'm not screwing around anymore. Answer your DAMN PHONE!

Aleshia!

Okay, I understand you might not want to talk to me. You at least need to let me know you're all right.

Aleshia?

Call me whenever you get this. I'm not going to be able to sleep until I hear from you.

"Somebody needs to tell him what happened to her," Olin said.

Dylan scrolled further down. "I want to see what he sent to her the night she was out with Tyler."

Those were immediately below the previous nine and said pretty much what Tyler had told them they did.

Call me back.

This is important.

I know you're not into me anymore, but I need to talk to you.

Seriously. Please. You'll want to hear this.

On and on they went. The last message Aleshia had responded to was weeks ago.

"Obsess much?" Dylan said, mostly to herself.

"At least we know Tyler was telling the truth," Connor said.

Dylan closed the conversation with James and checked the rest of Aleshia's recent messages. There was one confirming an appointment at Massage Envy and a verification code from Netflix. She also had a history of texts between her and Maddie. The most recent ones mirrored those she had received from James: Where was she? Was she okay? Why won't Maddie respond?

Prior to that, the exchanges were separated by weeks, sometimes months, and included little information about their lives. Usually, it was merely one asking the other if they would like to meet.

The most recent meeting, if the texts were to be believed, had happened about two weeks before Maddie went missing, and had taken place at Brick's, where James worked. At first, that made the small hairs on the back of Connor's neck stand up. Then he saw, as Dylan scrolled through the messages, that all of their meetings seemed to have taken place there. Which, now that he thought about it, wasn't so surprising. It was one of Maddie's favorite places to go. Hadn't James even said Aleshia had been in there before to see her sister? Yes, he had. That was how James and Aleshia had met.

But, either way, there they were—back at James again. The man who had liked all of Aleshia's Facebook posts and still had himself marked as "in a relationship." The man who had sent messages to Aleshia that, as Dylan rightly put it, seemed to border on obsessive. The man who had tried to explain those messages with a story about Maddie that couldn't be verified.

Dylan finished searching Aleshia's phone by going through her pictures and email, then dropped it onto the table and collapsed into the closest chair. "There's nothing there."

"Just the messages James sent," Connor clarified.

"Right," Dylan said thoughtfully. "There are those."

"He knew both women," Olin added, and Connor got the feeling Olin was thinking the same thing he was.

Dylan looked down at the phone. "I can see him going after Aleshia for breaking up with him. He's certainly the type, isn't he? But Maddie? Why would he go after her?"

Olin took a seat, too. "And if he is our guy, how are we going to prove it?"

CHAPTER 28

DYLAN DIDN'T WANT to go back to her apartment. She didn't want to be alone. So, Olin brought her some pillows and a blanket from his room, and she slept on the pullout sofa.

When Connor woke up, Dylan was already back at Aleshia's computer. She had folded the bed back into the sofa, stacked up the pillows, and made a pot of coffee in the small coffee maker on the counter.

"How long have you been up?"

She spun around quickly, surprised to see him there.

She must not have heard him come out of the bedroom, Connor thought. He had never known her to be so distracted that she forgot about her surroundings. What could be on that screen?

"An hour." She waved him over. "Come here. I want to show you something."

Connor did.

"Look."

She had James's Facebook timeline up on the computer. Connor recognized it from the research he had done yesterday. He had even seen the post Dylan was directing him to look at: a check-in at a Best Western in Savannah.

"So?"

"So? Look at the date. That's the day Aleshia disappeared."

When Connor had seen the post before, he had not paid it much attention. He had been far more interested in seeking out touchpoints between James's life and Aleshia's. A check-in at a hotel in Savannah had seemed meaningless at the time. However, now that Dylan had pointed out the date . . .

"How far away is that?"

"Four hours, I think. Maybe a little more."

Connor crossed his arms over his chest. "He has an alibi." They were back to square one.

"Actually, I'm not sure. That may be exactly what he wanted people to think. Four hours isn't that far away. He would still have had plenty of time to kill Aleshia. Besides, look at this." She scrolled up. "There's another check-in at a Starbucks here in Atlanta the next day. What makes it particularly strange is he doesn't seem to check in to a lot of places. I went through his timeline for the last three months and found only one other one—a bar called Shotgun Steve's."

"You think he was trying to create a digital footprint that would prove he couldn't be the killer because he wasn't in town?"

"Maybe. If I'm right, the Starbucks check-in was probably his way of announcing he was back. That way, if anybody had seen him around Atlanta the next day, nobody would question it."

Connor sat down next to Dylan. He noticed the post associated with the Starbucks check-in read "Hell of a night!" Was that a thinly veiled admission of guilt? There was no way for Connor to know, so he focused on the check-in itself instead. "You think he drove to Savannah, checked into Facebook, and drove back?"

"Could be. It's also possible he didn't go there at all."

Connor looked doubtful.

"Let me show you." She opened the Facebook app on her phone, went to where she could check in to a location, then typed in "New

York" and clicked. "Now I'm New York." She typed in "Boston" and said, "Now I'm in Boston. I'm a regular world traveler."

"I get it," Connor said. "We need to go talk to him again."

"You bet we do."

Connor looked at the time on the computer. It was later than he realized. "I have to meet Skylar soon."

"Olin and I can go talk to James. We'll ask him about that guy, too, Maddie was seeing while we're there, just in case."

Connor nodded. That made sense. There was no reason they all had to stay together. Besides, if they hadn't been on a clock before, they were now. "Is he up?"

"I haven't seen him yet."

Connor knocked on his door. "Olin. Shake a leg. We've got to get moving."

Olin groaned, said he would be out in a minute.

Connor returned to the table. "Did you call the hotel to see if they have any record of them staying there?"

"I don't think they would tell me. I'm sure there are some sort of laws about privacy or at least a policy that governs that sort of thing."

"You're probably right." Connor slid the laptop over so he could get to the keyboard. "They might tell me."

"Why would they tell you?"

Connor looked up the phone number for the hotel and dialed. He put his cell phone on speaker.

"Best Western. How may I help you?"

"Hi. My name is James—" Connor suddenly started to panic. He couldn't remember James's last name. He clicked over to Facebook and cleared his throat to disguise the delay. "Sorry about that. My name is James Hargrove. I was at your hotel Tuesday night."

"What can I do for you Mr. Hargrove?"

"I seem to have misplaced my iPad. Could you tell me if anybody there found it?"

"Just a moment, please." The receptionist put Connor on hold.

"What are you doing?" Dylan asked. "How's that going to help us?"

"She's either going to tell me I've called the wrong hotel or—"

"I'm sorry. Nobody has turned in an iPad. I can have somebody call you if it turns up."

Connor gestured to the phone as if to indicate that was the alternative he was about to mention. "That would be great. Thank you."

He hung up. "At least that rules out the possibility he never went to Savannah."

"It doesn't make him innocent."

"Absolutely not. Right now, he's the best lead we've got. But it's good to know which scenario you're dealing with when you talk to him, don't you think?"

CHAPTER 29

SKYLAR'S MOM DIDN'T come out of the bedroom until the next morning. When Skylar tried to check on her, she said she wanted to be left alone. Skylar tried to comfort her, to sit on the bed beside her, to tell her she had a way out of this mess. Her mom didn't want to hear it. She just told Skylar to get out, get out right now!

When she finally emerged, she was wearing a sweatshirt Leon had given her and a pair of mom jeans that were, in Skylar's opinion, too tight.

"I heard you banging around out here," she said.

The toaster popped. Skylar grabbed the two pieces of bread and slathered them with butter. "I didn't mean to wake you."

"It's fine." She looked Skylar over. "I thought you were off today."

Skylar was wearing a gray pantsuit, which she only ever put on when she was going into the bank. "I have a plan to get us out of this situation," she said.

"Leon told me."

He must not have told her all of it, or she would know why Skylar was going into the bank this morning. He probably didn't remember all of it. Leon had put away a lot of beers after Sam left. The empty cans still littered the coffee table.

Skylar wrapped the toast in a paper towel and kissed her mom on the forehead before heading to the door. She was meeting Connor in an hour, which was barely enough time to get everything done. "I'll call you soon and give you an update."

In her mind's eye, she could still see Sam's Escalade parked along the curb. She remembered his face as he'd climbed back into it yesterday, the tone of his voice when he'd said, "What the hell did I get in business with this asshole for?"

Leon's plan had gone to hell. Skylar's would not. This might be the last chance they would get to put things back on track. She wasn't going to screw it up.

She parked in the same loading zone Connor had parked in yesterday. If she was there long enough, a ticket might be inevitable, but she would be in and out quick. She didn't want to pay three dollars (which was the minimum the lot charged) and walk the two blocks to and from the bank when she would only be inside for a few minutes.

She put on her hazards and went straight for her office. She didn't want to talk to anybody if she could avoid it, barely even managed a "Hello" to the security guard when he nodded and said, "Good morning."

Her footsteps seemed impossibly loud on the tile floor, echoing around her in a way that made her feel like everyone would turn to look at her. She had worn these heels into the bank plenty of times but had never noticed how much noise they made.

Just get it done and get out, she told herself as she glanced toward the tellers to see if anyone was looking. They were not.

She grabbed the handle on the door to her office and pulled. It was locked like it always was when she wasn't there, and she fumbled for her keys.

Once inside, she sat down, turned on her computer, drummed her fingers on top of her desk while she waited for the machine to start up. Her boss didn't normally work on Saturday, so odds were he wouldn't be around to ask her what she was doing there. That was good since there would be no easy answer to that question.

But Lance was there. The douche bag who sat in the office across from hers. He was always staring at her. Always popping in to say, "How's it going?" or "Nice weather, eh?" (The latter was his go-to on days when the weather was clearly anything but.)

Skylar could tell Lance wanted to ask her out. Twice he'd looked like he was about to. He'd never actually got around to it, though. Probably just as well. She would have to tell him no, and that would make things awkward.

Finally, the computer was up.

She glanced over at Lance again to see if he was still looking at her. He was, just like he had been yesterday when Connor was in her office. However, now, unlike then, he was trying to be discreet about it. Maybe because he had a customer.

She navigated her way through a series of screens to the information she was after, grabbed the sticky notes from the edge of her desk and a pen from a drawer. It took only a few seconds to copy the data she had promised Connor.

When she was done, she turned her computer off again and stepped out of the office. It seemed like it was all going as well as she had hoped it would. Then she locked the office door, turned around, and found herself face-to-face with Lance. He had that goofy "I think I'm cool" smile plastered all over his face.

The customer—an elderly woman with a walker—was heading toward the exit.

"Sneak up on people much?"

He took a step back. "Only when there's somebody worth sneaking up on. How's it going?"

There it is. Lance had reached into his bag of greetings and pulled out one of his two favorites.

Skylar crumpled the sticky note into her hand, hoping he wouldn't see it. "I'm great."

He nodded, pretending to contemplate her answer. "Good, good. I'm good, too, by the way."

"Nice to hear."

"Isn't it?"

"I'm sorry. I really have to go," Skylar said, as she tried to move around him.

"I'm just curious," he said, stepping into her path. "Aren't you off today?"

"Yes."

"What are you doing here, then?"

Nosey son of a . . .

"It's personal." She would have needed a better answer than that for her boss. If Lance told him about her Saturday visit, she still might.

Lance held up his hands. "Okay, okay."

Skylar pointed to the door. "I really have to go." Then she stepped to the side again and, this time, followed it with a step forward, moving past Lance before he could block her path with another sideways step of his own.

She hurried to the door.

Lance went after her. "Skylar. Wait." He wasn't yelling, but his voice carried anyway.

She couldn't have him chasing her out onto the street. If Lance hadn't drawn too much attention to her presence yet, he certainly would if he followed her outside. Skylar stopped, spun around. "What? What? *What?*" she repeated through clenched teeth.

He took a deep breath. "I told myself I was going to do this Monday. And right when I made that decision, you showed up. It was like a sign, you know?"

She couldn't believe it. Was he really going to ask her out now? Like this?

"There's a Mexican restaurant I like. It's so cool. They have a live mariachi band and make guacamole right at your table. I think I first went there like five years—"

"Lance."

"Yeah?"

"Get to it."

He swallowed hard. "Would you go out with me?"

Skylar was prepared to say no. The word was already shaping itself on her lips when she froze. If Lance left this conversation happy, he would be on cloud nine the rest of the week. His goofy one-liners and annoying drop-ins would probably multiply, but he wouldn't question why Skylar was here on her day off. He certainly wouldn't think to mention it to anybody.

She could deal with one bad date and some unwanted attention if it would keep her off the boss's radar.

"Sure. Why not? When do you want to go? Next Friday? After work?"

Lance stammered toward an answer. Apparently, he had not expected her to say yes. "Uh, okay."

"Great. Gotta go. See you next week."

She started moving again, and—thank God—at least this time Lance didn't follow.

CHAPTER 30

OLIN EMERGED FROM the bedroom wearing the same clothes he had worn yesterday. He hadn't packed enough for a trip this long. Connor and Dylan filled him in on what they had uncovered, and then he left with Dylan to go talk to James again.

Dylan buzzed his apartment from the callbox for a full minute.

"I don't think he's home," Olin said.

"Probably slept over at some girl's house," Dylan said. "Wait. What day is it?"

"Saturday."

She snapped her fingers. "Brick's is open early on the weekend for brunch. Maybe he's there."

Olin shrugged halfheartedly.

"Well, since our only other option is sitting around here and waiting for him to come back, I think we should give it a shot."

It turned out Dylan was right. It also turned out they weren't the only ones who had come by that morning to talk to him.

"I'm going to circle the block," Dylan said, right before passing the parking lot.

Olin's head jerked around in confusion. He was trying to spot whatever she had seen. "What? Why?"

"Those two people coming out of the restaurant . . ."

Olin didn't have a good view of Brick's via the side mirror, so he spun around in his seat to look. He saw two men in suits leaving the restaurant.

"One of them is the cop who questioned Connor and me last night. The other one is probably his partner."

"You think they came here to talk to James?"

"No. I think they came here for the food." Dylan rolled her eyes.

"You don't have to get snippy," Olin pouted.

Dylan finished her lap around the block. She looked carefully for the detectives as she approached the restaurant for the second time. "All right, I think they're gone." She pulled into the lot.

Brick's had opened just minutes earlier. Olin and Dylan stepped inside. The restaurant had exposed brick walls and polished mahogany floors. Tiny lights had been strung along the ceiling. Only one table was occupied. A sign at the host stand instructed diners to seat themselves.

The lights along the ceiling reminded Olin of Christmas lights. He didn't like to think about Christmas. Even though every year, Connor tried to talk him into coming home with him to celebrate the holiday, Olin couldn't bring himself to do it. Christmas had been something special in his house—with homemade cookies and a massive tree in the foyer that reached all the way up to the second floor. It just wasn't the same without his parents.

James was behind the bar, leaning against a cooler with his hands in his pockets. He was wearing a pressed black dress shirt and black pants. A waiter at the only occupied table was dressed the same.

James looked bored. As if to emphasize that point, he yawned without bothering to cover his mouth.

"All right. Here we go." Then Olin looked over to where he thought

Dylan was standing to ask if she was ready and saw she was already on the move. He rushed to catch up.

Dylan took a seat on the stool directly in front of James. "Hi there."

He perked up. At the same time, Olin slid onto the stool next to her.

"You again. Did you find out anything about Aleshia?"

The police must not have told him they'd found her body, Olin thought. That had to mean they considered him a suspect, also. Olin had been worried about the detective's conversation with Dylan and Connor all night. He had hardly been able to sleep. He worried that if the police kept digging into their lives, they would eventually figure out they had broken into Maddie's and Aleshia's houses. (Sure, he hadn't entered Maddie's, himself, but he was still part of it, and he could still be charged.)

He felt guilty that he was more worried about what might happen to them than what *had* happened to Aleshia and *could* happen to Maddie. Then again, he didn't know either of these women. Bad things happened to people every day, and he didn't need any more of it coming his way. As far as he was concerned, he'd already had a lifetime's worth.

Maybe he was worried for nothing. Maybe the police were just chasing down every lead they had.

"What about Maddie?" James asked, when neither of them answered his first question right away. "Did you talk to the bank?"

"You're sticking with that, huh?" Dylan said.

"What do you mean?"

"We found the banker. She said she had not seen Maddie in a while."

James looked confused. "That's impossible. I know I saw her. You must have talked to the wrong person at the bank."

Olin had not considered that possibility. All they had was a physical description to go on, and only Connor had seen the banker. Maybe he had spoken to the wrong one. But even if that was true, there were a lot of questions James needed to answer, and when Dylan scoffed, he decided he'd better step in before this went sideways.

"What were you doing in Savannah the night Aleshia went missing?"

James's eyes narrowed. "I don't remember telling you I was in Savannah."

"You told Facebook," Dylan said. "So, we know."

"I guess we're back to you blaming me for Aleshia's disappearance again." He sighed. "The police were just in here asking me the same thing. Maybe you should start working together. Coming back to me like this—you can't do any worse than you are now."

"Please. Just tell us, okay?"

James pointed at Dylan. "This is the last conversation we're having like this. I don't need to be interrogated twice."

"All right. Sure. Fine."

"There's a band. The Night Stalkers. Heard of them?"

Olin and Dylan shook their heads.

"I guess I'm not surprised. They're not exactly mainstream. They're from Florida, and they don't come up this way very often. Some friends and I went down to Savannah to see them."

Dylan had shown Olin the same Starbucks check-in she had shown Connor. *Hell of a night!* Connor had wondered aloud if that was an admission of guilt, which had planted the same idea in Olin's head. Had James really been referring to the concert?

"You texted Aleshia from the show?" Dylan asked. She sounded doubtful, and Olin understood why. He couldn't imagine anybody sending messages like he had while they were watching a band.

"No. I sent her the messages after we checked into the hotel."

"Why didn't you text Aleshia as soon as you saw Maddie? What were you doing at the bank, anyway?"

"I stopped by to get some cash for the trip. As to your first question, there are a lot of reasons I didn't text Aleshia right away. First of all, Maddie was already gone. It's not like Aleshia could have headed down to the bank to talk to her at that moment, even if I had been able to reach her. Second of all, she didn't seem to be in any danger. And third, I hadn't talked to Aleshia in a while. For all I knew, she and Maddie were already in touch."

The only waiter Olin had seen showed up beside them and asked James for two mimosas.

"Frankly, I wasn't sure I was going to tell her at all," James said, as he grabbed two champagne flutes from the rack overhead.

"That's not how your messages made it sound," Dylan said.

"I had a change of heart. It was all I could think about on the drive down to Savannah. And the more I thought about it, the more I worried. Why would Maddie run off when I called her name? It couldn't just be because Aleshia and I were no longer dating. What was that about?" He shook his head as he poured champagne into the glasses. "If Maddie was hiding from me, was she hiding from everyone? It still doesn't make sense. Anyway, I decided whether Aleshia wanted to hear from me or not, it was something I needed to tell her. It was her sister, after all. If she already knew where Maddie was, so be it. If she didn't, I thought she might be glad I told her."

"So glad she'd get back together with you, right?" Dylan said.

"That's not what it was about."

Dylan winked.

"Seriously." He placed the mimosas at the end of the bar for the waiter to pick up. "Have you tried talking to Maddie's boyfriend? Maybe he knows something."

"Not yet. We don't know much about him. It would help a lot if you had a name."

"If I knew his name, *I* would have talked to him."

"Hey, James," the waiter said, now back at the bar. "Strawberry mimosas."

"On it." He poured the two drinks down the sink and started over.

While he worked, Dylan whispered to Olin: "Let's tell him what happened to Aleshia. I want to see how he reacts."

"Bad idea," Olin whispered back. "The police don't want him to know. We shouldn't step on their investigation."

"But—"

"Seriously, Dylan. You're already on their hit list. Let's not give them another reason to talk to you or Connor again."

Dylan had a certain look in her eye Olin had come to recognize. She got it whenever she was about to do something she shouldn't.

"Promise me you won't say anything," Olin hissed.

The look vanished. "All right, all right. It probably wouldn't tell us much anyway."

James walked down the bar and placed the new drinks in front of the waiter, who had not left since requesting the correction. He grabbed the drinks and returned to the table, which was still the only one occupied. "I'm so sorry," he said, loud enough for Olin—and thus James, whom it must have been directed at—to hear clearly.

James wiped his hands on a towel, subtly gave the waiter the finger. "Anything else?" he said to Olin and Dylan when he returned.

"You mind giving us the names of the people you went to Savannah with?" Olin noticed a certain tone when Dylan asked the question.

Based on James's response, apparently he had heard it, too. "I already gave those names to the police. Talk to them if you want that."

"Sorry," Olin said. "Sorry. She didn't mean it to sound like that."

"I know exactly how she meant it to sound."

"He's right. He did," Dylan agreed. Then she leaned forward. "James, please, look at me. You want to find out what happened to Aleshia. So do we. We want to find out what happened to both of them. I promise we won't come back and bother you again. But before we go, can you tell me if there is anything else you might remember that would help us? Did Aleshia tell you about any problems her sister might be having? Did you see anybody other than Aleshia or Maddie's boyfriend come in and talk to her at any point?"

James leaned back against the cooler. His hands went back into his pockets. He looked off into the distance for a moment. "I can't. You know how she is, Dylan. She didn't have a lot of friends, as far as I could tell. Hell, she might not have had any other than that guy."

Olin felt his phone vibrate in his pocket. He pulled it out to check the caller ID. It was Connor. As far as he was concerned, they were done here. He thanked James for his time, once again promised they would tell him if they found out anything, and walked away from the bar to take the call.

Dylan held out her hands. *What the hell?* She turned back to James. "If you're responsible for this, you'd better hope the police figure it out first." Then she hurried to catch up to Olin. "I wasn't done talking to him."

"There's nothing else we're going to get out of that conversation. Yeah, he's kind of—"

"Creepy."

"That doesn't make him a killer. He has an alibi for the night of the murder. If that falls apart, the police will figure it out. And maybe he was telling the truth about what happened at the bank. We didn't see who Connor talked to. Maybe he talked to the wrong person."

Olin answered the phone before it rolled over to voicemail.

"What did you find out?" Connor asked from the other end of the line.

Olin relayed the information James had told them and then asked, "Are you sure you talked to the right person at the bank?"

"I don't know. It's not like we had a name. She was the only person there who matched the description."

"The description was fairly generic."

Connor didn't respond.

"After Aleshia's—" Olin cut his eyes to Dylan. "After what happened to her, the police are going to be looking hard to find the person responsible. I think, if we're going to do this, we should focus on finding out what happened to Maddie."

The way Olin saw it, they would be approaching the same problem from a different angle. He had done this plenty of times as an accountant. Numbers that didn't add up one way might add up another. Was the company's cashflow positive or negative? Were they in the red or the black? To most people, that would seem like an easy answer. He had learned it was often about perspective. Did you count the money that was owed as well as collected in your positive cash flow? Did you remember to deduct the depreciation on your building? The maintenance on your vehicles? There was no reason they couldn't apply that same sort of thinking here.

He had said some time ago he thought Aleshia's and Maddie's disappearances were related. Now everyone seemed to believe it. Solve one and you solve the other. One plus one equals two.

He did not have to explain all this to Connor, though. Connor got it right away.

"I think you're right," he said. "Did James tell you anything else about the guy Maddie was seeing?"

"Unfortunately, no."

"Is Dylan nearby?"

"Hold on." Olin and Dylan got back in the car. He put the phone on speaker. "She's right here."

"How would you feel about going back into Maddie's house, Dylan?"

"Fine. Why?"

"Last time we were there, we set off the alarm when we left."

"I'm sure when the police went out and didn't find anybody, they chalked it up to a false alarm. Those things happen all the time."

"I doubt that's what they thought when they found the rope," Connor said.

"Just tell me what you're thinking."

"There might be something there about the guy she was seeing."

Dylan strapped on her seatbelt. "That makes sense. We'll go there now. The police might not have even gone inside. But if they did— and if they made it far enough into the house to see the rope—it's not like they would have posted a guard out front. Any news from Skylar?"

"She should be here soon."

CHAPTER 31

S KYLAR MADE HER way across town to the Grand Hyatt. On the way, she called her mom to give her an update. When her mom didn't answer, she called her stepdad.

The phone rang several times. She wasn't sure he would answer. He might still be sleeping off the hangover. But he did. There was still a bit of a slur in his voice when he said, "Hello?"

"I've got what I need from the bank," she said.

"Good."

"I'm going to meet Connor now. Fingers crossed."

Leon mumbled something unintelligible and hung up. He rolled over in bed and looked at the clock. It was almost ten. He should get up, he told himself.

He rocked forward, put his feet on the floor. His head started to pound. He wished he hadn't had so much to drink yesterday. Sam's visit had rattled him. He knew if the man came back before he had Sam's money, things were going to get ugly.

But Skylar had a plan. God willing, that plan was going to get them out of this shit storm.

He put his hands on his head and closed his eyes until the pounding subsided a little. He went into the living room. "Honey? Skylar called."

No answer.

He was alone. His empty beer cans still littered the coffee table. Looking at them made him want to throw up. He turned away, shouted again for his wife.

She must be at Ashford Park, he thought. She would go there often to sit and think, to try to calm her nerves. There was no point in trying to call her—she wouldn't answer—and there wasn't a reason to call her anyway. Not until Skylar located Maddie.

For now, it was best to let her be.

CHAPTER 32

CONNOR WAITED ON one of the large sofas in the lobby for Skylar to arrive. While he sat, he occupied himself with his phone. He searched for any recent news stories on Aleshia's murder or Maddie's disappearance to see if he might uncover a new clue. There were none.

He heard the *clickety-clack* of high heels on the tile floor and looked up.

Skylar was coming straight toward him. She was wearing a pantsuit similar to the one she'd had on yesterday. Connor assumed that was because she'd had to stop by the bank before coming to see him.

"Were you able to get it?" he asked.

"I wouldn't be here if I wasn't."

Connor gestured toward the elevator. "Come with me."

Skylar subtly glanced around the suite when she entered. She didn't even know hotels had rooms like this. It was big enough to be an apartment. Hell, it was almost as big as her whole house. Maybe, if they couldn't find Maddie, she could figure out how to get some money out of Connor.

He closed the door and went over to a table with two laptops on it. He gestured to one of the chairs. "Have a seat." Then he opened up the laptop in front of him, turned it on. "Can I have the information?"

Skylar fished around in her purse. When she couldn't find what she was looking for, she removed her cell phone so she could better see inside, placed it on the table, and tried again. Finally, she pulled out a crumpled sticky note and gave it to Connor. It had two long series of digits on it. The one on top was prefaced with the letters "RT." The one on bottom: "AT."

"Routing and account numbers," Skylar said, clarifying.

She had already explained to Connor that Maddie had been regularly transferring money from her accounts at Southern Trust to another at First One Financial and that those transfers had only begun recently.

"You checked the date of the first transfer?"

Skylar nodded. "They started a few days after Ms. Thompson went missing."

Despite Skylar's confidence that Maddie had initiated those transfers, they did not assure Connor she was alive. They could have been done by anybody who had access to her accounts. Her killer (if she had been killed) could have beaten that information out of her before taking her life. But wherever that money was going—whether it was an account in Maddie's name or an account in someone else's—it was bound to get them closer to finding out what had happened to her.

That was where he came in.

All Skylar could give him were the numbers on that sticky. There was no way for her to tell whose account it was.

"I can get it," Connor had said on the call when she relayed that information. But it was not going to be easy. He needed to find a hole in First One Financial's security.

Everybody had one.

In 2012, hackers had wormed their way into the LinkedIn network and made off with more than one hundred and seventeen million passwords. In 2014, they had gotten into J.P. Morgan Chase and, that time absconded with the personal information of more than seventy-five million customers. Next: the U.S. Office of Personnel Management, where in 2015 they had seized the detailed records of everyone who had worked for the government over the previous fifty years, including those with top-secret clearance.

Not even the institutions we think of as the most secure are impenetrable, as was proven in 2016 when a fifteen-year-old boy published to the dark web details about every undercover FBI agent.

If hackers could get into those places, Connor could get into First One Financial.

But it would take some time. And, if he was being honest, a little luck.

Once the computer finished starting up, he began the process of locating the First One Financial servers. After that, he would start looking for open ports.

He could feel Skylar staring at him. It was distracting, making him uncomfortable. "This could take all day," he said.

"That's okay."

She didn't seem to get the point, so he tried again. "If you want to turn on the TV, I'll let you know when I'm in."

"I'm fine."

Connor considered being more direct, but he hardly knew this woman. He hoped she would eventually tire of looking at Connor and his computer screen and go do something else. After all, there wasn't anything exciting about what he was doing. Certainly not to someone who wasn't familiar with the process.

From Skylar's perspective, the commands he entered must have appeared arcane, the results nebulous. On top of that, they were being sent and received via a simple black interface with white text, so it wasn't even interesting to watch.

Thirty minutes later, however, she was still there. The uncomfortable silence between them had swollen into a behemoth, making it increasingly difficult for Connor to think. If she wasn't going to leave him alone, he would have to find a way to break it.

Maybe a little idle chitchat would do the trick.

"Where are you from?" he asked, without taking his eyes off the monitor.

"Atlanta. I grew up here."

"What about your parents?"

"Them, too. Well, my mom did. My stepdad is from New York. He moved down here ten or fifteen years ago."

"What happened to your dad?" Connor asked absentmindedly. When he didn't get a response, he stopped pecking away at the keyboard and looked at Skylar. He could tell he had struck a nerve. "I'm sorry. It's not my business."

"It's fine. I didn't really know him. He took off when I was little. My mom was too much for him to handle. She has a lot of problems. She tells me it's nerves." Skylar shook her head. "I don't know. I wish she would see someone about it. My stepdad's been good to her, though. He takes care of her as well as anyone could. She's lucky to have him."

Connor wasn't sure what to say. He was, however, sure it would be rude to keep his attention on the computer after a comment like that. He let his hands fall to his sides, turned in his chair to face Skylar.

"I think it's because Mom had a hard time of it as a kid," she went on. "She doesn't like to talk about that. I know she has a sister who got all her parents' praise, all their love. They treated her like a princess. Meanwhile, Mom was getting locked in her room . . ." Skylar looked down at her hands. "Sometimes for days at a time, and that wasn't the worst of it."

Connor tried not to think about what the worst of it might have been, but he couldn't help himself. It was impossible not to imagine the beatings and the verbal abuse. Who knew if it even stopped there? If Skylar's mom didn't like to talk about it, she probably hadn't told her daughter about the things that truly were *the worst*.

Skylar shook her head. "I shouldn't be telling you all this." She gestured to the computer. "How's it going?"

"Slow. Like I said, it could take a while. You never know with this sort of thing."

"Then go ahead. Get back to work. None of that matters, anyway."

Connor considered whether he should say something else and decided not to. It wasn't his place. At least now, though, he understood why this reward was important to Skylar. She hadn't come right out and said she needed the money so her mom could get treatment, but it seemed to Connor she had implied it.

When Connor had spoken to Skylar on the phone yesterday, he believed Aleshia was still alive, that while finding Maddie would not be the end of the process for Skylar to claim the reward, she might still be able to do so once the search for both women was over.

At the time, he had also hardly cared whether she got the reward. He was annoyed that she had only been willing to help them find Maddie if she had a chance of getting paid.

Now that he could see the world through her lens, he felt differently.

With Aleshia dead, there was no longer a reward available, of course. (Not that Skylar knew that.) But maybe he and Olin could do something to help her anyway, when they were done.

He would have to think about that more later. Right now, the only thing he had room for in his brain was First One Financial.

There has to be a way in somehow.

He turned his attention back to the computer.

CHAPTER 33

ALEX SHAW AND his partner made Brick's their first stop this morning. Neither of them liked working on a Saturday. Howie especially hated it, and it showed. Even his "Hello" when they first approached James Hargrove sounded irritable.

This case, however, could not wait. Somebody had killed Aleshia, and they had reason to believe he might kill again. They needed to find him before that happened.

James was as polite as anyone could be. He called them both "sir" and answered their questions in full. Even offered up the names and numbers of those he had gone to Savannah with before the detectives could ask.

Alex and Howie had agreed they should not have told Connor and Dylan that Aleshia was dead, and likewise agreed they would not tell anyone else until they were able to make an arrest. *Especially* not an obsessive ex-boyfriend. They needed to keep the cards they had close to their chest. If James was their killer, the less they said, the greater the odds were he would accidentally drop a clue that would point them to the evidence they needed.

But by the time they were done talking to him, that didn't seem to have happened.

When they got back to HQ, Howie collapsed into his chair. "I'll start calling James's friends to verify his story, but I don't think they'll tell us anything different."

Alex didn't either. A subject didn't offer up witnesses like that unless they could verify his story. While there was always the possibility the witnesses were actually accomplices, that would be rare with a crime like this.

When Howie was done, he and Alex would almost certainly declare James innocent.

"While you're doing that, I'll type up the interview," Alex said.

Howie nodded and started making calls.

Alex pulled a folder out of his desk drawer. It contained all of the information they had on the case so far. Most of the detectives he knew preferred to keep everything in digital format these days. Alex did not. While he would use the computer to check email and type up his reports, he didn't trust them the way his colleagues did.

IT claimed the data was backed up regularly and stored in "the cloud." He didn't really know what that meant. Even if he did, he was confident he wouldn't consider it as reliable as paper.

No matter what might happen to the computer or "the cloud" (and, yes, he always put those two words in quotes whenever he thought about them), paper would always be there.

Before typing up the report, he reviewed the autopsy notes for the third time, and again stopped at the phrase "blunt force trauma." Aleshia had been killed by a blow to the back of the head, but he still had no idea what the weapon was. A shovel, perhaps? Or a rock?

Those were just guesses, though. So far, they hadn't found anything that could help them answer that question.

Or any of the others they had, for that matter.

Their only piece of physical evidence was the nose ring the CSI team had uncovered on the beach. And to be fair, they couldn't rule out the possibility that it was unrelated.

Alex put the folder to one side of his desk. He hunted-and-pecked his way around the keyboard until the report was done.

Subject: James Hargrove
Case #: 391-8201450

Subject works at Brick's, located at 255 Peachtree Ave., Atlanta, GA 30305.

Detective Howard Muller and I approached the subject at his place of employment at 9:23 a.m. Subject stated he was in Savannah, Georgia, at the time of Aleshia Thompson's disappearance and subsequent murder. Subject claimed he was there to attend a concert at The Blackwood Theater and stayed at the Best Western, 412 W Bay St., Savannah, GA 31401. The concert was presented by rock band The Night Stalkers.

Reservations for subject have been verified with hotel. Subject also provided a list of witnesses for independent confirmation of his whereabouts.

Subject appeared concerned for victim. No indication of lying.

Prepared by:
Detective Alex Shaw

Alex printed off the report and added it to the file, then turned his attention to his email. He had received two since yesterday. The first was from the CSI team. The attached preliminary report provided Alex with nothing he didn't already know. Almost nothing. The nose ring, it turned out, was not a nose ring, at all. It was a belly button ring, produced and sold by online retailer BodyArt. However, the DNA they were able to extract from it did not match anyone they had in the system.

Alex was about to call the retailer to request a list of the customers who had ordered the jewelry when he clicked on the second email and realized that lead might not be the best one he had.

His request for a court order to track Aleshia's phone had been approved.

He told himself it was unlikely the phone was still on. But he would be able to see where it had been and, more importantly, its last known location. The kind of information could be good as gold.

CHAPTER 34

SKYLAR DIDN'T SAY another word about her mother, and Connor didn't ask. He felt like he had trodden into territory that was far too personal. He still felt uncomfortable with Skylar looking over his shoulder. Since she wasn't going anywhere, the best he could do was pretend he was alone.

Getting into a bank was not like taking down a website—but Connor was motivated.

He had always considered his hacks to stand securely on the highest ethical grounds. The bad actors out there disseminating misinformation and encouraging hate might be protected by the First Amendment, but that didn't make what they were doing okay.

Connor had always known, no matter what he did, that he could not stop these sites for long. The way he figured it, if the disruption of service attacks and the warnings he posted to these sites saved even a few people from falling down a rabbit hole of lies that could ruin their lives, then his time had been well spent.

Now, the risk was not even metaphorical. Maddie's life might literally be on the line. If there was ever a time to hack into someone's system—even a bank's—this was it.

"How's it going?" Skylar asked.

Connor turned to look at her and realized she had moved her chair even closer to the computer than it was before. She was leaning forward, squinting at the screen. Trying to make sense of the commands he sent and the subsequent responses.

"Are we getting close?"

Connor had no idea. He had already told Skylar this could take all day. He wasn't sure how he could repeat the point without sounding condescending. Then he understood what she was really asking. She wanted a sense of his plan. She wanted to know what he had done already, what he was going to do next.

Connor did his best to explain what he was up to, but the talk about "open ports" and "running services" seemed to go over her head. Still, she nodded thoughtfully when he was done.

"As far as how close we are, I don't really know. We're not in until we are. That's kind of how this works."

While Skylar didn't seem to understand the more technical parts of the conversation, Connor got the sense she must have understood enough of them for this last point to hit home in a way it hadn't when he had simply told her it could take all day.

"Got it," she said, then gestured for him to get back to what he was doing.

Connor returned his attention to the computer. He reviewed the last response he received. His pulse suddenly picked up.

Was that the back door he was looking for?

Aleshia's phone had last pinged from the Grand Hyatt in Buckhead. Of all the places Alex might have expected to find it, that was not one of them.

He opened up the case file on his desk again and flipped through it until he found the notes on his interview with Connor and Dylan. That was what he'd thought: Connor was staying at the Grand Hyatt. Could he really be that stupid?

Alex called the Grand Hyatt to confirm Connor hadn't checked out. Although he thought it unlikely, it was possible Connor left the phone behind by accident. Maybe the detective's conversation with him and Dylan had spooked them into running. Maybe, in that state of mind, they had been careless.

The receptionist confirmed he was still there.

"Do you know if he's there now?"

"I'm sorry. I couldn't say."

"Is he staying in the room by himself?" Alex thought it was possible—even likely—Connor and Dylan were dating.

"I couldn't tell you that either."

He hung up and grabbed his jacket off the back of the chair.

Howie was on his feet, pacing behind his desk, ready to go. "Well?"

"The receptionist wasn't sure if they were in the room. I guess we'll find out when we get there."

The detectives headed to the parking lot. Alex did not say he would drive. He didn't have to. Ever since he told Howie he drove like an old lady, Howie refused to take him anywhere. It was perhaps the only source of tension between them.

Connor did not want to tell Skylar he might have found a way in yet. Because even if he had, he couldn't be sure the door would get him access to the information he needed. He didn't want to give her false hope.

He worked his way through the steps to verify he had indeed found the opening he was looking for.

Skylar put her hand on her stomach. "I'm getting hungry. Do you have anything around here to eat?"

"Try the mini-fridge."

Skylar got up. Connor could hear her crossing the room, opening the fridge. He kept his eyes and thoughts on the computer in front of him.

I'm in!

Next, he needed to see if he could get to the information he was after. He started working through another series of commands. Each one would have to be tweaked and re-tweaked for the computer he had hacked into. This was—as he'd once told Olin—as much an art as it was a science. A mix of knowledge and intuition.

He heard the fridge close behind him. "There's nothing there."

Connor turned around in his seat. "All right. They've got a little shop in the lobby. You can probably get something there. Or at the restaurant, depending on how hungry you are."

Skylar shrugged. "Okay. I'll be right back." She grabbed her purse, headed toward the door. "You want anything?"

Connor had already turned back to the computer. "I'm good." Then he hopped up, grabbed a spare keycard from the packet the hotel had given him. "Here. Take this. So you can let yourself in when you get back." He didn't need another interruption.

Skylar took the card and left without further comment.

She hadn't eaten since breakfast, and two slices of toast didn't get you very far. She could feel the acid churning in her stomach. Skylar didn't want to leave Connor alone for long. It was important to be there when he found the information he was looking for. The last thing she needed was him calling the hack a failure and keeping the account details to himself.

She made her way to the elevator and then down to the lobby. To her right, she saw the restaurant. It was as luxurious as the rest of the hotel, which would no doubt be reflected in the prices and the time it took to prepare the food.

To her left was the little shop that sold snacks and toiletries. Barely a hole in the wall that she suspected saw less than a handful of shoppers a day. The man behind the register stared absentmindedly out at the lobby. His eyes moved just enough that Skylar could tell he was watching the guests as they traveled this way and that, perhaps silently pleading with them to visit his little store if only so he would have someone to talk to for a moment.

All Skylar needed was something small. Even a candy bar would get her through for a while.

As she turned toward the little store, she saw two men enter from the street. One was lean, tired-looking, his hair a mess. The other was twice his girth and two inches taller. Neither one seemed like they belonged here. Something about the way they moved, maybe. Their eyes scanned over every person within sight, and not the way the clerk's did. It was like they were looking for someone.

It was like they were cops.

Skylar realized that must be exactly what they were just as the overweight officer looked at her. She hated cops, and while she had no reason to think they would have come to this hotel looking for her, she still felt uneasy.

The officer's eyes moved away, and Skylar quickly moved out of their path.

It was going to be a bad day for somebody, she thought as they stepped into the same elevator she had just exited.

Connor could hardly believe his luck. Once he'd gotten into the First One Financial network, the rest was easy. He even managed to launch an internal application that would allow him to browse client records, open loans, credit accounts. If he were the nefarious sort of hacker who went looking for this sort of thing, he could wreak havoc on their entire system.

When he was done here, he would drop them an anonymous note warning them about the vulnerability, he decided.

First things first, however. Connor entered "Madeleine Thompson" into the search bar, pressed Enter. The results came back before he had time to worry that the computer might not find anything.

He clicked on Maddie's name. The next screen presented him with a list of accounts and, more importantly, an address. He could tell right away this was not the address associated with her house. This had a suite number. It had to be a condo or an apartment.

Connor pulled his phone out of his pocket, opened the Notepad app, and copied down the address.

He was ecstatic. Maddie had a second home, a second bank account. This had to mean she was alive, didn't it? That she'd disappeared voluntarily?

But if so, why?

Then there were all the other questions: Why didn't she tell her sister where she was? Was Aleshia's death related to Maddie's disappearance? What did it all mean?

And then one more occurred to him that hadn't before: Was

Maddie *involved* in her sister's death?

Connor cautioned himself against that line of thinking. Objectively, all they had was a new address to check out. The condo/apartment could end up being as empty as Maddie's house. They wouldn't know anything more than they did already until they got there.

But it was still good news. Olin and Dylan needed to know. He closed the Notepad app, clicked the phone icon, and was just about to call Olin when Skylar's cell phone rang, drawing his attention from his screen to hers.

The phone had been on the table beside the computer ever since Skylar sat down next to him. He remembered noticing the case—bedazzled with green and gold—when she took it out of her purse to find the slip of paper with the account number on it but hadn't thought about it again.

The phone displayed a name and a face, no doubt pulled from Skylar's address book. The name—Erin—was unknown to him. The face, however, was not.

He picked up the phone so he could get a closer look at the screen. He must be mistaken, he thought.

That couldn't be . . .

The closer he got to the image, the more certain he was that he was right.

"What the hell?" he mumbled.

It was Maddie.

CHAPTER 35

CONNOR RECOGNIZED MADDIE'S picture from Facebook. There was no mistaking it. What was she doing calling Skylar?

He considered answering, but then what would he say? He needed a minute to think, and before he could decide what to do, the caller hung up.

Connor placed the phone back on the table. Had Skylar joined the investigation not to help them find Maddie but to monitor his progress? Throw him off the scent if he got close?

It didn't make any sense. No matter how he looked at it, the pieces didn't seem to fit together. However, he had a more pressing problem, and that was whether he should tell Skylar what he'd found when she got back to the room. And perhaps more pressing still: whether he should ask her about the phone call.

He could spend another couple of hours pretending to hunt down Maddie's information while he weighed the pros and cons of telling her he found the address he was after.

But the phone call—that happened while she was out of the room. Keeping secrets was always a bad idea, in his experience; a while back, when he'd found a stash of money after his parents were abducted, he'd kept that information to himself. That had turned out to be a huge mistake, and the longer he'd held onto the secret, the harder it had become to bring up. So, he either had to address this phone call immediately or not at all.

If he went with the latter, he could tell her he had been in the bathroom when the phone rang. Simple and believable.

What was the right move?

A knock on the door startled him out of his thoughts. Skylar must have lost the key to the room while she was downstairs. His time was up. He had to make a decision.

Another knock. This time louder, followed by his name. "Connor Callahan."

He recognized the voice as the detective who had questioned him last night. Connor had no idea what Alex was doing here. It couldn't be good.

"Hold on," Connor said, as he scrambled over to his computer and shut it down. He looked at the machine on the table next to his. Aleshia's. He couldn't let the detective see that, either. He grabbed both of them, dashed into his bedroom, and stuffed them into one of the dresser drawers. Then he grabbed Aleshia's phone and hid it with the computers.

The detective continued to pound on the door, now demanding he open up.

Connor wiped his sweaty palms on his jeans. Whatever was about to happen was only going to get worse the longer he waited. He grabbed the knob, turned.

Alex pushed the door from the other side, charging into the room as Connor stumbled back. He was followed by a second detective Connor hadn't seen before.

Skylar grabbed a Snickers from the small shop in the lobby. The clerk seemed delighted to have someone to talk to. He gleefully asked how her day was and what she was doing in Atlanta. Her answers were curt. When she pulled her wallet out of her purse to pay, she realized her phone was upstairs. Now she had a second reason to get back to the room as soon as possible.

Alex did not like how long it had taken Connor to answer the door. By the time he got inside, he was pissed. He slammed Connor up against the wall, face first, then looked around to see if Connor was alone. The room was huge.

"See if Naese is here," he said to Howie, who was already charging toward the closest bedroom.

"What the hell's going on?" Connor said.

Alex told him to shut up.

"All clear," Howie said, after he checked both bedrooms.

"Is that your cell phone?" Alex asked Connor, referring to the one on the table in the bedazzled case.

"No, it's—"

"Ms. Naese's?"

"No. It's—"

"Bag the phone, Howie."

Alex pulled out a pair of cuffs. "Hands behind your back." Then he told Connor he had been charged with concealing evidence and read him his rights.

Skylar slid the key Connor had given her into the door and was just starting to open it when she heard someone inside reciting the Miranda warning.

"You have the right to remain silent. Anything you say can and will be used against you in a court of law . . ."

That had to be the cops she'd seen in the lobby. Had someone at the bank figured out they were being hacked? Had the police been able to track Connor down that quickly? Or was this about something else? She wasn't sure. Whatever it was, she didn't want to get mixed up in it.

Skylar quietly withdrew the key and slipped down the hall to the emergency stairwell. She stepped inside and then held the door open a crack so she could hear what was going on back in the room. What she heard, though, was nothing. Not for a minute or so.

Then a door opened. From where she was, she could not tell if it was the one to Connor's room. Since the stairwell was halfway between his room and the elevator, she eased the door shut and waited one long breath before opening it again and having another look. By now, anyone leaving Connor's room would have had plenty of time to get past the emergency exit.

She saw the same officers she'd seen in the lobby leading Connor away in handcuffs. The more heavyset of the two pressed the button for the elevator, while his partner kept one firm hand on Connor's arm. There was some conversation between them. She was too far away to make out what it was.

When the elevator doors opened, she slipped back into the stairwell long enough for them to get on board and the elevator to depart.

With the hallway clear, she returned to the room. She hoped against all reasonable odds Connor had found the information he was looking for before the police arrived and had written it down somewhere. As soon as she stepped inside, she was sure that was not the case. There was no paper on the table where she would have expected to find it— or anywhere else immediately visible, for that matter. That wasn't the only thing missing. Both laptops were gone, too. So perhaps Skylar was right when she wondered if the police had tracked Connor down because he hacked into First One Financial.

Then she realized she had a bigger problem because her cell phone was also missing. She had no idea why the police would have taken it. Maybe they thought it was Connor's. Whatever the reason, if they found out what was on it, she was totally screwed.

CHAPTER 36

ONNOR'S MIND WAS spinning. It had been ever since Alex and his partner charged into the hotel room. When he opened the door, he had simply expected more questions. Now he was here—back in a little room at the police station, this time facing charges. He had tried to tell the detective the cell phone he was asking about belonged to Skylar. But once the detective charged him with concealing evidence, he decided the best thing he could do was exactly what Alex told him to do—shut up.

He didn't know if the detective was really there for Aleshia's cell phone or if he was asking about the phone simply because he thought it was Dylan's. He could just as easily have been looking for Aleshia's computer. Or maybe the charge wasn't for physical evidence, at all. Maybe they'd found out Connor and Dylan had been in Aleshia's house or Maddie's house . . . or both.

Could he be charged with concealing evidence if what he kept from the police was information?

He wasn't sure. He would just have to wait and see.

Alex entered the room again and sat down at the table across from Connor. This time, he did not offer coffee or anything else. In fact, the only courtesy he extended Connor was when he removed the handcuffs.

"Last time we talked, you told me you had come down here to help Dylan find Aleshia," he said.

"That's right."

"You said you were looking for Madeleine because you thought if you found her you might also find Aleshia."

"Yeah." Connor felt like the detective was leading him somewhere, perhaps trying to box him into a specific set of facts, and he wasn't sure why. So far, everything Alex said to Connor had been the truth. It made him uneasy, and the emotion showed in his voice.

"You want to cut the crap?"

"What are you talking about?"

"Tell me why you are really looking for Madeleine."

Connor shook his head, confused. "I already told you."

"See, that's the thing. I don't know if I believe someone would fly all the way down from New York just to help look for a missing friend. Even if I did, I certainly don't believe that same someone would conceal any evidence they found from the police."

"What do you think I'm keeping from you?"

Alex tapped the table with his pointer finger. "You know damn well what you've got."

Of course Connor did. But since he had kept a number of things from the police, he needed Alex to tell him what he knew. He didn't want to get into any more trouble than he might be in already. He kept his mouth shut, waited for the detective to speak again. Fortunately, when he did, Connor was able to put an end to the guessing game.

"What are you doing with Aleshia's cell phone?"

Connor flashed back to the arrest.

"Bag the phone."

The detectives must have thought Skylar's phone was Aleshia's, and who could blame them? Alex had clearly tracked Aleshia's phone to the hotel. (Connor should have expected that.) Since he already knew

Connor was staying at the Grand Hyatt, the conclusion he seemed to have drawn—that Connor was somehow involved in what had happened to Maddie and Aleshia—was entirely reasonable.

Connor realized he could use that to his advantage. "I don't have Aleshia's phone."

"That's the line you want to stick with? You saw my partner grab it before we left the room, didn't you?"

"That isn't Aleshia's."

"Really? Whose is it?"

"My girlfriend's."

"Seriously?"

"Her name's Skylar. Check it out. You'll see."

"What's her last name?"

Connor tried to remember. He had seen it on the plaque by her office. It was the kind of thing a boyfriend would know, so he had to answer. He remembered the child's rhyme he had been singing to himself while he waited to speak with her. He put himself back in the moment, walking quickly through all the times he had sung that rhyme to himself: chair, pen, form, bank . . . Hall! It was Hall!

He repeated the name to Alex.

The detective leaned back in his chair, studied Connor like he was trying to decide whether Connor was telling the truth. Then he jumped up and charged out of the room. "Lock him up," Connor heard him say before the door shut behind him.

CHAPTER 37

DYLAN PULLED UP to Maddie's house.

"Looks quiet," Olin said from the passenger seat beside her.

Dylan wasn't sure what else he'd expected to see. She had already explained that it wasn't as if the police were going to leave an officer posted out front.

She parked outside the garage, just like she had last time. "Let's go."

"You know I still can't get in."

"The front door's unlocked, remember?"

"The alarm . . ."

She saw what he was getting at. She had assumed that, after the police came, the company would have turned the alarm off. But maybe they'd reset it, instead. "I'll go through the doggy door again. If the alarm's off, I'll call you and let you know."

Dylan pulled her gloves out of her purse and put them on. She went back over the fence, began to wriggle through the doggy door. She was able to move twice as fast this time now that she knew what to expect. But knowing what to expect didn't stop her from scraping her hips again as she pulled herself inside. Once she was back on her feet, she turned to look at the alarm panel on the opposite wall. The glowing red light she'd seen last time indicated it was once again armed.

She called Olin. "Looks like you were right."

"I guess I'll be lookout again."

"I'll be out soon."

Dylan hung up and began to make her way through the house. She wasn't sure what she was looking for, exactly. Evidence of a boyfriend, for sure. But that could be a lot of things. Probably best to start in the bedroom, she decided. Maddie had no toothbrush in the toothbrush holder, which obviously meant there wasn't one for the boyfriend there, either. Still, if they were close, she might find some of his clothes in her closet or a jacket he had left behind.

She wasn't sure what she would do with this sort of evidence if she found it. While it would verify James's story, it wouldn't get her any closer to knowing who the mystery man was. She would just have to take it one step at a time.

As she headed to the stairwell, she glanced toward the living room and froze. The rope she had tossed up to Connor through the skylight was gone; the skylight was closed. Would the police have done that?

Dylan didn't think so. It seemed like that would have been a job for the homeowner.

Either Maddie had come back and done it herself or she had someone looking after the place. Maybe the same mysterious man Dylan was searching for now.

Out of curiosity, she rerouted to the front door. The deadbolt was once again secured. That definitely wasn't the police.

She'd entered the house with little hope of finding anything useful. Now she was determined. If all she left with was a man's clothes, she would find a way to get a DNA test done, if that's what it took.

Dylan took the stairs two at a time and went straight for the bedroom. She didn't remember seeing a man's clothes when she was in here before, but she also hadn't been looking for them that time.

She checked under the bed, went through the closets, found nothing. She thought about some of her ex-boyfriends and the things they had left behind. Toiletries (which she had already excluded). A favorite book. Even a watch once. They were always little things—less forgotten than left behind to make sure they had a reason to come back.

Anything like that would be hard to spot.

Dylan continued to work her way through the second floor until she was out of places to look. She found nothing she could say for sure belonged to the boyfriend. She went back downstairs. Then she had an idea—the studio.

She suspected Maddie spent a lot of time there. It was the equivalent of her office. Many people kept photographs of loved ones or other mementos on their desks. Perhaps she would find something similar in Maddie's studio.

When she entered, she noticed the hooks to the left of the door were bare. Last time Dylan was here, this was where she'd found the rope Maddie used for her frames. Whoever had cleaned up made sure to take not just the rope Connor used to climb down from the roof, but all of it.

In the center of the room, there was a paint-stained workbench and an empty easel. Blank canvases of various sizes were stacked up along one wall. And all over the place, in various stages of completion, were paintings as disturbing as those Maddie had hanging in her living room; they were mounted to the walls, leaned one against the other, squeezed into every nook and cranny.

The workbench was covered with paint cans and brushes.

Dylan searched everywhere, closely examined every painting. She wondered if any of the men in them might be the one she was looking for. But, just like upstairs, she ended the search unable to draw a direct line between the mystery man and anything in the studio.

She was about to give up, to head back through the doggy door, when a photo on the fridge got her attention. It was small, held in place by a magnet. She stepped closer so she could get a better look at it. A takeout menu for the Great China restaurant, also stuck to the fridge with a magnet, partly obscured the photo. She pushed the menu out of the way.

Dylan recognized Maddie right away. She was standing in the parking lot outside the Mercedes-Benz Stadium. A tall man stood beside her. He had one arm over Maddie's shoulders, and they were both grinning like teenagers in love.

That had to be the man James had told them about, Dylan thought.

She swiped the picture off the fridge without giving a second thought to whether she should. Cupping it in one hand, she shimmied back through the doggy door.

She scrambled back over the fence, hurried around to the front of the house, and held the picture out so Olin could see it. "Look! Look what I found." She sounded both excited and out of breath.

"You think that's the guy?"

"It better be. I've been through the whole house. There's nothing else. Well, nothing else that could point us to our guy. The front door Connor and I came out of yesterday—it was locked, and the rope he used to climb down from the ceiling was gone." She paused to catch her breath before continuing. "Someone's been in there cleaning up."

"You think it was Maddie?"

"Maybe. I don't know. It could have been him." She held out the picture again.

"How are we going to use that to figure out who he is, though?"

"That shouldn't be hard. We can—"

Olin's phone rang. "Hold on. That's probably Connor." He pulled it out of his pocket. The caller ID showed a number with an Atlanta area code. He frowned at the screen. "Strange."

"What?"

"I don't know anybody around here, so who would be calling me from Atlanta?"

Dylan could imagine several scenarios. In the worst of them, someone was calling Olin to notify him Connor was dead. Whatever it was, there was only one thing to do. And Olin had better do it fast since the phone would roll over to voicemail any second. "Answer it."

Olin did. He put the call on speaker.

A computer-generated voice told him, "This is a collect call from"— a pause, then they heard Connor say his own name—"at the Fulton County Jail. Will you accept the charges?"

It wasn't the worst thing Dylan had imagined, thank God.

"Yes," Olin said.

A moment later, Connor was on the line.

"The police arrested me. I'm in jail. They tracked Aleshia's phone back to my hotel."

"Connor—"

"Don't say anything. Just listen. Apparently, that's where it last pinged from, so they think I have it. Obviously, I don't. But they saw Skylar's phone on the table when they came in the room, and they grabbed that thinking it was Aleshia's. Don't tell her about that, okay? And don't tell her about anything else, either. I don't want to get her involved in this. I'll catch up with you once they figure out how badly they screwed up."

Connor hung up before Olin or Dylan could respond.

There was a lot of information packed into that brief statement.

Connor had said "*my* hotel." The police must not know Olin was staying there, too, and apparently, Connor intended to keep it that way.

Dylan also noticed the way he spoke about Skylar was . . . well, *off*. He said he didn't want to get her involved in "this." But she was already involved. She might not have gone with them to find the phone, but she had come through with the information Connor needed to hack into First One Financial. So, what exactly did Connor mean?

"Don't tell her about anything else, either."

Had he learned something troubling about Skylar since this morning?

Dylan shook her head. She wasn't going to figure it out. There was only so much she could parse out of that brief statement. Best not to tell Skylar anything at all, like Connor said, until they found out what he'd meant, she decided.

Which led her back to the most important part of Connor's statement. He had made a point of telling them the police had taken Skylar's phone instead of Aleshia's. He had also made a point of saying they didn't have Aleshia's phone. Often, calls made from jail were recorded, and she suspected that was his cryptic way of saying the following: Aleshia's phone is still in the room. Go back and get it before the police do.

CHAPTER 38

ALEX CHARGED OUT of the interrogation room, went straight to see his partner. The officer he had spoken to on his way would take care of getting Connor booked in and processed.

Howie was on his feet, pacing around the observation room.

"Can you believe that crap?" Alex said.

Howie stopped pacing. "What if he's telling the truth?"

"That the phone belongs to some girl named Skylar Hall?" He made a face. "Where is she, then? She wasn't outside the bank. She wasn't in the hotel room. You looked around when you were there. Did you see anything that might suggest there was a woman staying with him?"

Howie thought about that for a moment. "That place was big for one person. Why would Connor need two bedrooms in a place he was staying in by himself?"

"Why would Connor need two bedrooms if he was there with his girlfriend?"

Howie shrugged.

"Did you see anything that would belong to a woman or not?"

"No, not that I can remember."

"And if there was a woman staying with him, why would she go somewhere without her phone?"

Howie again declined to answer.

Alex took a seat at the table. Neither of them said another word for a full minute—long enough for Alex to collect himself. No matter what he had said to Howie, he wasn't lashing out because Connor had lied. Suspects lied all the time. It went with the job. Hell, it was half of what made the job interesting. The suspect would lie, Alex would prove it, then the suspect would lie again, squeezing himself tighter and tighter into a corner of untruth until there was no corner left. It was like a giant game of chess.

He was lashing out because he feared Connor was telling the truth. He hadn't asked Connor if the phone was Aleshia's when they were in the room. He just assumed it was. He and Howie both had.

If it wasn't, it would mean they had Connor locked up on charges for which there was no evidence. That was the sort of thing that could land them in some seriously hot water.

Once he calmed down enough to think rationally, he said, "Did you already log the phone?"

Howie pulled the phone, still bagged, out of his pocket. "Not yet."

"We need to find out if this is Aleshia's." He snapped his fingers. "I have an idea." Alex hurried down the hall into the bullpen, gesturing for his partner to follow.

He found Aleshia's number in her file and dialed it using his desk phone. Then he and his partner watched the cell, waiting for it to ring. This had to work, he told himself. As long as it rang, everything would be exactly the way it was supposed to be. They would have the killer in jail. They would have the evidence to hold him. The world would make sense.

But it didn't.

CHAPTER 39

ALEX FELT HIS stomach drop. He and Howie shared a look. It was a genuine *Oh, shit* moment, and Alex didn't need to ask to know that was exactly what Howie was thinking.

This wasn't Aleshia's phone.

They had to get back into Connor's hotel room and find it. The right way to do that was to request a warrant. Alex was confident he could come up with an excuse to get one without revealing the real reason they needed it. But warrants took time. If Skylar really existed (and at this point Alex believed she might), they needed to get back in that room before she had a chance to clear it out.

He looked at his watch. Not even ten minutes had passed since he stormed out of the interview room. Connor would be somewhere in the middle of the booking process, likely having his fingerprints or photos taken.

"Come with me," he said. "I think I can get us into that room."

With Howie on his tail, Alex navigated a labyrinth of hallways that took him to Booking.

"Connor Callahan?" he asked the desk clerk, and the clerk pointed toward the door that would lead them inside, as if to say he was still being processed.

"I need to see what he came in with," Alex clarified.

As soon as Connor had been escorted across the floor, the officers would have packed up his possessions to ensure they were returned upon his release. Perps came in with all sorts of things in their pockets—sometimes even evidence. Asking to see what he had wasn't unusual.

Without a word, the desk clerk stepped through a door.

When he returned, he was carrying a small plastic bin. There were two labels across the front. One read "Case Number 947-8273720." The other had Connor's name on it. Alex thanked the officer and carried the bin around the corner. With Howie hovering over him, he used his finger to slide the contents around so he could see everything. A wallet, keys, change, loose receipts. Alex took the wallet out, handed the bin to Howie. Inside, among the credit cards, he found what he was looking for: a digital room key.

He discreetly slid the room key into his pocket. Then he put the wallet back in the bin and returned the bin to the desk clerk.

Whenever an officer removed an item from one of these bins, they were supposed to fill out a form so that the chain of evidence was preserved. Since Alex wouldn't want to explain why he had removed the card if asked, he had no intention of doing that. For the same reason, he also had no intention of returning it. The card had no financial value. So, if one day in the distant future, Connor complained that the card was missing, no one would care. More likely than not, they would simply assume he hadn't had it on him when he was arrested, that he was mistaken if he believed he did.

"Did Connor get his phone call yet?" Alex asked the clerk.

The clerk nodded. "First thing."

Alex cursed. "We got to go."

Alex had no doubt they were in a race against time. Connor would have certainly called Skylar or Dylan to tell them what had happened. One or both of them might be on their way back to the hotel right now. If he didn't get there first, that evidence would be gone for good. The dots Alex could connect between Aleshia and Connor might be good enough for him. However, they would never stand up in court. He *needed* that phone.

He didn't have to explain this to Howie. There was a reason Howie kept his mouth shut when Alex slid the keycard into his pocket. Howie got it.

They weren't bad cops. Neither one of them would plant evidence or pay off a witness to bring their suspect down. But sometimes—like now—the rules seemed so onerous that working within them was just about impossible. Connor should not be allowed to walk free because they had picked up the wrong phone when they were in his hotel room.

The way Alex saw it, going back there was more about bending the rules than breaking them. They were just cleaning up their mistake.

Alex placed a removable siren on top of his car and sped through all the lights. Parking lot, lobby, elevator, hallway—the whole thing was a blur. Once they were outside Connor's room, he pounded on the door to make sure it was empty. "Police! Open up!" When no one did, he used the keycard to let himself in.

He opened the door slowly. Howie reached one hand under his blazer and grabbed hold of his Glock. Alex wasn't sure they should expect trouble, but they were both ready for it.

At first glance, everything appeared to be exactly how they'd left it.

Alex waved a finger in the air to tell Howie they should make sure no one was hiding anywhere before they started their search. They fanned out across the room. Alex cleared the closet and Howie the bathroom. Then each went to a bedroom and examined that.

"Clear," Alex said, when he was done.

"Clear," Howie repeated.

"Let's find that phone."

CHAPTER 40

DYLAN KEPT HER foot on the gas. She laid into the horn when she got caught behind a slow driver and sped up when a light turned yellow. Twice, she miscalculated and had to slam on the brakes to avoid careening into an intersection after the light had turned red.

Olin had a death grip on the grab handle above the door the entire time. He told her to "Stop!" and "Slow down!" and, the second time she had to slam on the brakes, he said, "We're not going to do Connor any good if you get us killed."

Dylan didn't respond to any of his comments. She didn't know how much time they had, and she couldn't take the chance the police would get back to the hotel first. One slow driver, one light might mean the difference between whether or not Connor walked out of the police station a free man. It might have implications for her, too, since Alex had questioned them both.

When they arrived at the hotel room, she took a quick inventory of what she could see. Both laptops were gone. So was Aleshia's cell phone.

Connor had made it clear the police didn't have her phone. It had to be around here somewhere. Dylan just needed to figure out where. "Go check your room," she said to Olin. "I'll see what I can find in Connor's."

Olin responded with a casual two-finger salute and did as instructed.

It didn't take long before Dylan had worked her way around to the drawer where Connor had stashed the laptops and cell phone. She stuffed the phone into her pocket, picked the laptops up, and held them to her chest. Connor had clearly been hoping the police wouldn't find any of it, so she did not intend to leave even his computer behind.

"I found the phone!" she said, as she exited the bedroom. "Got the computers, too!"

Olin appeared from the other bedroom. "Good. Let's get out of here."

Dylan couldn't have agreed more. They had beaten the police back here, but who knew by how much? Then the door to the suite opened, and Dylan feared they were about to find out.

But the woman facing them didn't strike her as a cop.

"Hi," the woman said uncertainly.

"Who are you?" Olin said.

"Skylar. I'm . . ." She glanced from Olin to Dylan, like she wasn't sure who she should address. "I'm here to help Connor find Maddie." Then her head rocked forward an inch as she focused all her attention on Dylan. "I saw you at the bank yesterday, didn't I? You were with Connor, right? You were parked outside in the loading zone."

"How do you have a key to the room?" Dylan asked.

"Connor gave it to me so I could let myself back in after I got something to eat downstairs. When I was gone, the police showed up and arrested him. I think someone at the bank must have figured out what he was up to and reported it." She pointed to the laptops Dylan was holding. "Are those Connor's?"

"Why?"

"I thought the police had taken them when he was arrested. Where did you find them? And what about my phone? I left it in the room when I went downstairs, and when I came back, it was gone. Did you find a phone with the computers?"

"No."

Skylar looked disappointed. "Have you opened them up?" she said, referring to the computers again. "Do you know if Connor was able to get any information about Maddie out of First One Financial?"

Connor had told Dylan not to say anything to Skylar if she saw her. In this case, she couldn't even if she wanted to. "I don't know."

"Have you looked?"

"No, I—"

Skylar reached forward to grab the laptops. "Let's look."

Dylan twisted away. "Not now. The police could be back any second."

"Why?"

She shouldn't have said that, Dylan realized. It would be impossible to answer without telling Skylar about Aleshia's phone. Of all the things she was not supposed to tell Skylar, that was the one Connor had called out by name. She would have to make something up. All she could think to say at that moment was, "It's just a hunch he has."

It sounded lame even to her, and Skylar clearly didn't buy it. "If he got into First One Financial and you're keeping that from me—"

"I'm not. Really, we have to get out of here. Connor thinks the police might have arrested him over the hacking. He thinks they're going to come back looking for his computer. We don't want to be here if that happens."

That story had problems, too. If the police really had arrested Connor over his hack into the bank, they would have stayed in the hotel room until they found the computer. But this version was better than calling the possibility of their return "a hunch." As long as Skylar didn't think too much about the story, it might sound plausible.

Still in the doorway, Skylar glanced toward the elevator, as if the police's arrival might be imminent. "All right. Let's at least get down to the lobby before we look."

Dylan and Olin stepped into the hall behind Skylar.

Dylan couldn't say why but being this close to Skylar made her uneasy. Like she was within striking distance of a rattlesnake. Was it just Connor's mysterious warning that had her on edge? She didn't think so. It wasn't the fact that Skylar was only here for the reward, either. That might be true of a lot of people in her situation.

Whatever it was, the question would have to remain unanswered for now. Even if she had the information to figure it out, she didn't have the time.

They were passing in front of the emergency stairwell when the elevator dinged.

Skylar looked back at Dylan and Olin. The expression on her face made clear she was afraid of the same thing Dylan was: the police were back.

"In here," she said, pushing open the door to the stairwell.

Dylan did not have to be told twice. She hurried into the stairwell as the elevator doors started to part.

Olin, however, did not move. "What are you doing? It's just a guest."

Dylan could see enough of the two men on board to know he was wrong. It was too late, though, for Olin to come with them without drawing attention—and way too late to explain to him he was wrong. "Be cool," she said. "Meet us in the lobby."

Skylar shut the door.

He'll be okay, Dylan told herself. *They don't know what he looks like. They don't even know he exists.*

"Seems you were right about the cops," Skylar whispered, and Dylan realized she would only have said that if she recognized at least one of them, also.

"You know them?"

"They're the same men who arrested Connor."

Of course. That made sense. If she hadn't seen the police lead him away, how else would she know he had been arrested?

Dylan and Skylar started down the stairs.

Olin spun toward the hotel room, then away from it. He wasn't sure what to do. Dylan seemed to think these two men were cops, but he doubted she had gotten a good look at either of them. Presumably, if they were, they would be the same two officers she had pointed out at Brick's. Unfortunately, with the car in motion and looking over his shoulder, he hadn't been able to pick out enough detail then to say for certain now whether she was right.

Did it matter, though?

Not as long as he followed Dylan's advice, he told himself. He just had to *be cool*. Act like a normal guest. What would a normal guest do? They would walk past the detectives (if that was indeed what they were) with hardly a glance.

Dressed as they were, they could have been businessmen in town for a conference. Olin shifted to the side to make room for them as he headed toward the elevator. At the same time, one man stepped behind the other.

Olin resisted the urge to make eye contact, even as every muscle in his body seemed to tense up. As they passed within inches of each other, he thought he saw the larger man turn his head to check Olin out. Then the man's arm moved forward. Was he about to grab Olin?

Don't run. Don't react. It's in your head.

Then, just like that, they had passed each other.

Olin realized the forward movement of the man's arm was nothing more than the natural swing that occurred when walking.

He took a deep breath, pressed the button for the elevator, and—as much as he wanted to keep his gaze straight ahead—he couldn't help looking back to see where the men were going.

They stopped in front of Olin's room. One pulled out a keycard and slid it into the lock.

So, Dylan was right, after all. They were detectives.

The elevator dinged. Olin stepped in and continued to watch the detectives until they were inside his room. Then the elevator doors closed, and once again he took a deep breath.

He was only a few floors up, but the ride to the lobby seemed to take forever. He hated being on the wrong side of the law, even if—as Connor had pointed out multiple times—they were doing what they were doing for the right reasons.

When the elevator doors opened again, he saw Skylar and Dylan waiting for him.

"Here. Let me take those," he said to Dylan and scooped the laptops out of her arms. She had been carrying them long enough. Then he looked around to make sure he didn't see anybody else who might be a cop.

Dylan handed over the laptops. "Let's get out of here." She headed toward the parking garage. As much as she wished Skylar would turn around and go her own way, she knew that wasn't going to happen until the woman got to have a look at Connor's computer. That, she had decided, was fine with her. His computer was password protected. So was Aleshia's—which mattered because Skylar seemed to be under the impression they were both Connor's. And since they looked a lot alike, she'd probably want to check out both of them.

They navigated the dimly lit underground garage to Dylan's car. She gestured to the lid of the trunk. "Put them down," she said to Olin.

Olin seemed reluctant.

"It's fine," she said, hoping her look would tell him everything he needed to know. "Let's see if we can find out what Connor's got."

When Olin didn't move right away, she grabbed the laptops from him. She placed them on her trunk, opened the first one, and turned it on. They were met with the login screen. "That's right. I forgot. We're going to need Connor to get us in."

Then, predictably, Skylar said, "I think he was using the other one."

Dylan was sure that wasn't true, since it was Aleshia's. She turned it on anyway and was once again stopped by a login screen. "We're stuck until Connor gets out on bail, it looks like."

She didn't think a bail hearing would happen before Monday. She also didn't think Connor would be locked up that long. Once the police searched the room and realized Aleshia's phone wasn't there, they would likely have no choice other than to let him go. But the lie would get Skylar out of their hair for a while, and once they could hook up with Connor again, they could find out why he didn't want them talking to her.

"Go home," Dylan said. "Once Connor gets out, we'll be in touch with you."

"You'd better," Skylar said.

CHAPTER 41

SINCE ALEX WAS already in one of the bedrooms, he started there first. He found a suitcase tucked in the corner with nothing inside. Button-down shirts and slacks were neatly folded in the dresser. He rifled through them and came up empty again.

Over the next twenty minutes, Alex and Howie covered every inch of the suite.

"It's not here," Alex mumbled several times as they neared the end of their search.

"No, it's not," Howie agreed when they were done.

"You looked everywhere in that bedroom, right?"

"Of course."

Alex knew that if Howie said he had looked everywhere, he had. But he still couldn't help himself. He had to double-check.

The second bedroom was a mirror image of the first, with the bed dressed in white linen and nightstands on each side. A dresser catty-corner. A TV mounted to the opposite wall.

Alex went through the room methodically, and while he didn't find the phone, he did find something unexpected: more men's clothes. These were not like those in the other bedroom. They were balled up and wrinkled and still packed in a suitcase at the foot of the bed.

Alex had only had two interactions with Connor, but now that he thought about it, these looked more like the kinds of clothes he would wear than those in the other bedroom. Their pool of suspects seemed to be getting wider by the minute.

But without the phone, he wasn't sure any of that mattered.

And, dammit, there was no phone!

CHAPTER 42

DYLAN NAVIGATED HER way through the hotel parking lot to the exit.

"I can't believe you just opened up the laptops like that for Skylar to see," Olin said.

"Would you relax? I knew we wouldn't get past the login screens. She wasn't going to see anything I didn't want her to see."

Dylan slid her parking ticket into the machine at the exit and paid. Olin checked the side mirror for the twentieth time since they started moving to make sure the police weren't behind them. Then he glanced down at the phone in the cup holder closest to him. Aleshia's phone. "Do you think they'll let Connor go?"

"I hope so."

The wooden arm rose. Dylan pulled out onto the street.

"Why do you think he doesn't want us talking to Skylar?" Olin asked.

"I have no idea. Let's just focus on what we can do right now."

"That is?"

"Find out who the guy in that picture is."

Olin checked the side mirror another time. "How are we going to do that?"

"There are websites out there. They can do image scans; some even use facial recognition software. It's not always perfect, but it might give us what we're after."

"So, we need to get the picture into a digital format."

"Exactly."

Olin nodded. He seemed to understand what their next move would be. There was only one way to get a physical picture into a digital format. They would have to scan it.

There were only a few places you could go to do something like that. One such place Dylan knew about was the FedEx on Milton Avenue. They could not only scan it, they could blow it up into a print large enough to hang above the sofa, if Dylan wanted them to.

Other than the long line, the whole process couldn't have been easier. An employee scanned the image on one of the machines behind the counter and sent it to Dylan's email address. They were in and out in fifteen minutes flat.

Dylan cranked her seat back, then grabbed Aleshia's laptop from the backseat. "Let's see what we've got." She opened the computer and logged in.

"I thought you said you couldn't get past the login screen."

"I said we *wouldn't*. When Connor got into Aleshia's computer, we changed the password in case we needed to get in again. What I did with Skylar in the parking lot—that was for show. Come on, Olin. Keep up."

Then Dylan's phone rang. It was a call she needed to take.

CHAPTER 43

CONNOR WAS LOCKED in a holding cell with eight other men. The police hadn't told him how long he would be here or what was going to happen next. He hoped he wasn't going to have to spend the night. Not that he would sleep, if he did. These were not the sort of men you closed your eyes around.

Especially not that one over there in the corner. He had been staring at Connor ever since the police locked him up. Maybe it was because Connor didn't look like he belonged. He had been the odd man out much of his life, but never felt it more than he did at this moment.

He stood up, approached the bars. From here, he could see a large room with more benches and more men. These men had yet to be processed. In the middle of the space, there was a raised, wraparound desk that allowed the police behind it to observe the entire area.

"Officer!" he called.

From behind him: "Man, they ain't gonna answer you."

Another voice: "Sit down, shortbread."

One of the cops behind the desk looked straight at Connor, and then went back to what he was doing.

Connor had been hoping they would let him make another phone call. He wanted to see if Dylan had managed to get Aleshia's phone out of the hotel. Seemed like that wasn't going to happen. Once the police had finished processing him into the system, they were done with him.

"I told you. Now sit your ass down."

Disappointed, he was about to do just that when the same cop who made eye contact with him a second earlier answered a phone call and then sauntered over to the cell. "Connor Callahan?"

Connor raised his hand.

"Looks like today's your lucky day."

Connor stepped outside into the sun and started walking. He would have to call an Uber to get to where he needed to go. Right now, he just wanted to put some distance between himself and the police station.

Cars whizzed up and down the four-lane road. He could smell the exhaust. The crisp winter air cut through his thin jacket.

He had his cell phone in one pocket and Skylar's in another. When he was two blocks away, he pulled his cell phone out of his pocket and called Dylan.

"You're out?" she said.

"Yes. I take it you found Aleshia's phone?"

Connor had expected Alex or his partner to speak to him at some point before he left the station. Neither of them had. The police had sent him back out into the world with no more than a guess as to why.

"We did. Got the computers, too. Did you find what you were looking for?"

"Maybe. I mean—I got an address. I'm going now to check it out."

"We'll meet you there."

Connor turned to put his back to the wind. "Did you find anything at Maddie's?"

"A picture."

"Of the guy?"

"We think so. Looks like they might have gone to a baseball game together."

"Did you get a name?"

"No."

"You know how you can track it down," Connor said. It was more of a statement than a question. Dylan was better than he was at that sort of thing, so if he knew, she almost certainly did, as well.

"Of course. We were about to do that now."

"All right. You do that. I don't know if the address is going to get us anywhere or not. For all I know, it could be a P.O. box." Those at places like the UPS Store sometimes disguised the box number to make it look like a real address. Since the one on Maddie's account included a unit number, he worried that might be the case here. "I'll let you know what I find."

"Why didn't you want us talking to Skylar?"

"I think she might know more about Maddie than she's letting on."

"Really?" Dylan said. "Why?"

Connor wasn't sure how to answer that. When he was locked up (and he wasn't worrying about the big guy in the corner watching him), he'd spent a lot of time trying to make sense of the phone call Skylar received. The answer remained elusive. Why would Skylar offer to help them find Maddie if she already knew where she was? It wouldn't be for the reward. And why would she have Maddie's number saved under the name "Erin"? Could it be so if someone happened to see the screen when Maddie called (like Connor had), they wouldn't see her name? But then why have her picture saved with it? What was their connection?

He hoped, if he did find Maddie at the address on the account, she would be able to explain it. Until then, he figured he should probably keep that information to himself. It wouldn't help them answer their core questions, and Connor worried it might prove a distraction for Dylan. He could imagine her confronting Skylar, demanding answers Skylar wouldn't give, when she had better things she could be doing with her time—like finding out who the man in that picture was.

"It's hard to explain. I'll tell you later," he said. "Just see if you can find out who that guy is for now. Divide and conquer."

Dylan didn't seem to like that answer, but she accepted it. "All right."

"I'll talk to you soon," Connor said before he hung up. Then he ordered a ride through the Uber app.

CHAPTER 44

AFTER CONNOR HUNG up, Dylan slid the phone into one of the cup holders between the seats.

"What's going on?" Olin said.

"Connor's got an address."

"Great."

"He's going to check it out now."

"We're not going with him?"

"We're going to see what we can find out about the guy in that picture." Dylan turned back to the computer in her lap.

Olin wasn't ready to let it go. "Why aren't we going with him?"

"We're not sure he's going to find anything." Then she repeated the same two points Connor had made to her. "What if it leads to a P.O. box? We need to divide and conquer."

This seemed to satisfy Olin. He nodded toward the computer. "All right. Let's do it."

Dylan loaded the image from her email to the desktop. She had to go through several sites before she found what she was looking for. Most of them did a simple reverse image search, which was just a matter of comparing the ones and zeros that composed the image to other ones and zeros across the web. She needed something smarter. Whosthat.com seemed like it would do exactly what she wanted.

Olin fiddled with the heat while he waited. "You sure this is going to work?"

"Don't be so negative."

Dylan uploaded the image. After a minute or so, the website notified her it had found forty-two possible matches. It was "Only $19.95 to See Them Now!"

Fine.

Dylan pulled out her credit card. Before she could enter the information into the payment screen, Olin passed her his. "Use this."

Olin was generous with her and Connor in a way that she had never gotten used to. But it was easier to accept the card and say "Thanks" than to insist on using her own, so she did.

The website returned the list of possible matches. No names. No addresses. Nothing identifiable from a glance. Just a list of URLs and a tiny image next to each showing a match that was too small to be useful.

"Looks like we'll be here for a while," Dylan said.

Olin looked across the street at the Waffle House on the other side. "You hungry?"

Dylan was not. But the Waffle House would give her some room to stretch out, she realized. Scouring through these results with the computer in her lap was going to be a pain in the ass. "Sure. Let's go."

CHAPTER 45

THE UBER LET Connor out in front of a tall glass building in Midtown. There was a lot of foot traffic here—something, it occurred to Connor, he hadn't seen since he'd left New York. He approached the building. A doorman pulled open the door.

The lobby seemed to occupy two full floors. Massive modern lights hung over a raised seating area in the middle of the room. On the other side of it, two receptionists, a man and a woman, stood at a marble desk, shoulders back and at full attention. They both smiled at Connor and the woman nodded a welcome.

Connor nodded back. He moved as quickly as he could to the elevators behind them, hoping they wouldn't ask any questions.

So far so good.

He pressed the button to go up. The doors opened onto an elevator that was just as opulent as the lobby. He pulled out his phone and double-checked the address. Suite 1427. Usually, that meant the fourteenth floor. Playing the odds, he pressed the corresponding button.

It lit up and immediately went out. Strange. He tried again. The same thing happened. He noticed a black scanner, about the size of a credit card, above the keypad and realized what was going on. The reason the receptionists had not asked if he lived there was that there was nowhere he could go if he didn't.

Connor pressed several other buttons, just to be sure. The light on each turned off as soon as he let go of it.

For barely a second, he considered staying on the elevator, waiting for someone to call it up. That was crazy. There were thirty floors in this building. Odds were the elevator wouldn't get called to the floor he wanted to go to, and they were just as good the stairwell would be secured with the same sort of scanner the elevator was.

Looked like he was going to have to talk to reception, after all.

He stepped off the elevator and rounded the corner to the front desk. The man and woman behind it were still standing at attention. Both were attractive enough to be models, Connor thought. In a place like this, that probably wasn't by chance.

"Hello, sir," the woman said.

"What can we do for you?" the man asked.

"I'm here to see one of your residents."

"Name?"

"Maddie Thompson." Connor still didn't know whether she actually lived here. If the bank account at First One Financial had been fraudulently opened by someone else, that name would get him nowhere. But this did *look* like the kind of place Maddie would live, and since he had no other name he could give, he hoped for the best.

The woman looked something up on the computer that was positioned just below the edge of the desk. "You are?"

"Aleshia's friend."

"I need your name, sir. I have to notify Ms. Thompson of your arrival."

So, the good news was Maddie did indeed have a place here. The bad news was he would never get upstairs to talk to her. Even if she was home, she wasn't going to let a stranger up. Worse still, it could spook her into disappearing out a back door, and then they might never find her. There was a reason she had gone into hiding, after all.

Maybe if Dylan could find out who the guy in that picture was, he could come back and try again. For now, he would just have to find a way to make an exit without raising an alarm. That wasn't going to be easy, though. If he hightailed it out the front door, the receptionists might tell Maddie about his strange behavior. That would concern her as much as a call announcing an unknown visitor. More, actually.

He had to say something.

To hell with it. He would have to go with the lesser of two evils. "Tell her it's Connor Callahan. Make sure you also say I'm Aleshia's friend. I'm here because her sister is worried about her."

As far as Connor knew, the police had not yet located Maddie. She probably didn't know what had happened to Aleshia. If Connor got upstairs, he would have to tell her. But first, he had to *get upstairs*, and his name alone wasn't going to do it. Which was why he had invoked Aleshia's name to begin with.

Come to think of it, though, this was actually better than his original plan. If the receptionist had called up to say Aleshia's friend was here, it implied the visitor was a stranger. Hopefully coupling that news with his name would also imply the visitor wasn't a threat.

He wasn't sure if he was telling himself that because he had no other choice or because he bought into the logic. Since it *was* the only choice, it didn't matter either way, so he didn't dwell on the decision.

The receptionist placed a call. Thirty seconds passed. She returned the receiver to its cradle. "I'm sorry. Ms. Thompson is not picking up."

Connor waved a dismissive hand. "That's fine. I'll try her later." He turned toward the exit, relieved he did not have to find out whether his logic would have held up. Now he could do what he should have done to begin with—sit outside and wait.

If she was out, she would eventually come back.

The building was within sight of a bar called the Rustic. The place looked exactly like its name suggested it might and came complete with a patio out front. He found a table with an unobstructed view of Maddie's building and took a seat facing the street.

He was far enough away, he thought, that he wouldn't draw unwanted attention, but still close enough to see everyone who went in and out of the building.

With his elbows on the table and his hands clasped together, he studied every woman who went anywhere near the entrance. He had to consider the possibility that Maddie had dyed her hair, so he couldn't assume he was looking for a brunette. His best indication would be the woman's build, and then, if he could see it, her face. That wasn't much to go on, but it was all he had.

While he waited, his mind drifted back to the discussion with the receptionists. He had assumed the police hadn't located Maddie yet, and thus she wouldn't know her sister was dead. But how hard could it be for them to find her? All they had to do was follow the money. Had they even tried?

Connor knew that was only one of many questions he might never get answered, and of all of them, it mattered the least. He put it out of his mind.

Then he ordered a beer so he would look like he belonged and pulled out his phone so he would look busy. He didn't want people to think he was some kind of creeper. But from the time the phone was on the table in front of him until he thought he saw someone who might be Maddie, he hardly looked at it.

CHAPTER 46

SKYLAR ENTERED THE house and found Leon back on the sofa, watching a baseball game. He was wearing the same grungy undershirt he had on yesterday, as well as the same New York Mets cap. The beer cans that had been spread across the coffee table this morning were still there. He moved only his eyes to look from the TV to her. "You find Maddie?"

Standing in the doorway, Skylar looked around the room, toward the kitchen and the hall. "Where's Mom?"

"You know where she is."

Ashford Park, Skylar thought.

Her mom said she went there to think, but Skylar knew that sort of thinking could be bad. It was the same sort of thinking that had preceded her last breakdown and had started only a week or two before the sleepwalking.

She closed the front door. "There's a problem."

Leon muted the TV, leaned forward. "What do you mean?"

"Connor's been arrested."

"Before or after he got the address?"

Skylar collapsed onto the sofa next to him. "I don't know."

Leon rocked forward. "What do you mean you don't know?"

"I went to the lobby to get a snack, and when I was gone, the police came up to the hotel room and arrested him. I got back just in time to see it happen."

"You left him alone?"

"If I had been there, they would have arrested me, too."

The chaotic energy coursing through Leon moved into his legs, and he was on his feet now. "Oh, this is not good."

"It gets worse."

"How could it get worse?"

"When the police arrested Connor, they took my phone."

Leon's hands balled into fists. He looked like he wanted to hit something. He looked like he wanted to hit *Skylar*.

The rational part of Skylar knew he wouldn't. He was a good man. He had put his life in danger to try to help Skylar's mom. Even when he was at his angriest, he had never lifted a hand toward either of them. Still, when he suddenly moved in her direction, she pulled back.

But he wasn't after her. He was after one of the empty beer cans. He grabbed it, threw it at the wall. The can clanked meekly against the wood paneling and fell to the floor. "Do you know how bad things are going to get for us if they see what's on your phone?"

"Of course I do. Please, Leon, calm down."

"Calm down? That's your answer?"

Looking up at Leon from the sofa, Skylar felt like a child who'd been caught sneaking out at night. (Which, years ago, she had been. And Leon's tenor and tone in that conversation were not all that much different from this one.) However, she was not a child anymore. She was a part of the plan, and in deeper than Leon had ever been. She was not going to be talked to this way.

As if to make that point, Skylar got to her feet as well. "That's my answer. This"—she gestured at the space between them—"isn't going to get us anywhere."

Tall and lanky, Leon still towered over her. But he seemed to get the point that he shouldn't speak to her like he had. He put his hands on his hips and turned away, then started pacing the room. "So, what are we going to do?" he finally asked.

"About the phone?"

"Yes, about the phone," he snapped. Then, perhaps because he could sense Skylar's annoyance, he apologized.

Skylar took a beat. "I don't think they can get into my phone without my password. It will probably be fine." Since Connor's arrest, Skylar had remembered seeing news stories from time to time about high-profile cases and the iPhones they featured. As far as she could remember, the police had been unable to crack them. She couldn't be sure that was still true, and she couldn't be sure Apple wouldn't help if asked. However, she was sure that whatever the police wanted with Connor, it had nothing to do with her phone. They had almost certainly picked it up by accident. As long as the police realized that before they got into the device, she would be all right, she told herself.

She tried to relay that same fragile confidence to Leon. "When Connor makes bail, they'll probably give it to him along with the rest of his possessions and we'll be able to get it back then."

"What about Connor? Do you think he can get it into it? He's good with computers, you said."

"I don't think so."

But even more than the possibility that the police might get into it—that was what worried her now. Connor *was* good with computers. Was he better than the police? She wasn't sure. Either way, he wasn't bound by the same rules. If he wanted to get into it—and if he could—nothing was stopping him.

"So, the police have your phone."

Leon was speaking more to himself than Skylar. She answered anyway. "Yes."

"And Connor might have Maddie's address."

"Maybe."

"And there's nothing we can do until Connor gets out on bail."

Skylar shook her head. "I don't think so."

"When is that supposed to happen?"

"Monday."

Leon had been moving slowly toward the front door when Skylar answered. He suddenly stopped and spun around. "Monday?" The sharp edge he had had in his voice before was back.

"That's what Dylan and Olin think."

"Who?"

"Connor's friends. They're . . ." She shook off the explanation. It could sidetrack the conversation, and, more importantly, "It doesn't matter."

Leon's pacing eventually led him to the chair at the small computer desk. He pulled it out at an angle and sat down in such a way that he could still see Skylar. "What if Sam comes back before then?"

Skylar understood his concern. She was worried about the same thing. So worried, in fact, she had half-expected to see Sam's Escalade when she'd pulled up to the house. But there wasn't any more they could do about that than they could about Connor, so she told Leon the only thing she could. "He was just here yesterday. You told him you were waiting on permits. He seemed to buy it, right? We've got some time."

Leon frowned, nodded. "I hope you're right."

"I am."

"You know what we're going to have to do if this falls apart."

Skylar did. She'd been able to hold him so far. She'd already done a lot of things she regretted. Most of them she could bury deep in her subconscious and, with time, perhaps forget entirely. And with a little luck, she and Leon would be the only two who ever knew what she had done. But there would be no hiding from the thing Leon wanted her to do. She would have to run. They all would.

"It's not going to fall apart."

CHAPTER 47

DYLAN SLOGGED THROUGH the forty-two possible matches Whosthat.com had returned. It was tedious work. She wished they could log on to Connor's computer so that she and Olin could divide the list. As it was, all Olin could do was sit on the other side of the booth and watch.

A waitress wearing the Waffle House's trademark black-and-blue uniform stopped by their table more than a dozen times. Some of those visits were expected: she took Olin's order, brought him a plate with eggs and bacon, refilled their water glasses. Most of the time, though, she seemed like she was there to spy on what Dylan was doing.

Dylan addressed the issue first by subtly turning the laptop toward the window. That didn't seem to discourage the waitress. She would still stop to see if they needed anything while she awkwardly craned her neck to the side to try to see the screen.

On the last of those visits, Dylan had finally had enough. She spun toward the waitress, who in turn straightened up, shifted her gaze away from the computer. "Would you like to pull up a chair and join us?" Dylan said sharply.

The waitress's mouth opened like she wanted to say something. When she didn't, Dylan added, "We'll let you know if we need anything."

The waitress responded with only an uncomfortable smile before quickly stepping away.

"That was unnecessary," Olin said.

"Just be glad I didn't tell her what I really wanted to say," Dylan said, as she returned to her work.

Twenty minutes later, she spun the computer around and told Olin to "Scoot over." Then she came around the booth to sit next to him so they could both see the screen.

"The list we got back was all over the place. Some of the matches came from Facebook or LinkedIn. Others came from corporate websites. One even came from Cupid's Corner."

"Where?"

"That dating website Aleshia was using. Anyway, it took some doing, but I was able to figure out enough about these people to whittle down the list of possibilities to a mere four." She pointed to a list of names on one side of the screen.

"Impressive."

"That wasn't the hard part. Because the images we got back were from all over the web, they were also from all over the world. I was able to exclude the images that came from other countries right off that bat, and that cut the list by twenty percent."

"How did you do that?"

Dylan explained that most commercial websites in the US ended with a ".com." This was called a top-level domain. In the United Kingdom, that same top-level domain would be identified as ".co.uk." Since Maddie clearly wasn't commuting to the United Kingdom or any other country to go on a date, Dylan was able to rule those links out immediately.

Cutting the list further took a scalpel instead of a hacksaw, but even then, it wasn't too hard. While some of the images might have been a match when seen by a computer, they were easy to filter out with the human eye.

That had gotten her to twelve results.

At that point, Dylan had started to worry she wouldn't have any left by the time she was done. Still, she'd plowed ahead, looking up business addresses for those images she found on corporate websites and cross-referencing social media platforms to find the city and state for the rest.

That got her to three. All located in Atlanta, Georgia.

She then used publicly available data to identify matching addresses. In two of the three cases, she found multiple results with the same name, and she solved that problem by leveraging the person's age to narrow down the results to only the most likely. One was a man named "Joseph Brown," which was so commonplace she was forced to put two of the possible addresses on her list, ticking her total back up to the four she had now.

Still, four wasn't too bad. They could get through that quickly.

"I've already emailed the list to myself," she said. "Let's go check them out."

"Sounds good to me."

Dylan closed the computer and, on her way out the door, caught the waitress giving her the evil eye. Dylan sneered in response.

The first house they approached could properly be classified as a mansion, Dylan thought. It dwarfed even Maddie's house. "This looks promising," she said, as they pulled up the long and winding driveway.

Olin looked from the house to Dylan. "What makes you say that?"

Dylan hadn't thought she would have to explain her comment, but apparently, she did. "Well, Maddie's father was famous. She probably traveled in certain circles. Seems like this guy might be traveling in those same circles, don't you think?"

Olin shrugged.

The driveway led them to a roundabout that circled a massive fountain. Stone steps, reminiscent of nineteenth-century Vienna, took them to an oversized front door. Dylan knocked. "You think he has a butler?" she asked, while they waited for someone to answer.

"He's not Batman," Olin said. "Does anybody even have butlers anymore?"

"I think he has a butler."

Then the door opened. A young boy in a striped tee shirt was standing on the other side. "Can I help you?"

"Is your dad home?" Dylan asked.

The boy turned around. "Daaaaaaaad!" He ran off, leaving the door open.

A gorgeous black-and-white foyer stretched out before them.

A minute later, a man appeared. He was wearing a Polo shirt tucked into a pair of pleated tan slacks and had the sort of pinched expression Dylan associated with old money. "Can I help you?"

One look at him, and Dylan was certain this wasn't their man. He had an unappealing swagger, a cockiness that made her want to recoil. And that voice . . . *ughh*. It was like a scratchy whine.

Maybe somebody else could overlook all that, but Dylan had known Aleshia well, and if Maddie was anything like her sister, Dylan doubted she would fall for a jerk like this. Besides, this man was wearing a thick gold band on his ring finger that was impossible to miss. He didn't just have a kid—he had a family, and that definitely wasn't something Maddie would put up with.

But she and Olin had come all this way, so she asked anyway: "Do you know Maddie Thompson?"

His pinched expression tightened further. "Who?"

"Maddie Thompson," Olin said, as if Dylan hadn't been clear the first time.

"I'm sorry. I have no idea who that is. Can I ask what this is about?"

"Is this Two-Seven-Two Riverlake Avenue?" Dylan said.

"Riverlake Road," the man said.

Dylan smiled sheepishly. "Sorry about that."

"But—"

Dylan grabbed Olin by the arm and started to pull him away before he could finish his sentence. "We've got the wrong address."

The man grunted and closed the door.

"What are you doing?" Olin said. "We were looking for Riverlake Road. We were at the right address."

"I know. That wasn't our guy."

"How can you be sure?"

They reached the bottom of the stairs. Dylan let go of Olin's arm. "A lot of things. Most important—the wedding ring. Maddie wouldn't be wasting her time with someone who was married, and we don't have time to waste talking to the wrong person. Let's try the next name on the list."

The next two addresses took them to houses that were far more modest than the mansion, and neither of the men at those addresses claimed to know who Maddie was. But this house—the small ranch they were parked in front of now—was the most modest by far.

The siding needed a good wash, and several boards needed to be replaced. The shutters needed to be repainted. The yard was two months past time to mow it and had odd, scattered bald spots. Barely visible along the front of the house was evidence of a flowerbed that had long since been taken over by weeds.

"This doesn't seem right," Olin said.

Dylan was inclined to agree. But the man who lived here was also the last one on their list. They might as well talk to him. "When we're done here, we can call Connor and tell him we struck out. Maybe he'll have something for us by then. If he doesn't, and if he asks, I don't want to tell him we left any stone unturned."

"All right." Olin's tone suggested he had already resigned himself to the failure this mission was doomed to be.

Dylan stepped out of the car and approached the front door. Olin followed.

A man wearing a grungy undershirt and a Mets cap answered her knock. "Yeah?"

Dylan could hardly believe what she was looking at. The other three men she had approached today *might* have been the one in Maddie's photo. But this man—Leon Hall—looked *exactly* like the one posing with her outside the Mercedes-Benz Stadium.

She tempered her emotion, told herself it might just be the shadow from the Mets cap obscuring his face. If he took it off, would he still bear the same resemblance to the man in the photo? Plus, there was the problem of the wedding ring again. This man had one, too, and Dylan was still certain Maddie would not get involved with a married man.

"We're trying to locate Maddie Thompson. Are you familiar with her?"

Leon didn't answer, but Dylan saw a flash of something behind his eyes.

She asked again, "Do you know her?"

"Who are you?" he responded.

Olin opened his mouth to speak. Dylan beat him to it. "She's a friend."

Leon slowly shook his head without taking his eyes off Dylan. "No. I don't. Can I ask why you think I would?"

"You look like someone she knew," Olin said.

That wasn't the answer Dylan would have given, since it might lead him to ask again what had brought them to his house. Maybe when he opened his mouth, that was indeed the question he'd first planned on asking. Then he hesitated and asked instead, "What happened to her?"

"She's missing."

Leon ran his tongue over his teeth as he seemed to consider this. With measured words, he said, "I'm sorry. I wish I could help you."

"That's okay. Thanks for your time." She and Olin headed back up the driveway.

"That was weird," Olin whispered.

"Yeah."

Then a voice from behind them shouted, "Hey!" It was Leon again. They both turned around.

"Let me know if you find her, all right? I hate the idea that there's this missing woman out there somewhere."

Dylan smiled awkwardly. "Will do."

Leon shut the door.

"Very weird," Dylan said to Olin.

"What were those questions about?"

"Did you see the resemblance?"

"Yeah."

Olin and Dylan reached the car. After they got in, Dylan said, "I wasn't sure if it was just me."

"No, I saw it. I think that's the guy in the picture. Why was he pretending he didn't know her?"

Dylan, too, wanted the answer to that question, as well as so many others. What was Maddie doing with a guy like that? Dylan couldn't see it. And what was that last question about—asking them to tell him if they found her? Didn't he know how strange that sounded?

The answers to some of her questions were easier to guess than others. Like what Maddie was doing with him if he was married. To that, the answer was simply this: Maddie didn't know. Leon could have taken off his wedding band when they were together. His skin was pale. If he had a tan line from the ring, it might not be easy to see. He certainly wouldn't be the first guy to pull a stunt like that.

But how had they met? That was harder. Maddie was an introvert. Dylan could imagine her limited social engagements might have put her in contact with the first man they had spoken to, but Leon? Had he approached her at a bookstore? An art show? A gas station? Maybe that had been the case, but it seemed unlikely that she—or any other woman—would say yes in any of those situations, if she even responded at all.

And if they were dating, why would he pretend he didn't know her? Could it be that his wife was somewhere in the background, and he didn't want her to find out? Dylan thought she had heard footsteps deeper in the house, so it was possible.

If that was true, it would also explain the strange question at the end, which, when seen through this lens, wasn't so strange. Leon didn't want his wife to know he was seeing another woman, so he denied knowing her. But he also cared about Maddie, so he wanted to know what had happened to her.

However, Dylan did not *know* whether that had been Leon's wife in the background. Leon might have been pretending he'd never met Maddie because he was trying to hide the information from Dylan, like she had originally thought.

She explained her reasoning to Olin.

"So, you think he's involved or what?" Olin said.

"I'm not sure. Either way, I think it's safe to say he knows more than he's letting on."

She called Connor. He didn't pick up.

"What do you want to do?" Olin asked.

Dylan thought about that. Until Connor got back to them, Leon was the only lead they had. "Let's stay here for now. Maybe we'll see something."

CHAPTER 48

CONNOR'S PHONE WAS back in his pocket when Dylan called. He didn't hear it ring or feel it vibrate. The traffic was too loud. He was in motion. Seconds earlier, he thought he'd seen Maddie on the other side of the street. She was still a block away from the entrance to the building, and from this distance, he couldn't be certain it was her. The woman's hair was shorter than Maddie's had been in the pictures they'd looked at. She was wearing big movie-star sunglasses that hid much of her face. The features he could see—her nose and lips, in particular—were impossible to examine in detail from so far away.

He had to trust his gut.

The only firm indication he had that he might be right was the Golden Retriever the woman had on a leash.

He slapped a ten-dollar bill on the table, hopped over the small wooden fence dividing the patio from the sidewalk, and started to cross the street. He weaved through the traffic, holding out one hand to ask oncoming cars to slow down and ignoring the horns. Once he was across the street, he waved to get the woman's attention. "Excuse me."

She didn't respond. There were a lot of pedestrians around them. Maybe she thought he was calling out to someone else. The distance between them continued to shrink. He tried again. "Excuse me!"

This time, he thought he saw her head shift in his direction. They were close now. If he didn't stop her soon, she would breeze right past him.

"Maddie!"

The woman sped up.

That had to be her, Connor thought. He stepped into Maddie's path. He tried to tell her he just wanted to talk, that he was here because Dylan had asked him to come. But the dog was already barking and, try as he might, he didn't think she could hear him.

What happened next happened fast.

Maddie pulled on the leash, trying to control the Golden Retriever, trying to turn around, to go in the other direction, to get away from Connor. The dog fought her for every inch. He was pulling so hard he looked like he could rip Maddie's arms right out of their sockets.

Connor worried what might happen if the dog got loose. He imagined those giant teeth coming down on his arm, taking a bite out of his side. But he had come so far. Maddie was right here. He couldn't walk away.

Then the leash slipped out of Maddie's right hand, and she could not hold the dog back with only her left. It lunged at Connor.

After Alex got back from the hotel, he had requested warrants for Connor's and Skylar's phone records. Aleshia's cell might no longer be in Connor's room, but that didn't mean Alex couldn't draw a line connecting the pair to it.

With nothing better to do, he sat at his desk, refreshing his email every five minutes while he waited for the warrants to get approved. Howie told him that was pointless—when an email came in, he would get an alert. Alex knew that was true. However, he doubted the email refreshed in real time, and he didn't want to wait any longer than he had to.

Refresh.

Refresh.

Refresh.

Howie stood up. "I'm going to get some food. You want to get away from that thing for a while?"

Refresh.

"No."

"You want me to get you anything?"

"No."

Howie shrugged. He slipped on his coat. "Suit yourself. See you in twenty."

Alex didn't answer.

Refresh.

Refresh.

An email appeared in his inbox. The warrants had been approved.

The dog landed heavily, forepaws first, on Connor's chest. Connor stepped back, terrified, and the dog stepped with him. Then, instead of barking, growling, or biting, he started licking.

Connor's terror turned to relief so fast he almost laughed. "Okay, get down. Get down, boy," he said, momentarily forgetting about Maddie. He took hold of the dog's forelegs and lowered him to the ground.

The Golden Retriever was panting like he had a new best friend.

In retrospect, Connor should have expected that. Dylan wouldn't have charged into Maddie's backyard so carelessly if her dog was vicious.

He also should have expected that when Maddie had lost control of the dog, she would run. Because that was exactly what she did. She already had half a block on Connor. He wasn't sure what to do. He couldn't leave the dog here, wandering around the street on his own.

The doorman.

He was only steps from the entrance to Maddie's building. If he hadn't been between her and the doors, certainly she would have taken refuge inside. Had she done that—especially if she had made it onto the elevator—he would have had no way to get to her. The receptionists might not be able to stop him, but they would call the police, who would. You could bet your last dollar Detective Alex Shaw would hear about that, and any hope Connor had of convincing the detective he was there to help would be gone.

He moved quickly to the glass doors at the front of the building, thrust the leash into the doorman's face. "Take him," he said. "He's Maddie's."

The man waved his hands back and forth in front of his chest like he didn't want to have anything to do with Connor or the dog.

"Take him!" Connor demanded, and perhaps because he was so insistent, this time the doorman grabbed hold of the leash.

Connor turned to run after Maddie. The half-block she'd had on him before had become a full block. He sprinted, pushing his legs as fast as they would go. Maddie turned right at the intersection, and so did Connor. He was gaining on her slowly, he thought. However, he wouldn't be able to keep this up for long. He was thin, wiry. But he was not an athlete.

He wished Olin were here. Olin was built for just this sort of thing. His only hope was that Maddie had no more endurance than he did.

They both kept running. Maddie looked back only once. Tall glass office buildings rose to the sky along both sides of the street. She turned another corner. This block was longer than the others. Connor should have been able to see her in the distance. He couldn't.

Confused, with heart pounding and taking deep, desperate breaths, he stopped. Maddie couldn't have made it to the next intersection. She had to be hiding somewhere, hoping he would run right past her without seeing her.

Connor shouted her name. No answer. "I just want to talk to you! I'm on your side!"

There weren't a lot of people on this street. Those that were looked suspiciously at him, keeping their distance. He realized calling out to her like that was a bad idea. If he kept it up, he was going to draw unwanted attention, and Maddie wasn't going to believe him anyway.

He would have to find her. More office buildings rose up around him. Connor glanced into each lobby he passed. He saw banks of elevators, attached shops and restaurants, all closed, and unattended reception desks. The doors he tried were locked. Perhaps that was no surprise since it was a Saturday.

Up ahead in the distance, Connor could see retailers that would be open. But if Maddie hadn't been able to make it to the end of the block, she certainly couldn't have made it to them. The only plausible place left was the parking garage attached to the office building on his right.

As he got close to the entrance, he noticed it was open to the public on weekends, and as such, had plenty of cars—and plenty of places for Maddie to hide. He would have to approach this methodically.

He began quietly circling the first floor, looking around every car and listening for any sounds of movement.

When Alex reviewed the phone records, he was hit with his second *Oh, shit* moment of the day. He tried to call Howie to tell him what he'd found. The call rolled over to voicemail, and before he could leave a message, his own line beeped. Call waiting. He looked at the number and knew right away he had to take it. He switched calls, listened for a moment. "I'll be right there," he said, already heading to the elevator.

He would have to catch up with Howie later.

CHAPTER 49

DYLAN HAD CIRCLED the block, and she and Olin were now watching the house from a safe distance. So far, nothing had happened. She checked her phone to see if Connor had returned her call. He had not.

Olin slid his seat back to make himself more comfortable. "Do you think . . ." He hesitated, like he didn't want to ask the question. Then he pushed forward. "Do you think he killed Maddie?"

"I don't think so," Dylan said. She had already imagined the only scenario she could come up with that would end with Leon killing Maddie. It went like this: Maddie found out Leon was married. She confronted him. At first, he tried to deny it. That only made her angrier. Things got out of hand. He responded in kind. The confrontation continued to escalate. And that was that. Maddie was gone.

While it was plausible—things like that happened more often than they should—it didn't sit right with Dylan. For one thing, she didn't think Maddie was dead. While someone *might* be able to set up a bank account in Maddie's name and slowly siphon off her money, that would take a degree of sophistication she didn't think Leon possessed. And even if he did, would he also have gotten rid of her dog? Would he have changed the phone number on her security system so he would get notified if someone broke in? Would he have gone back to her house and cleaned up after Connor and Dylan had left?

That seemed like too much. Even if you assumed Maddie had disappeared because she was afraid he would kill her, why would he have killed Aleshia?

He was a cheater, sure. But that was all they knew. If he was involved, it had to be in some other way.

Dylan was still trying to figure out what that "way" might be when a black Escalade passed them and parked in front of the house. Three men stepped out. All three were wearing suits.

The driver was large, heavyset. He carried himself in such a way that suggested he was more muscle than fat. He ran his fingers through the few strands of gray hair he had on the top of his head as if trying to keep the hair neatly parted like he had in his youth.

The other two men were even bigger.

If Dylan had seen them in any other setting, she wouldn't have thought much about them. They looked like any number of middle-aged businessmen she'd seen over the years. But showing up here, now, dressed like that . . .

"What's going on?" Olin said.

"I don't know. It's not good, I'll tell you that."

The driver signaled for one of them to go around back while the other followed him to the front door.

Inside, Skylar was sitting on the sofa. She had changed out of her work clothes and was now wearing black sweatpants and a loose tee shirt. They were her comfy clothes, her standard home attire.

Leon was in the kitchen, scouring the fridge for another beer. Skylar knew he wouldn't find one. He'd finished everything last night. But she was going to let him look as long as he wanted because she was pissed.

She had heard the conversation at the door. She had recognized Dylan's voice. How the hell had Dylan made the connection between Leon and Maddie? More important: Why the hell would Leon ask her to tell him if she found anything out? Didn't he understand how suspicious that must look?

Skylar had been tiptoeing around those questions so far. They were both on edge, and she couldn't see how bringing them up with Leon would do any good. He wouldn't know how Dylan had made the connection between him and Maddie. And it wasn't as if he could take back the question he asked her when she was leaving.

But by the time he came back into the living room, she had held her tongue as long as she could. Her anger had boiled over into a rage. Mostly because she worried that if Dylan had made the connection between Leon and Maddie, she might also have made the connection between *her* and Maddie.

"What the hell's the matter with you?" she snapped.

"What?"

"Asking Dylan to let you know if she found anything out about Maddie? A woman you said you don't know? Who does that?"

"What's it going to hurt? Right now, you're stuck waiting on Connor to get out of jail. Why not ask her to let me know if she finds something out? Sure seems a lot better than sitting here doing nothing."

He didn't get it, and she was about to go off on him. He also looked like he was about to tear into her. Then someone knocked on the door and they both froze.

"Do you think they're back?" Leon whispered.

Skylar shook her head. They wouldn't be back that fast, she didn't think. She moved to the window and peeked between the blinds. She saw the Escalade parked along the curb. A sense of dread overtook her anger. "It's Sam."

"I told you he might come back," Leon said.

"What do you want to do?"

Now Sam's voice came through the door. "I know you're in there. I can hear you. You'd better let me in, or things are going to get a lot worse."

Leon looked nervously at the door, and then back at Skylar. He waved his hand at her, fingers down and out, shooing her into the hallway.

She shook her head. She didn't want to leave Leon on his own.

Then Leon pointed to the hall, mouthed the word *Get*, and she reluctantly stepped out of the room. Once she was out of sight, Leon took a deep breath, went to the door, and opened it.

"Looks like you and I have got a problem," Sam said as he and one of his associates entered.

That was all Skylar needed to hear to know things were about to get very bad. She wasn't sure what to do. Maybe she could go out the back door, she thought, and—

Suddenly a loud bang echoed through the house. It sounded like a gunshot and had come from the rear of the property. It was followed by two more in rapid succession. These latter two were comparatively soft, and together she knew exactly what they meant. One of Sam's men had shot the lock off the door and then kicked it open. They were surrounded.

Dylan and Olin watched the two men step into the house. "We need to get closer," she said.

"Are you crazy?"

"We were waiting to see if anything might happen. I would say this qualifies. Maybe it's related to Maddie and maybe it's not—"

Olin gave her a look.

"Okay, it's probably not. But we shouldn't make any assumptions. Let's just go have a look. We'll be careful."

Olin still didn't seem satisfied. Dylan sighed. She had tried to convince him as much as she was going to. If there was anything to learn, she might miss it if she spent too much time sitting out here. "I'm going," she said, as she opened the car door. "Come if you want."

"Wait—"

She didn't. Dylan scurried across the yard, instinctively bending at the knees and the waist, as if it would make her harder to see. She collapsed against the siding, directly underneath the window.

To her surprise, Olin dropped onto the ground beside her. "This might be stupid, but I'm not letting you do it on your own."

She smiled. Then she held a finger to her lips, telling him to be quiet. The men who had entered the house had left the door open a crack behind them. She hoped she was close enough to hear what was happening inside.

The voices were muted. She had trouble understanding what the men were saying. Something about money, she thought. Who was giving it to whom, she had no idea.

Then there was another voice. A woman's voice.

Although it was probably Leon's wife, Dylan still wanted to make sure. She straightened up cautiously, peeking her head above the edge of the window frame. Like at Aleshia's, the blinds were drawn. But they weren't entirely closed, so instead of picking out details along their edges, she could see through the slits between them.

The two men in suits who had entered the house from the front door had their backs to the window. Leon was on the other side of the sofa, facing them. Farther away, standing near a doorway that looked like it might lead into a hall, was the only woman Dylan could see. The man the driver had sent around to the back of the property was standing behind her and holding her by her hair.

Once Dylan realized who the woman was, her breath caught. She dropped back to the ground. *Oh my God!* she mouthed.

Olin held his hands out to his sides, lifted them slightly. *What?*

"It's Skylar," she whispered.

"Are you sure?"

Dylan nodded. "What the hell is Skylar doing in there?"

CHAPTER 50

THE GARAGE WAS dimly lighted. The shadows between the cars stretched into each other, creating dark pockets that were hard to see into from a distance. As far as Connor could tell, nobody was hiding between the cars and the exterior walls. He slowly moved up the first ramp.

To his right, there was an alcove for the elevators and a door that led to a stairwell. Connor detoured into it long enough to be certain Maddie was not behind a wall.

Then he pushed the door to the stairwell open. Garbage littered the ground at the bottom of the stairs. There was nowhere in here for someone to hide.

He returned to the ramp, continued going up. He imagined how terrified Maddie must be. He again felt the urge to call out to her, to tell her that he was a friend, that everything was all right, that he just wanted to talk. But if she didn't know where he was, that would give him away for sure. And what good would it do? He had to find her, to get hold of her long enough to make her listen.

He continued up the ramp, looking between the cars and underneath any trucks that might provide enough clearance for her to slide underneath.

Somewhere in the distance, he heard the drip, drip, drip of water. Perhaps condensation forming on a pipe, he thought. It was so soft he wouldn't normally have noticed it. But here, now, he was acknowledging and identifying every sound, because just like he would betray his location if he called out to Maddie, she might betray hers in a way much more subtle. A shoe scraping along cement as she shifted her weight. The clang of jewelry against the trunk of a car. It could be anything. If it happened, he didn't want to miss it.

At the top of the ramp, the cement leveled off and looped around. Another ramp took Connor higher. From the street, he had estimated the garage contained four floors. Two of the overhead lights were out, making the shadows darker, the trucks harder to see underneath.

He stepped past a hatchback—a white Toyota Corolla that was sandwiched between two larger vehicles. He heard a whisper of sound so faint he wasn't sure whether he had imagined it, and it was far too faint to identify. He stopped moving, held his breath to see if he would hear it again.

When he didn't, he considered his options. If it was Maddie, sliding behind vehicles, mirroring Connor's progress in reverse so he wouldn't see her, she had to be behind the hatchback. There would be nowhere she could go without exposing herself. As long as Connor didn't start moving toward her, she would almost certainly stay where she was.

Quietly, Connor knelt down so he could see underneath the vehicle. He wanted to confirm his assumption before settling on his next move. He saw a pair of white sneakers and straightened back up.

"Maddie," he said, speaking as calmly as he could. "I need to talk to you. Do you know Dylan Naese? Aleshia's friend? She asked me to come down to Atlanta to help her find you. You and Aleshia both. Do you know what happened to your sister?" Connor decided against saying she had been murdered. If Maddie didn't already know about it, he probably shouldn't be the one to tell her. Certainly not like this. So, he settled on his next best option—the only thing he would know if Detective Shaw hadn't filled him in. "She's gone missing, too. Dylan's worried about you. I'm worried about you. Why did you disappear?"

Connor waited for her to answer. A minute passed, maybe two. "Please come out, Maddie. I know you're there." He took a step toward the hatchback.

Then Maddie spoke. "I've got pepper spray! Stay back!" However, she remained out of sight.

Connor retreated to his previous position. "Does this have anything to do with that guy you were dating?"

Another long pause.

"How do you know about him?"

"James Hargrove mentioned it. Aleshia's ex? He said you met him at Brick's a couple of times, and Dylan found a picture of you and him at a baseball game."

"You were the ones in my house?"

"We weren't there to cause trouble. We were just trying to find out what happened to you."

"My sister isn't missing. She's dead."

At first, Connor wasn't sure how Maddie would know that. If she was in hiding, if she wasn't in touch with anyone, who would have told her? Then he remembered his visit to the police station with Dylan and Olin to ask about her case. The officer had seen something on his monitor. He had even gone to talk to somebody about it before he returned to tell them he could not provide any information. They must have known where Maddie was the whole time.

When he was at the Rustic, Connor couldn't figure out why it had been so hard for them to find her. Apparently, it hadn't been. So, why hadn't they told Aleshia they knew where she was?

"If you want to help me, leave me alone."

"Why did you disappear? Does it have anything to do with what happened outside of the Ink Well?"

Another pause. "They came back. At least one of them did, anyway. Did you know that? He broke into my home in the middle of the night. I guess he thought I'd be asleep. But I was in the studio. I don't always sleep well, so I do a lot of work at night. I couldn't tell who it was. The guy—he was wearing a mask, just like he was in the parking lot. He chased me through the house. I'm lucky I got out. I told the police about it. Spoke to a detective and everything. They're still looking for him, but they didn't have a lot to go on."

"That's why you disappeared?"

"I didn't feel safe. Not even in my own home. What choice did I have?" Maddie still hadn't shown herself. At least she didn't sound so afraid anymore.

"Do you know what they wanted?"

"No. I wish I did."

"Why didn't you at least tell Aleshia what you were doing?"

"I was going to. Eventually. I . . . I don't know. I needed time. I wasn't ready to talk to anyone. If I had known they might go after her, too, I would have told her. I would have asked her to come stay with me right away." Another pause. Then she added meekly, "I wish I had."

At one point, Connor wondered why Maddie would open an account at another bank. Now he knew the answer. She wanted to disappear entirely—at least until the police figured out who was after her. That meant changing everything, right down to her bank account. She didn't want to take any chances.

"We can help you find out who's after you," Connor said.

"Why would you do that?"

Connor could have answered that question in a lot of ways. They would do it because Dylan would want them to. They would do it for Aleshia. They would do it because they had already started looking. But perhaps the best answer he could give right now was the simplest. "Because somebody abducted my parents."

He realized Maddie might think he was implying those abductions were related.

"That was a long time ago now," he clarified. "The point is: I didn't know who took them or why, and I know what it's like to live with that fear."

Maddie rose from behind the hatchback. She had removed the big movie-star sunglasses and was cupping them in her left hand. Connor still couldn't see her face well in these shadows. The little he could see suggested she was overwhelmed by emotion. Sad and afraid, sure. But also somehow hopeful, relieved. Maybe, Connor thought, it was because she had been dealing with all this on her own for so long, and now after what he had said, she thought she had an ally.

Then again, maybe he was projecting those emotions onto her. Whatever she felt, though, he figured he couldn't be entirely off-base since she had finally shown herself.

Maddie opened her mouth, about to say something else, when a blue sedan came roaring up the ramp.

Connor darted toward Maddie, afraid the asshole behind the wheel wouldn't be able to stop in time. But the asshole—Detective Alex Shaw—slammed on his brakes when he was within feet of Connor and was out of the car not a second later. He grabbed Connor, slammed him against the hatchback hard enough to knock the wind out of him. He pulled Connor's hands behind his back.

Connor could feel the handcuffs lock into place, first around one wrist and then the other. He wanted to say something, but it was all happening so fast, and Alex was already talking, asking Maddie if she was all right, if Connor had hurt her.

Connor's mind was spinning. What the hell was going on? Then another piece of the puzzle fell into place. He remembered the look Alex gave Dylan when they were being questioned at the station. Alex had said he wanted to talk to them about Ms. Thompson. Dylan had asked if he meant Aleshia or Maddie. The way he had looked at her— Connor didn't get it then. Now he understood the detective Maddie said she'd spoken to must have been Alex. He was the one who told Maddie her sister was dead. That meant not only did the police, as an organization, know where Maddie was the whole time, but that Alex, specifically, did, as well.

When Maddie was on the run from Connor, she must have called him. Connor could picture her, crouched down behind the Toyota Corolla whispering into the phone while Connor was still out on the street trying to figure out where she had gone.

Maddie moved closer to the action, insisting she was fine, that calling Alex was a mistake. Really. "He's not who I thought he was. He's trying to help."

"I'm afraid that's not true."

Maddie looked confused. "He said—"

"I'm sure he said a lot of things. He said a lot of things to me. Why don't you ask him about the girl he's with?"

"Dylan?"

"Skylar."

"Who?"

Alex pulled Connor off the car by the handcuffs. "Tell her."

"I'm not sure what you want me to say." Then Connor looked at

Maddie. "Skylar works at Southern Trust. She was helping us track you down."

"That's not entirely true, is it?" Alex said.

Probably not, Connor thought, remembering the phone call she had received from "Erin" right before he had been arrested at the hotel. He was already certain from Maddie's Facebook photo that she was the woman on Skylar's phone. Standing this close to her, he had no doubt. He didn't know how to explain that.

"We got a court order for your phone and hers. We know everywhere you've been. Like Maddie's house. You were the one who hung that rope down through the skylight, weren't you? What were you doing there?"

Connor didn't want to answer that. He shot a pleading look at Maddie, asking her to keep her mouth shut. It seemed like she would, perhaps if only to see how this would play out. "We went to see if she was home."

"Uh-huh. So, you didn't break in."

"No."

"Let's say that's true. Do you want to know where Skylar's phone was a few days ago? At Aleshia's. Right before she went missing, and right before you came into town. You know where she went after she left there?"

Connor had a feeling he did.

"Straight up Highway Nine. Guess who went with her? Aleshia. You see what I'm getting at here?"

Connor didn't answer.

"In fact, when I track the movement of all these phones, they paint a pretty damning picture. Tell me if this is right. Skylar killed Aleshia at her house—I don't know why yet. We'll find out eventually. Then, in a panic, she loaded Aleshia's body into her car. Who knows what she planned to do with it at that point? Maybe she wasn't thinking straight. Regardless, at some point—probably when she was on Highway Nine, she figured out Aleshia had her phone on her and dumped it. My guess is that's when she reached out to you. There's no record of a call. With all the apps these days there doesn't have to be. Anyway, she reached out to you or Dylan or both of you, and you came into town to clean up the mess."

"It's not like that," Connor said.

"Wait, let me finish. So, you came into town. You dumped the body because Skylar wasn't strong enough. She probably could have manhandled Aleshia into her trunk, but getting her way out on the beach like that?" He shook his head. "Then you told her it wasn't a good idea to leave Aleshia's phone on the side of the road. Maybe it had fingerprints or DNA on it or who knows what? So, you went and got it and brought it back to your hotel. Meanwhile, Dylan put in a missing person report to try to throw us off the scent. What you didn't count on was that the body would float back to shore. How am I doing so far?"

"Not very well," Connor said, and instantly regretted it. Antagonizing Alex would not make things any better. Since he had already said it, he kept going. "After Aleshia went missing, I came down to help Dylan find her. Dylan knows her Apple password."

That was a lie. If they hadn't broken into Aleshia's house and then her computer, they would never have found the phone. But he didn't think admitting to additional crimes was the way to go right now.

"We went looking for her phone because we thought if we found it, we might find her."

"Why didn't you tell me you had it?"

Connor twisted his head toward Alex and lifted his arms enough to draw attention to the handcuffs. "Why do you think? As far as Skylar goes, I met her at Southern Trust because Aleshia's boyfriend told us she saw Maddie there, and she inserted herself into the investigation."

"I haven't been back there since—" Maddie began.

"She said she wanted to help us find her," Connor continued. He was so wrapped up in what he had to say, he hadn't realized Maddie had spoken at all. "I was willing to take all the help I could get. Then, right before you came into my hotel room, someone called Skylar's phone." He looked at Maddie. "The name was Erin. The face that came up with it was yours. I don't know what that was about, and it doesn't sound like you would either."

Back to the detective: "You must have seen the missed call. I've still got her phone in my pocket."

Alex reached in and grabbed it. He pressed the power button to have a look at the screen. From where he was, Connor could see the missed call notification.

"You'll have to log in to see the caller. But after what you told me, it sounds like Skylar's the one you need to talk to if you want answers."

"Why were you looking for Maddie?"

"Same reason we were looking for Aleshia's phone. We didn't think it could be a coincidence that the two women disappeared a month apart. At first, we thought if we found either one of them it would help us find the other. Then, after what you told Dylan and me about Aleshia, it became even more important. We were worried Maddie might be in danger, and as far as we knew the police weren't doing anything about it."

Connor wished he hadn't said that last bit, either. Dylan must be rubbing off on him. Then he had another thought. It was obvious, but he still felt like he needed to say it. "I wasn't even in town when someone came after Maddie before. So why would I have anything to do with it now?"

CHAPTER 51

EVERYTHING CONNOR WAS saying made sense. Well, most of it. The phone call he claimed Skylar had received was out there, but it would also be easy enough to verify. Had Alex been looking at this whole thing all wrong?

He was starting to think the answer was yes.

Alex's theory, as it stood now, involved too many people: Dylan, Skylar, Connor. Not to mention the masked man who had attacked Maddie in front of the Ink Well and at her home. Their relationships did not seem strong enough to bind them together in a conspiracy of this size.

He remembered a quote that he often applied to his cases when a theory seemed to be spiraling out of control: *The simplest explanation is usually the right one.*

If he applied that logic here, he had only one choice.

"Do you know where Skylar is?" Alex said.

"I don't. Dylan might." Connor had intentionally left Olin out of the conversation so far since the detective didn't seem to know about him. "If you take these cuffs off, I could call her and ask."

Alex snorted out a small laugh. "I could call her and ask, too." Then he paused, pulled his keys out of his pocket, and took the handcuffs off anyway.

236

Connor rubbed his wrists. "Does this mean you believe me?"

"It means we're going to play this thing out and see where it goes. Make no mistake, you're staying with me the whole time, you got it?"

"Of course." Connor wouldn't have it any other way. He had come too far. He wanted to see this investigation through to the finish line. Skylar's phone had been in his left pocket. His was in his right. He pulled it out and called Dylan, put the call on speaker.

"Yeah?" Dylan sounded like she was whispering.

"Are you all right?"

"Yes. Fine. We found the man Maddie was dating."

Connor glanced at Alex. He could tell the detective was intrigued. Connor had skipped that part of the story because it wasn't germane to the accusations Alex was throwing at him. He would have to fill the detective in when they got off the phone. First, though, he asked, "Do you know where Skylar is?"

"She's here."

"What? Where?" Alex said.

"Who's that?" Dylan said.

Connor held the phone closer to his mouth. "It's Alex. I don't have time to explain but . . . I think you could say we're on the same side now."

Alex nodded reassuringly.

"It's starting to look like Skylar might be the key to all this," Connor continued. "Where are you?"

"With Leon. That's the name of the guy Maddie was dating. We're outside his house right now. They're both there. And some big-ass guys just showed up. I'm not sure what's going on. We're trying to figure it out."

Connor didn't have to look at the detective to find out what he would want to know next. "What's the address?"

"I'll send it to you. I can't hear what they're saying. I have to go."

Dylan hung up.

Connor was now certain of several things: Skylar and Leon were in this together. Likely he was even the man who had attacked Maddie outside the art studio and broken into her home. She had said he had worn a mask. Maybe he would have done that anyway. If he was worried she might recognize him, he definitely would have.

But that wasn't all. Skylar—

"Come on," Alex said, gesturing for Connor to get in the car.

"We don't know where we're going yet."

"Wasn't that your phone that just dinged?"

Connor glanced at the screen. Apparently, it was. He must have been too deep in his own thoughts to hear it.

He opened the message to confirm it was from Dylan. As he hurried over to the passenger door, he said to Maddie, "Thank you. We'll be in touch." Then, just before he closed the door he added, "Oh, and your dog is with your doorman. I'm sorry I scared you."

CHAPTER 52

SKYLAR HEARD THE back door bang into the wall and slipped into her parents' bedroom in search of a weapon. There were heaps of clothing on the floor and a whole assortment of junk on the nightstands. Still, even among all that stuff, she didn't have any options other than a couple of coat hangers. Maybe she could take out an eye with one of them if she was lucky, but even that seemed unlikely.

She felt a hand slide up into her hair and take hold before she was able to pull away. She knew it was the man who had entered through the back door. "Let's go," he said, as he pulled her into the hall and then pushed her forward into the living room.

"I'm glad you could join us," Sam said. "I was just telling your father here that I've got a friend who works down at City Hall. I don't like to bother him much, especially on a Saturday. But our conversation yesterday just kept *eating* at me, so I asked him if he wouldn't mind doing a little checking on those so-called permits. I can't say he was any more excited to be doing this on a weekend than I was, but he owed me, so . . ." Sam frowned. His voice took on a mocking tone. "Would you believe it if I told you that nothing was filed? I thought, 'That can't be. There must be some mistake. Leon knows what a bad idea it would be to screw me over like that.'"

The man behind Sam rolled his shoulders around in his blazer. When he did, Skylar could see a gun stowed in a shoulder holster. She didn't think that was an accident. Then she looked at Leon and could tell he had seen it, too.

"What name did you give them?" Leon asked, trying to sound far more cool and collected than he was able to.

"Excuse me?"

"When you asked about the permits."

"I gave them your name."

A nervous smile. "Oh. That was your mistake. They're not under my name."

"Really?"

"That other investor I told you about—he filed them."

"Ah, yes. Him." The sarcasm was back. "I should have thought about that. Alas, I don't know his name. What is it?"

"It's, uh . . ."

Sam raised his eyebrows.

"Frank."

"Frank what?"

"Frank Sticks."

"Frank *Sticks*?"

Leon nodded, and Skylar almost groaned out loud. He couldn't have come up with a name that sounded any more fake.

Sam took two steps toward the TV and placed his hand on top of it. "Are you sure that's his name?"

"I'm sure."

Then, Sam's fingers wrapped around the edge of the TV and he pulled it forward. The TV fell off the stand, crashed into the coffee table. The screen shattered. The table shook. And the remaining beer cans still standing upright collapsed with a clatter. "Give me my money!"

Dylan got off the phone with Connor. "He's on his way."

Olin was about to respond when she held up her finger again to silence him. The voices were still muffled. Getting a word here or there wasn't going to cut it. She would have to move closer. "Stay here," she told Olin.

"Where are you going?"

She pointed to the door, then started to creep along the edge of the house. The door was still open a few inches, and the closer she got, the more she could understand. The man who had been driving the Escalade was named Sam. Leon owed him money. Sam was pissed and had already broken the TV to show them he meant business. From what she could gather, it sounded like Leon had borrowed money to open a restaurant, then kept that money for himself.

Dylan wasn't surprised by any of it. Leon seemed like exactly the kind of person who would do something like that, and Sam was exactly the kind of person he would borrow the money from. Maybe she should just let Sam beat the crap out of him.

"There is no second investor," Sam said.

The man behind him reached under his jacket and pulled out the gun. He let it hang by his side.

Skylar was afraid for herself and for Leon. She wanted to do something to put a stop to this. Maybe she could have if she'd acted sooner. Now that the man behind Sam had drawn his gun, it was too late. The man behind her still had her hair knotted in his hand. He might let go if she jabbed him in the gut with her elbow. But before she would be able to get away, to do anything substantial to help herself or Leon, the gun would come up. The man holding the weapon might even fire it. Perhaps not at her, since she was so close to his partner, but Leon would make for an easy target.

"I thought about going to the police," Sam continued. "That's a slow process. It could be a year until you go to trial, and I'm supposed to just sit back and watch you walk around a free man until that happens? Because I'm sure you'd be offered bail, and you'd use my money to post it. Talk about adding insult to injury. Besides, if I did that, I still wouldn't have my money back. In fact, I'd *never* get it back. Really, I don't want to make things hard for you. Give me my money and you can go run your scam on some other sucker. How does that sound?"

Leon had his hands raised in the air. His attention shifted between Sam and the gun. Skylar hoped he did not continue to lie about the restaurant. She wasn't sure how they were going to get out of this, no matter what he said, since most of the money was gone. However, she was sure, at this point, that lying was not going to make things better.

Fortunately, he seemed to realize the same thing. "I don't have it," he said.

"You don't?" He was mocking Leon again. "Color me surprised."

"I can get it, though." Leon said. "I just need more time."

Sam smiled in his unnerving way. He moved closer to Leon. The man with the gun stayed where he was. When Leon and Sam were almost a foot apart, Sam, who had to look up at Leon to meet his eye, said, "Excuse me," and Leon wisely took several steps back toward Skylar.

Sam pulled his own gun fast, swung it left to right across the room.

Skylar screamed; she couldn't help herself. Leon ducked. Sam fired three shots at the computer, point blank range. One bullet went through the monitor. The other two drilled holes into the console, turning the machine into an expensive paperweight.

"You don't have a lot here. Sooner or later, I'm going to get to you."

"Listen," Leon said. "There's a woman. Maddie Thompson. Have you heard of her?" Any attempt at composure was gone, and Skylar worried he was about to tell Sam everything. "She's Andrew Thompson's daughter. The painter? Anyway, she's loaded. I had a plan to get my hands on that money. To do it, I needed to get close to her, and she wouldn't have looked twice at me. Not if she knew who I really was. I needed to make it look like I belonged in her world. So, yes, I lied to you. I didn't know where else I could get the money. There wasn't a bank in the world that was going to loan it to me. I was going to pay you back, I swear. With interest."

"So where is this money?"

"Things didn't go exactly as planned. She disappeared."

"Because of you."

"What? No. *No!*" Leon shook his head feverishly. "What happened was . . . So, I started following her on social media, looking for my way in. Eventually, I saw she had signed up on this dating site her sister had recommended. It's called Cupid's Corner. I had gotten a good idea of what she liked from her feed, so I sent her a message. We went out on some dates. Things were going well. Then someone breaks into her home and she freaks out. The police weren't able to figure out who it was, and one day she just disappears. But now there's this guy looking for her. We think he can find her. Skylar's gotten close to him, and when he finds her, we'll know. We'll be back on track soon."

"Let's see if I got this right," Sam said. "You're screwing me over, so you can screw this woman Maddie over. Now you want me to believe that when you're done screwing her over, you're going to give me my money back?" He looked at Skylar. "And you were in on it."

Leon had left out some important pieces of the story. The guy who shot the computer hadn't seemed to notice. But Dylan had. Leon had glossed over the part about *how* he was going to get Maddie's money. He had also skipped the attack in the parking lot and implied he didn't know who had broken into Maddie's home.

Dylan had trouble believing those events were unrelated to Leon's plan. She suspected, in truth, Leon had gotten close to Maddie to learn her routine. Then he used that information to either orchestrate those attacks or commit them himself. And the reason he hadn't simply grabbed her while they were on a date? That was easy. What if it went wrong? Maddie had turned the tables on the man in the parking lot and escaped when he came after her in her home. If Leon had tried to kidnap her while they were on a date and failed, she would have known exactly who to blame when she went to the police.

Had he been successful, though, he likely would have forced her to initiate wire transfers or give him her bank card and her PIN. Then what? Kill her, Dylan assumed. He wouldn't have been able to let her go after that.

Something clicked. When they started the investigation, they assumed Aleshia's disappearance had to be related to Maddie's, and they'd still assumed it was even after they had learned Aleshia was dead. Leon was the reason why. He must have gone to Aleshia's house intending to force her to tell him where Maddie was.

Maybe he'd killed her on purpose and maybe not. Either way, Dylan was certain they had found the man responsible.

"I can't say I trust you," Sam said to Leon. He pushed past him, grabbed Skylar by the jaw. Skylar started to reach up, to try to pull away, when the man behind her let go of her hair and grabbed both of her arms.

"Maybe I should take a piece of you with me for my trouble," Sam said.

Dylan wasn't sure what that meant. Was he going to cut off a finger? Was he going to do something worse? Would he kill her? If Connor hadn't called, Dylan might have just stayed where she was and let it happen. Whether you wanted to call it vigilante justice or karma— Skylar had it coming.

But he *had* called, and Alex was with him. Maddie deserved the kind of justice she would never get from Sam. She deserved a trial. She deserved to know exactly what these two were up to and who else might be involved. Without that information, could she ever properly grieve for her sister? Could she ever feel safe?

Dylan turned around. She expected to see Olin still crouched against the wall under the window, but he was only inches away. Like her, he was on his hands and knees, trying to hear the conversation.

"We have to stop this," she whispered.

"How?"

Dylan turned back toward the living room window. "I don't know." If they had a gun, at least they could level the playing field. As it stood, however, she was certain they would be on the losing end of any confrontation.

Dylan was about as close to the ground as she could get, and the door was only open a crack. Skylar finally spotted them, though, and when she did, Dylan could see her pleading for help.

Dylan studied the room, trying to assess the situation. If she could sneak up behind the big guy blocking the door, she could probably take the gun out of his hand before he realized what was happening. The problem with that was getting through the door. She would have to open it, at least a little. The big guy with his back to her wouldn't notice, of course. Neither would Sam—all of his attention was on Skylar. But the thug holding Skylar's arms behind her back would definitely see her enter, and he'd warn his partner.

They needed a distraction.

Suddenly, she had an idea. She told Olin what she needed from him, and he crept away. He looked back once. When he did, she gestured for him to hurry. So far, Sam had done no more than threaten Skylar. Sooner than later, though, things would escalate.

Sam continued to study Skylar's face like he was assessing its value. "Are you sure you don't have my money?"

Dylan heard a crash deeper in the house. The sound of glass breaking. Everyone turned to look.

Good job, Olin, she thought. He had done exactly what she'd asked him to.

Sam let go of Skylar. "Who the hell else is here?" he asked Leon.

"Nobody. Nobody, really! I don't know what that was."

"Go check it out."

The man holding Skylar's arms also let go and headed down the hallway. At the same time, Olin—panting, short of breath—reappeared beside Dylan.

"It's now or never," Dylan said, but Olin was already pushing the door open, moving toward the man with his back to them. Dylan shouldn't have been surprised, because when it mattered—really mattered—Olin was there to do what needed to be done. She just wished he had coordinated his action with her.

She cursed under her breath and followed.

The man must have heard the door open or felt a breeze because he started to turn, to raise his gun. Dylan dropped to her knees and grabbed the weapon, while at the same time Olin slammed into his back, knocking him off balance. For less than a second, he and Dylan were caught in a tug of war. But when Olin threw his weight against the man, he let go of the gun, reached forward for something to grab hold of.

Dylan did not have much experience with guns, but she knew how to hold one. She had been to a shooting range once for lessons. Research for a book, she'd said.

She wrapped both hands around the handle and trained the gun on Sam. He, too, was just starting to turn toward the commotion.

Skylar must have seen the opportunity for what it was because she immediately ripped his gun out of his hand. Then Leon jumped on top of him, forcing him to the ground.

Dylan heard the thud of heavy footsteps moving in their direction. The man at the back of the house was coming back.

Skylar spun the gun toward him and fired. Once. The man fell to the floor, half in and half out of the living room. His head and outstretched arm were visible from Dylan's vantage point.

"Move!" Skylar shouted at Leon and fired again. The bullet hit Sam in the shoulder, spun him around. A second shot through the torso finished him. He fell to his knees, grabbing hold of the sofa as he went down, and eventually collapsed.

At the same time, the man by the front door had regained his balance. Dylan and Olin were standing beside him—Dylan with the gun hanging by her side and wide-eyed, Olin equally immobile. Both seemed to be overwhelmed by the violence Skylar had unleashed on these men.

The man stepped backward toward the door, then turned to run. He didn't make it past the threshold before Skylar fired her fourth bullet into his back.

Dylan worried they were next. She braced herself.

And Skylar did indeed spin the gun toward them, but she didn't fire. Keeping them in her sights, she said, "Drop it."

Dylan immediately let the gun fall to the ground.

"Kick it over here."

That would have been difficult even without the bodies in the way. As it was, the small room was a virtual obstacle course of horrors. Dylan kicked the gun intending to slide it under the sofa and out the other side. Perhaps in another situation, she would have aimed to kick it just hard enough to get it under the sofa but no farther. However, this did not seem like a time to be, as her mother would have said, *cute*.

The gun came to rest against Sam's shoulder.

"Pick it up," Skylar told Leon.

He did.

Then Skylar nodded toward the hallway. "Come on," she told him. "We need to go."

CHAPTER 53

SKYLAR LED LEON toward the back door, stepping awkwardly around Sam's goon as she went. She saw the rock on the floor and the shattered glass around it. The window beside the back door was broken. That was the noise that had drawn the man's attention earlier.

Thank you, Dylan, she thought.

She didn't like that Dylan and Olin had tracked down Leon, that they now knew she and Leon were working together, that they had stuck around watching the house (why else would they be there now?), but she sure was glad they had come charging through that front door when they did. She didn't want to imagine what Sam might have done to her and Leon otherwise.

"This way," she said, signaling for Leon to follow her around the house.

They needed to get out of there fast, and they weren't doing that without a car. Skylar could have led Leon out through the front door, but that would have meant doing an awkward dance with Dylan and Olin as one pair moved further into the house and the other pair moved closer to the exit. This seemed faster and easier.

"I'll drive," Skylar said. "Give me your keys." They were going to have to take Leon's F-150. Skylar had left her purse, and thus her keys, inside. She'd also left her wallet, and thus her license, in there, but that wasn't going to stop her from driving. She had just killed three men. Driving without a license seemed comparatively inconsequential, and she was in no mood to sit idly in the passenger seat while Leon took control.

They were in this situation largely because of him. Five simple steps and, now that she thought about it, he couldn't get even one of them right. Borrowing the money from Sam (the one step she gave him credit for) had almost gotten them killed.

And Step Two, getting close to Maddie, was a bust. He had bought the right clothes (Prada and Burberry), rented the right vehicle (a Mercedes S-Class he had since returned), said the right things (thanks, partly, to Skylar's guidance), and taken her to the right places (Bones and Fogo de Chao). He had charmed her like a pro.

When it came to using the information he'd learned, however, he had dropped the ball again.

Skylar remembered sitting with Leon in this same F-150 outside the Ink Well. That would be the best place to grab her, he had said. They knew exactly when she would be there, exactly when she would leave, and she would be out in the open when she went from the studio to her car. It would be easy.

He had, of course, been wrong.

Skylar had cursed him up and down after he had fumbled his way back into the truck, pawing at his eyes and saying he needed water to rinse away the pepper spray.

Then he screwed up again when he broke into her house. Skylar had not been there for that. She hadn't thought she would need to be. The plan had been to sneak in through a window he'd unlocked when he was visiting Maddie earlier that day. After that, he just had to creep up to her bedroom without waking her, douse a rag with the chloroform

Skylar had bought for him online, and knock her out. It should have been easy.

Skylar had suggested it would be smarter to stay overnight and do it then, but he said if he did, a neighbor might tell the police they'd seen the Mercedes there, and he would be stuck explaining to them why he hadn't called when someone broke in. And if he did speak to the police, no doubt he would be their first suspect. They would pull at the threads of his life to test the veracity of his story, and when they did, it would undoubtedly unravel.

He couldn't take that chance.

Turned out his way wasn't any better, though. He might not have ended up talking to the police, but he also hadn't left the house with Maddie.

She was awake when he broke in, he told Skylar. He chased her through the house with the chloroform-soaked rag in one hand and managed to grab hold of her twice. Both times, she twisted away before he could get the rag over her mouth. She ran out the front door and went straight for the neighbor's house across the street. Leon's only choice then was to leave before anyone thought to write down his license plate.

"This won't be our last chance," he had assured Skylar when he returned home. But Maddie had disappeared without a word days later, and for a while there, it looked like he was wrong.

Without Maddie, steps three through five could not be done. At least, not as they were planned.

Leon passed over the keys once they were inside the vehicle. The truck was old. It took Skylar two tries to start the engine.

"You know what we have to do now," Leon said, as Skylar pulled out onto the road.

She did. Their plan had been a good one when it started. It had seemed simple and elegant. But in the end, it was all about balancing the scales, and there was more than one way they could do that.

She was finally ready to flip the switch on the nuclear option, the alternative to steps three through five, the choice that meant they would have to run, because after killing Sam and his men, Skylar would have to run, anyway.

"Call Mom. See if she'll answer."

"You know she's not going to pick up—"

"Call her!" Skylar knew Leon was likely right. She was also done listening to him. She had already blown up her life cleaning up his mess, and since the nuclear option depended entirely on her, she was running the show until they were somewhere safe.

Leon pulled his phone out of his pocket, dialed a number, and held the phone to his ear.

Skylar resisted the urge to speed through every stop sign she saw. The last thing she needed was to get pulled over right now.

Leon returned the phone to his pocket. "See? Like I said. She's not going to answer."

That was okay, Skylar told herself. Ashford Park was only a few miles away. Her mother would take the bus whenever she went there. It would take her an hour to get to the park, but she had always said the trip was almost as peaceful as the park itself.

Skylar didn't get it. She had never found a bus ride enjoyable. But she believed her mom did, because on more than one occasion she had known her mom to get on the bus and just ride for hours at a time.

She liked to pretend she was going somewhere far away, she said. A place where she had no problems. Skylar knew what she meant. It wasn't merely a fantasy. It was something closer to regret. When she said that, her mom was thinking about the pivotal decision that led her to where she was now and how different her life could have been. But it wasn't *her* choice that had led her to this point in her life. That pivotal decision had been made by somebody else. It wasn't fair that she should have to live with the consequences of it.

At least she wouldn't have to live with them for much longer.

In the Ford, Skylar could get to the park in fifteen minutes, even with the stop signs.

CHAPTER 54

DYLAN SIGHED WITH relief when Skylar and Leon stepped into the hall without shooting them. She listened to their footsteps fade to nothing. She knew they'd gone out the back door. They were going to make a run for it. After killing three men, Skylar didn't have much choice.

Dylan couldn't let that happen. Connor and Alex wanted to talk to her. She was, as Connor had put it, "key to all this."

Dylan maneuvered her way around the body in the hall as well as she could without looking directly at it. She felt something sticky underfoot. Blood, she realized, when she finally looked down.

She wanted to vomit.

She forced herself to turn away, to keep going.

"What are you doing?" Olin said.

"We can't lose them."

Olin made a sound that she took as frustrated acknowledgment she was correct. "Okay, but what do you think you're going to do?"

This time, Dylan didn't answer because she didn't know. She was playing this by ear. Perhaps if she could see where they were headed, she might have an idea.

She looked cautiously out the back door, afraid they might not have gone anywhere at all yet. When she didn't see them, she stepped into the backyard. Looked left, right. The backyard was a shallow stretch of weeds that ended at a sagging chain-link fence in all directions. Beyond it was another house whose yard was not much better.

What the hell? Where are they?

They couldn't have disappeared. Then Dylan heard a car start, and she had an answer. "Out front!" she shouted, hoping Olin would hear her.

She ran along the side of the house but stopped short of coming around to the front of the property until the Ford drove away. She noted the vehicle's color—red—and the first three digits of the license plate—ARH. It would be enough to find them again as long as she and Olin didn't fall too far behind.

Olin stepped out the front door. Dylan scrambled over to her car, called for him to follow. He climbed into the passenger seat and was still buckling his seatbelt when Dylan put the car into drive.

"What's your plan?" he asked, as she peeled out onto the road.

"I don't know."

"Well, don't get too close."

She looked at him. "Duh."

"And keep your eyes on the road!"

Dylan weaved back into her lane. She kept a lot of distance between her Volvo and the truck until they pulled out onto Arbor Street, a heavily trafficked thoroughfare that cut straight through the heart of the city. Here, she could hide with only a car between them.

Alex pulled up to Skylar's house.

"That's strange," Connor said.

"What?"

"I don't see Dylan's car. Where are they?" On the drive over,

Connor had finally decided he should tell Alex who Olin was since the detective seemed to be on their side. So, when Connor said "they," he didn't have to explain what he meant.

He could tell this observation didn't sit right with Alex, either. Alex stepped out of the vehicle and turned to Connor. "I'm going to see what's going on. You stay here."

"But—"

"I mean it." As Alex crossed the yard, he turned around briefly to point at Connor, as if to emphasize how serious he was.

Connor had almost said something similar to Dylan years ago when they had followed a killer deep into the woods. She wouldn't have listened. Now, in her position, he wasn't sure he would either.

There weren't a lot of reasons the car wouldn't be there. Olin and Dylan would not have left unless they had to, and they probably would have called to tell Connor why.

The other possibility—the one that worried him the most—was that they *hadn't* left. Perhaps the reason they hadn't called was that someone else had moved the car. That would mean something terrible happened.

Connor was about to call Olin to see what he could find out when Alex pushed open the front door of the house and immediately drew his gun.

Connor thought he saw a body on the floor just beyond the doorway.

Screw this, he said. His friends might be in there.

He unbuckled his seatbelt, got out of the car, and approached the house slowly, listening for trouble. So far, nobody had started shooting. Once he stepped onto the porch, he could see enough of the man sprawled out on the floor to know he had been shot in the back. He peeked into the living room and saw more dead bodies, but no Alex. The detective must have moved into the hall.

Connor stepped around the body, careful to avoid the blood pooling along its side. He tried to make sense of what he was looking at. Was this a shoot-out? A Mexican standoff or something?

Dylan said Skylar had been here with the man Maddie was dating. Was he among these bodies? Or were these the big-ass guys Dylan had told him about?

What the hell happened here?

Alex returned to the living room. His gun was back in its holster. "I told you to stay in the car."

"Did you find . . ." Connor swallowed hard. He could barely bring himself to ask the question. "Did you find anybody else back there?"

"No." Then he asked Connor the same question Connor had wondered about moments earlier. "Any of them the guy Maddie was dating?"

Connor shook his head. "I don't know."

CHAPTER 55

SKYLAR PULLED INTO the parking lot at Ashford Park, hoping this was not one of those times her mom had decided to aimlessly ride the bus. She'd seen a white Volvo behind her once and worried they were being followed. But she had also thought the same thing about a black Kia and a beige Taurus. The stress of the situation was making her paranoid. The only people who might be behind her right now would be Olin and Dylan. After what they had seen at the house, she didn't think they would be stupid enough to follow her.

"I'll be right back," she told Leon, and Leon, staring down at the gun in his hands, responded with a barely a nod. He'd been quiet ever since they left the house. She wasn't sure what that meant. Nor did she have time right now to figure it out.

Skylar jogged past the playground, where children screamed joyfully as they chased each other in endless circles. On the far end of the park, the gravel path that looped around the playground gave way to a collection of nature trails that meandered through the woods beyond it in unpredictable ways.

It would take hours to search them all. Fortunately, Skylar knew exactly where to find her mom if she was here. There was a bench a quarter of a mile down the main trail overlooking a stream.

Skylar went straight to it.

As she hoped, her mom was there, sitting with her back to the trail.

Skylar slowed to a walk. She didn't want to alarm her mom by coming up on her too fast. She thought her mom might look over once Skylar was within her peripheral vision. She didn't. She was lost in her own world of "what-ifs" and "never-weres."

"Mom."

"Oh, hi, honey. I didn't see you there."

"Mom, we need to go."

"Why? What's going on?" The frown lines around her eyes and mouth deepened.

Skylar had to tell her. She sat down on the bench, tried to deliver the news as gently as she could. "Things haven't gone the way they were supposed to. We're still going to get the money. We're going to make things right. But you can't go home. We're going to have to find a new place."

"Is it because of Sam?"

Skylar nodded and hoped her mom would not ask any more questions. She did not want to tell her about the men she killed. Her mom had been okay with the idea of taking Maddie's life after they kidnapped her. That would be justice, she'd said. But she had explicitly said she didn't want any more bloodshed than was necessary.

Her mom turned back toward the stream.

Skylar gave her a minute to process the news. Then she said, "Mom."

The woman sighed, pushed herself off the bench slowly. "I know. Let's go."

Dylan parked far enough away from Skylar's Ford that she wouldn't draw attention. Using the rearview mirror to keep an eye on the truck, she saw Skylar step out and jog into the park. "What's she doing?"

Olin didn't respond. Dylan hadn't expected him to. Only time could provide an answer.

They sat in silence, each watching a mirror. Olin's phone rang. "It's Connor," he said and answered with the call on speaker.

"What the hell happened here?" said the voice on the other end of the line.

Dylan knew right away that it wasn't Connor, but she needed a couple of seconds to figure out it must be Alex. She quickly explained the events that had transpired at the house.

"Where are you now?" Connor said.

"Ashford Park. We followed Skylar and Leon here. We didn't want to lose them."

Alex: "What are they doing there?"

Olin: "We don't know yet."

Dylan: "About ten minutes ago, Skylar went running into the park. She left Leon in the truck. She hasn't come back yet."

Alex: "Christ—"

Olin: "Wait." He spun around so he could see out the back window. "Look. She's coming back."

Dylan spun around, too. "He's right. She's back, and she's not by herself. There's a woman with her." Dylan leaned forward and squinted, as if that might help her see better. "Is that Maddie?"

"Impossible," Alex said. "We were just with her. She's back at her apartment."

"You found her?" Dylan asked.

"We always knew where she was. She was never lost. You three were just sticking your noses where they didn't belong."

"That sure looks like her," Olin said.

"I told you it can't be."

"Hold on." Olin used his phone to take a picture and texted it to Connor.

"Well, shit," Alex said.

Dylan fastened her seatbelt. "They're moving again. We'll let you know where they go."

CHAPTER 56

THE UNDERWOOD MOTEL served a certain kind of clientele. It rented rooms by the day, week, and month, and had the kind of reputation that came with that. Skylar knew about it because everybody knew about it. Normally, she would steer clear of the place. But because they *did* serve a certain kind of clientele, she knew they didn't ask a lot of questions. For three people who needed to fly under the radar, it was perfect.

They just had to get through the weekend. Monday, Skylar would go into the office just like she would any other day, transfer all the money she could from Maddie's account to her own, then remove that money in cash from another branch. After that, she would deposit it into her mom's account, where it would be squeaky clean. (Or clean enough, anyway. Sooner or later, the police would figure out what she had done and freeze the account. But if they could get out of the country Monday afternoon and transfer the money again, it wouldn't matter.)

Skylar would undoubtedly be charged with various types of fraud. She would be looking at serious jail time if she was convicted, which was why she hadn't pursued this option before. That, and the fact that they would get their hands on only a small portion of the fortune her mom deserved. All of the money Maddie had in investments and other accounts would remain with her.

But Skylar was also going to be charged with multiple counts of murder now, so what did it matter? They would take what they could get.

The potential for a murder charge had existed well before Skylar shot the three men in her house. It had existed since she had gone to Aleshia's to ask her where her sister was. She'd knocked on the door with Leon's bottle of chloroform and a rag at the ready. Knocking her out had been a piece of cake. Getting her into the trunk of the car, however, was less so. She'd thought she would be able to manage the body on her own, but somehow Aleshia seemed ten times heavier than she should be. So, she called Leon to help her. Then she drove Aleshia up to an abandoned building on Highway 9 and tortured her for hours. Aleshia kept insisting she didn't know where Maddie was. Skylar didn't believe her. In the end, it cost Aleshia her life.

If she had seen the reward posted to Aleshia's Facebook feed beforehand, she never would have bothered.

Spending too much time thinking about that would lead her into her own world of "what-ifs" and "never-weres," so she didn't. What was done was done. All she could do now was make the best of it.

She had promised Leon if the police stopped by even once to ask about Aleshia, she would pull the cord on the nuclear option, but they never did. If Sam hadn't come around with his goons, she might never have needed to. Thanks to Connor, she had been *so close* to finding Maddie.

Now that was also a "what-if" and "never-was." She pushed it out of her mind.

The motel had several rooms available, all on the first floor. She selected the one at the back of the property and farthest from the street. The desk clerk—a small, greasy man with cracked lips and a sleazy smile—gave her a knowing look. "Have a good time."

Her skin crawled. However, she didn't want to make waves. For the right price, this man might be their only ally at the motel. She thanked him and returned to the truck.

"Nobody's leaving this room for the next two days, you got it?"

"Got it," Leon said.

Her mom nodded.

Skylar drove to the back of the building and parked in front of their room. It was small and hot. The striped wallpaper had yellowed. The carpet was worn thin. It was, without any doubt, the most depressing place she had ever been. But the worst part of it was the smell. It was nauseating and musty, as if the mold she was sure was growing behind the walls had vomited on itself over and over again.

She knew she would not get used to that smell, no matter how long she was here.

The room included two double beds. Leon took a seat on the one farthest from the door, propping his feet up and resting his back against the headboard. He patted the mattress, inviting Skylar's mom to join him, which she did.

Skylar pressed the remote on the TV and found a rerun of *The Wonder Years*. Her mom would like that, and Leon would tolerate it, so at least they would be occupied for half an hour or so.

She went into the bathroom and found two glasses by the sink. She checked the water to make sure it was drinkable. Once she determined it was, she returned to the bedroom and said, "I'm going to find some ice." The heat in this place was going to kill her. It was like the motel was trying to fight off a winter that never came to Atlanta.

CHAPTER 57

DYLAN CIRCLED THE Underwood's parking lot looking for the Ford Skylar was driving. She found it parked in front of a room at the back of the motel. There were plenty of open spots around it. She started to pull into one of them.

"I don't know that we should get this close," Olin said.

"We need to keep an eye on them."

"Let's go park by the lobby. It's the only way in or out of the lot. If they leave, we'll see them."

Dylan reluctantly returned to the front of the motel and backed into a spot that gave them a clear view of the exit. "Happy?"

"I guess," Olin said. Then he called Connor to tell him where they were.

The longer Dylan sat there, the less she liked it. What if they had seen her following them? What if this was a diversion? What if they planned to leave the room on foot?

She told herself all that was unlikely. However, she decided she at least needed to know what room they were in. When Connor and Alex arrived, she wanted to be able to point them to the right door.

"I'll be back," she said, getting out of the car.

"Where are you going?"

"To use the restroom," Dylan lied. "Keep an eye out." She didn't feel like getting into an argument with Olin about whether this was a good idea. She was going to do it, anyway.

"Be quick."

Dylan entered the lobby. It was an oddly shaped space with a green-and blue-tiled floor that might have been cool in the seventies. When Dylan had circled the building, she noticed a pair of glass doors that led into the lobby from the rear. She made her way quickly toward them. A desk clerk with crooked teeth and bushy eyebrows smiled at her in a suggestive way. Behind him, keys dangled from numbered hooks.

"Perv much?"

His smile immediately disappeared.

She pushed through the doors and turned right. Skylar's truck was perhaps a hundred feet away. She glanced at each of the rooms she passed to see if the lights were on or, if the curtains were open, whether anyone was inside.

By the time she had reached the truck, she'd passed two rooms with the lights on and curtains drawn.

That wasn't ideal, but at least she could tell Connor and Alex she had narrowed down the possibilities. As a cop, Alex could cut the list to one pretty easily by knocking on both doors.

She turned around, deeming the reconnaissance mission as much of a success as it could be. A door opened behind her. She spun back toward the sound as she also heard the clatter of an ice bucket hit the pavement.

Skylar was coming toward her fast. She grabbed Dylan by the shirt, pulling her back when Dylan tried to run. Then she got an arm around Dylan's waist, shouted for Leon.

The door opened again. As Dylan flailed about, she caught a glimpse of Leon standing in the doorway. She thought she saw surprise on his face. Then he was coming toward her. He took over for Skylar, lifting

Dylan off the ground. Dylan tried to kick, and Skylar grabbed her legs. She tried to scream, and Leon covered her mouth.

They carried her back into the room.

Skylar's mom pushed herself over to the farthest edge of the bed and pulled her knees to her chest. "Oh, no. Oh, no. Oh, no. What is—"

"It's okay, Mom. We've got this." To Leon, she said, "You still have the chloroform in the glove box?"

Dylan continued to writhe and kick.

"Should be," Leon said.

"Can you hold her?" Skylar asked.

"I think so."

She reluctantly let go.

Dylan kicked her feet into the carpet and bucked back against Leon, trying to push him off. He stumbled back. She kicked the bed frame, trying again. He released the hand he was using to cover her mouth and wrapped both arms around her torso.

Dylan started cursing up a storm.

"Just hurry!" Leon said.

Skylar dashed out and grabbed the chloroform from the Ford's glove box. The door to the room barely had time to click shut before she was coming back through it again. Leon now had Dylan pinned to the ground on her stomach.

Skylar grabbed a towel from the bathroom and doused it with the chloroform. She pressed it to Dylan's face.

"She's holding her breath," Leon said. "I can feel it."

"She'll have to breathe eventually."

Dylan tried to push herself up, twisted her head left, then right.

With her free hand, Skylar pressed the right side of Dylan's head to the floor. She kept the towel pressed firmly against Dylan's nose and mouth long after she stopped moving. "I want to make sure she's out for a while."

When Skylar finally removed the towel, Leon let go of Dylan's wrist and got to his feet. "What do you want to do with her?"

Skylar wasn't sure. She had let Dylan live before because she and Olin had helped her out of a bad situation with Sam. That was probably a mistake. Skylar shouldn't have let her sympathy get the best of her.

Funny, she thought, since it was sympathy for her mom that had led her down this path to begin with.

Actually, to be fair, it wasn't just sympathy when it came to helping her mom. Or love. It was also greed. *Justice for Mom. A whole bunch of money for all of us.*

"We've got some time to figure that out," Skylar said. "First, we need to go find Olin. If Dylan's here, you can bet he probably is, too."

"You're going to leave me here with that?" Skylar's mom said as Skylar and Leon headed for the exit. She was quite obviously talking about Dylan.

Skylar opened the door. "She's not going anywhere. Just stay put. We'll be back soon." Then she stepped out into the twilight. The halogen lamps mounted to the exterior of the motel were on. Night was coming upon them faster than she had expected. It must have been getting dark when she was out here earlier; she was just so surprised to see Dylan, she hadn't noticed.

"You go right. I'll go left," she said. "Check everything."

Skylar headed toward the front of the motel and glanced into the lobby. When she didn't see Olin, she continued the long way around the building.

He's got to be here somewhere.

She was within sight of Leon again when she found him, sitting in the passenger seat of a white Volvo. He was looking down at something in his lap. Maybe his phone. If the car was locked, she wasn't going to be able to get him out. There might be another option.

She signaled for Leon to go back the way he had come. When they were back in the room, her mom nodded toward Dylan. "She didn't move. I watched her the whole time."

"That's good, Mom." Skylar fished Dylan's phone out of her pocket and held the screen up to Dylan's face, hoping to unlock it. When that didn't work, she pulled Dylan's eyelids open and tried again.

That did the trick.

She sent a message to Olin: *Come through the lobby! Meet me around back! Hurry!*

Three dots danced along the bottom of the screen, like Olin was typing a response. They stopped.

"He's coming," she said to Leon.

They ran back outside. Without coordinating their moves, each took up a position on one side of the lobby doors.

Olin came flying through them a moment later. He seemed to realize immediately he had been tricked, tried to turn around.

Leon had his arm around Olin before he could get back into the lobby. Like they had done with Dylan, he lifted Olin off the ground and Skylar grabbed his legs. Olin was stronger than Dylan, harder to hold on to. But with Leon pressing the chloroform-soaked rag to Olin's mouth and nose, she could feel that strength fading quickly.

They carried Olin back into the room, dropped him on the floor next to Dylan.

"We have to get rid of them," Skylar said. "But not here."

Although the motel staff seemed to overlook a wide variety of crimes, Skylar was not certain murder would be one of them.

CHAPTER 58

ALEX PULLED INTO the parking lot of the Underwood Motel.

Connor pointed to a white Volvo. "That's Dylan's car."

Alex pulled into a spot next to it. "Where are they?"

Connor had an uneasy feeling he might know the answer to that question. Dylan was not one to sit still. She had probably gone looking for Skylar's room and dragged Olin with her. Alex wouldn't like that, so he kept it to himself. They were already walking a thin line with the detective.

Besides, he couldn't see what difference it would make. Sooner or later, they would turn up. Perhaps—he thought about Maddie—they were crouched behind a car watching the door to Skylar's room.

Maddie.

Alex had told Olin and Dylan she was at her apartment. But when he'd tried to call her after Connor hung up, she didn't answer. He had left a message asking her to call back, and she hadn't done that, either.

Was she the woman in the picture Olin had sent? Was that why she hadn't answered?

The picture was a little fuzzy, so it was hard to be certain. If it wasn't Maddie, the woman sure looked a hell of a lot like her, and that bothered him.

Connor shrugged at the detective to say he had no idea where Dylan and Olin were.

270

Then the detective got out of the car and made his way toward the lobby. Since he hadn't told Connor to stay put this time, Connor immediately followed.

The detective flashed his badge at the man behind the counter.

The clerk's creepy smile vanished, and the blood drained from his face. He said there had only been one person who checked in recently. A single woman. When he described her, she sounded like a spot-on match for Skylar.

Alex asked for her room number.

Connor thought the clerk might put up some resistance—citing privacy laws or something like that. He didn't. Likely, Connor thought, he didn't want any more attention from the police than he was getting right now.

While Connor and Alex waited for the clerk to pull up the room number on the computer, Connor sent a quick text to Olin, telling him he had arrived.

"Room forty-two," the clerk said. "It's that way." He pointed toward a pair of glass doors that led to the back of the building.

Alex thanked the clerk and left, went back to his car.

Connor followed him out just like he had followed him in. "Wait," he said. "Where are you going? This isn't the right way."

The detective spun around. "What do you think I'm going to do right now?"

Connor had to admit—he didn't know. He had assumed once Alex had the room number, he would go knock on the door, demand Skylar open up. Probably take her and Leon into custody right then and there. Maybe he would arrest that woman who was with them, too.

But that didn't seem to be the right answer. So, like he had with his thoughts on Olin and Dylan, he kept this to himself.

"First I'm going to call my partner and tell him where I am," Alex said, as he and Connor got back in the car. "Then I'm going to call for backup. If you think I'm doing anything else, you've been watching too much TV. We know Skylar and Leon killed the men in that house. We can bet they're armed. If I showed up all by myself, what do you think my odds would be of walking out of there?"

Then Alex started making calls.

Connor checked his phone for a response from Olin. There wasn't one. He started to worry, decided he had better make a call as well. But Olin didn't answer. Neither did Dylan.

This was bad. Even if they were crouched behind a car, watching the door to Skylar's room, wouldn't they answer?

Alex was still on the phone when Connor opened the car door. He put one hand over the microphone. "Hey. Where do you think you're going?"

"I'm going to have a look at the Volvo. I want to see something."

"Stay here."

"Are you going to arrest me for looking at the Volvo?" He could feel himself once again channeling Dylan.

The detective made a face, then his attention was diverted back to the call. Connor walked around the Volvo to the driver's side. He opened the car door, leaned in. He had worked out a theory that might explain why he was unable to reach his friends, and it was this: Dylan or Olin (or both) had left their phones in the car.

And if it was just one of them, perhaps the other phone was on silent. How many times had he missed a call for that very reason?

The theory was simple, reasonable.

And unlikely.

But he wanted to see if he was right before his imagination ran away with him.

He did a quick examination of the interior. He pushed the fast-food wrappers out of the way. He opened the center console, moved the makeup bag to make sure there was nothing underneath it. The glove box contained only an owner's manual and an insurance card.

So much for that.

The alarm his theory held at bay burst forth now as a fully formed emotion. What the hell had happened to his friends?

Connor feared he knew the answer to that. He passed back in front of the detective's car.

Alex opened his door. "Now where are you going?"

This time, Connor didn't answer. He went through the glass doors that took him into the lobby and exited the other side. He checked the closest room numbers to get his bearings and turned right. "Dylan! Olin!" Connor didn't want his voice to carry into Skylar's room, so he whisper-shouted their names.

No response.

He moved through the parking lot and tried a couple more times. Now he was certain he knew what had happened.

Alex came barreling through the lobby doors. "What do you think you're doing?"

Connor closed the distance between them. "I think Skylar and Leon found them."

"Your friends?"

"They've probably got them tied up in their room right now." *Or worse*, Connor worried.

"Backup is on its way. If they're in there, we'll be able to get them out. We'll bring in a hostage negotiator. It will be all right."

But all that took time, and Connor worried it was time they might not have. He couldn't take that chance. Olin and Dylan had always been there for him. They were like family. If they died while he sat out here doing nothing, he wouldn't be able to live with himself. He had gone up against a man with a gun before. He could do it again.

The only question was, how would he get into that room?

Connor started back toward the lobby.

"Good choice," Alex said. Apparently, he thought Connor was going to return to the car. He was about to find out how wrong he was.

Connor walked straight up to the front desk, scanning the keys hanging on the wall behind the clerk. In most motels, he would be surprised to see such an antiquated security system. Here, he was almost surprised the rooms weren't simply left unlocked.

He found the hook for Room forty-two. It was empty.

"I need your master key," he said to the clerk.

"Excuse me?"

The detective came up beside him. "Hey, Connor. Seriously, get back in the car."

Connor ignored him. "Give me the master key!"

The clerk looked pleadingly at Alex. "I can't do that."

So, there were some lines even this man wouldn't cross.

Connor reached across the counter, tried to grab the man's shirt. He didn't have any sort of plan other than once again demanding the key. If he could have stepped outside of himself, he would have seen the flaws in this plan. But right now, Connor was riding high on fear and anger. To him, there seemed to be only one path forward, and that was getting into Skylar's room.

Alex grabbed Connor by the waist—"Let the man go!"—and pulled him back.

Connor lost his grip on the clerk's shirt. He twisted, shook Alex off, retreated several steps. His hands were up, palms out, in a "stay back" gesture. He was ready to fight or flee if Alex tried to get hold of him again.

"Don't do something stupid," Alex said. He seemed happy to give Connor some space. For now.

Connor wasn't going to get his hands on that key, he realized. He knew Alex had a gun under his jacket and wondered if he could get to that, instead. With a gun, he could shoot the lock off Skylar's door. He quickly dismissed that idea as borderline suicidal.

There was still one way into that room, however. Now that he thought about it, it might have been his best option all along. If he had used a key, Leon and Skylar would have heard him coming. They would have had time to react. Somebody might have gotten shot.

But this . . .

It would depend on timing and human nature. But if it worked, everyone would walk out of that room in one piece.

He was on the move again, afraid that if he thought too much about it, he might talk himself out of what he had to do.

Alex was coming after him, telling him to stop.

Connor broke into a run. He was certain if the detective caught up to him, he would probably slap the handcuffs back on, if only to keep Connor under control.

The detective was barely feet away, reaching out for Connor, when Connor arrived at Room forty-two and knocked on the door.

With that, the detective threw his back against the wall, drew his gun. "What do you think you're doing?" he hissed.

"I told you my friends are in there."

Connor saw the peephole darken as someone looked out. He made sure his hands were visible. He did not want the person on the other side of that door to think he might be armed. "I'm alone. I'm just here for Olin and Dylan."

The door flew open. A man Connor didn't recognize dragged him inside. The door shut.

CHAPTER 59

SKYLAR AND LEON each had a gun aimed at Connor. His friends were on the floor—hopefully unconscious rather than dead. A woman, who as far as he could tell might be Maddie, was standing between the bed and the wall with her hands clasped in front of her. Connor held his up.

"I didn't know you were out of jail," Skylar said.

Connor pointed at the woman in the corner with just his eyes. "Is that Maddie?"

Skylar smiled and shook her head. "No. That's my mom."

Connor remembered James Hargrove had claimed he had seen Skylar talking to Maddie at that bank. But Maddie had said it wasn't her, and now he understood why. It had been this woman—Skylar's mom. Then he thought about the phone call he had seen come in to Skylar's phone in the hotel room, and that made sense, too.

"Erin," he said, looking at the woman.

She reacted in some sort of subtle, mousy way he couldn't quite put his finger on. It was enough to tell him, however, that he was right. And even if Connor had been imagining that reaction, Leon confirmed it when he said, "How do you know her name?"

"My phone," Skylar said. "You got into my phone, didn't you?" She had been holding the gun in only her right hand, a stance intended more to threaten than kill. Now she shifted her weight to place it evenly on both legs, wrapped her left hand over her right.

"No, I didn't. Really, I swear. How would I? Erin called after you left the hotel room to go get something to eat. It was right before the cops showed up. That's how I know."

"Mom, did you call me earlier today?" Skylar asked, without taking her eyes off Connor.

Erin nodded.

Skylar must have been able to see her mom out of the corner of her eye, because the next question was directed back at Connor: "Do you have the phone on you?"

He reached for his left front pocket.

"Slowly," Leon said.

He pulled out Skylar's phone.

"Throw it on the bed," Skylar said.

Connor did. He looked at his friends. "Are they okay?"

"Are you really alone?" Skylar said.

"Yes. Olin called me. He told me where he was. That was before . . ." He looked again at his friends. "I just want to get them out of here. We're not going to tell anybody where you are. I promise."

"So, you want me to believe the three of you will just walk away?"

"We will."

"You're not that type. Those two wouldn't have been here to begin with if that was true. If I let you out of here, you three will go straight to the police, won't you?"

"We won't. I'll make sure of it." There was no need to lie this time. They *wouldn't* go to the police when they left—the police were already here.

"Leon," Skylar said, "get the chloroform. We're going to have to take all three of them with us."

Leon stepped into the bathroom at the rear of the motel room. When he returned, he still had his gun in one hand. Now, in his other, he was also holding a towel, no doubt soaked with chloroform.

Connor had gathered from Skylar's comment they didn't plan on killing anybody in this room. That didn't mean, though, he was okay letting Leon get anywhere near him with that towel. Plans change. Once Skylar and Leon realized the police were here, who knew what might happen? If Connor wanted to help himself and his friends, he needed to remain conscious.

What was taking Alex so long, anyway? Connor had expected Skylar and Leon to pull him inside when he knocked on their door. He had also expected Alex, gun drawn, to follow. Now he was wondering how long Alex was going to wait. He remembered what Alex had said before he'd started making phone calls in the car.

First, I'm going to call my partner and tell him where I am. Then I'm going to call for backup. If you think I'm doing anything else, you've been watching too much TV.

Was he really going to stand outside until backup arrived?

Leon slowly stepped closer, like he was cornering a wild animal. He kept the gun at arm's length until it was touching Connor's temple. Then he moved in with the towel.

Connor instinctively tried to turn away, and Leon—perhaps also instinctively—tried to stop him. He grabbed Connor around the chest from behind, pressed the towel firmly to his mouth. Connor held his breath as he struggled to break free.

In a brief moment of clarity, he realized Leon had dropped his gun. He was already as sure as he could be that Skylar wouldn't pull the trigger in this room unless she didn't have a choice, which gave him a very narrow opportunity to turn this conflict to his advantage.

Connor fell to his knees, pulling Leon with him. Leon made a sound—something guttural and deep. It seemed like he thought Connor was going down for the count.

Connor knew he had only a second or two before Leon figured out what was really happening. He reached for the gun, touched it first with just the tips of his fingers. Leon tried to pull him away, but gravity was not on his side. Connor let himself fall farther forward. Close enough to wrap his hand around the weapon.

Leon let the towel fall from Connor's mouth as he grabbed Connor's wrist, and Connor took a much-needed breath.

"He's got the gun!" Leon shouted.

"Move out of the way!" Skylar said.

Leon did as instructed, letting go of Connor entirely.

Until that moment, even with the weapon in hand, Connor had not been sure he would be able to turn this around. Leon was strong. He had a good hold on Connor even after Connor had pulled him to the ground. If he had just held on . . .

Connor rolled over, rocked up, and aimed the gun in Skylar's general direction all in one single move. Then everything became still. All three of them did nothing but breathe. All *four* of them, actually. Erin was still standing meekly in the corner, watching the conflict unfold with wide-eyed alarm.

Connor thought he saw Dylan move a little. The chloroform must have been wearing off.

Connor had come into this investigation looking to answer not only the questions of what had happened to Maddie and Aleshia but also why they had disappeared. Some of those answers he now thought he could piece together on his own.

Sofia had mentioned the man who attempted to abduct Maddie

outside of the studio was picked up by someone driving a Ford F-150. That was the same kind of truck parked right outside the motel room. Clearly, Leon and Skylar had been after Maddie long before Skylar had tried to use Connor to locate her through her bank account. That meant the odds were good Leon was also the man who had broken into Maddie's home.

He could further assume they had gone to question Aleshia about Maddie's whereabouts after she'd disappeared and killed her when she was unable to tell them anything.

He didn't yet know how Leon had wormed his way into Maddie's life or how Skylar ended up working at her bank, but those questions hardly mattered right now. They weren't going to tell him why they had done what they'd done, and this might be his only chance to find out. Once Alex and his buddies got in here, Skylar and Leon would likely clam up for good.

Obviously, it had something to do with the woman in the corner. She couldn't look more like Maddie if she tried. Was she a sister? A twin? If so, how come nobody seemed to know about her?

Connor's breathing slowed. He asked his first question to Erin. "Who are you?" Then, without waiting for an answer, he asked his second to Skylar, "Why did you do all this?"

Connor wasn't sure Skylar would answer, but after a long pause, she did.

"Erin deserved more than what she got." Skylar pointed to herself and Leon. "We all did."

"What do you mean?"

"I don't have to tell you Erin and Maddie are sisters, do I?"

"Why doesn't anybody know about her?"

Skylar took a step closer to Connor, perhaps trying to decide whether he had the nerve to fire. Connor wasn't sure he did, but he closed one eye and tilted his head like he was taking aim.

She stopped moving. "I don't know how much you know about Andrew Thompson."

That was Maddie's father. "I know he was well off."

"That's an understatement. But he wasn't always that way. Not long after he got married, his wife got pregnant. Andrew was an art teacher back then, and they barely had enough money for themselves, let alone their kid. Unfortunately, he wasn't having just one kid, he found out."

"Twins," Connor said.

"Exactly. They didn't feel like they could afford that, so they put one of them up for adoption."

The puzzle was coming together fast now. "That was Erin."

"She bounced around between foster homes. Sometimes the parents were abusive. Sometimes they ignored her. Most of them only took her in for the check. I'm sure there are plenty of good families out there that adopt children. She just didn't get any of them."

"It messed her up. She didn't deserve that."

"How did you find out?"

"She did one of those DNA tests to learn about her family."

Connor thought he remembered seeing a letter from some such company in a stack of mail next to the computer in Skylar's house.

"So, Leon and I thought we could make things right. Maddie had her time in the sun. It was Mom's turn."

"I don't understand. How—"

Connor was about to ask how she thought they were going to pull that off, when *finally* Alex came through the door with his backup officers trailing behind him.

CHAPTER 60

THE OFFICERS FANNED out, shouting instructions at Skylar and Leon. Drop your weapon. Hands on your head. Skylar and Leon did as they were told. As Skylar raised her hands to her head, her shirt lifted enough for Connor to see a Band-Aid over her belly button.

Then, just like that, it was over.

EMTs rushed in to tend to Olin and Dylan. After checking their vitals, they told Connor they were taking them to the hospital just as a precaution. "They should be fine once the drug wears off."

They were.

Over the next several weeks, Dylan stayed in touch with the detective, and, through her, Connor got most of his remaining questions answered.

Leon flipped on Skylar for a reduced sentence. He explained that after Erin learned she had a sister, Leon and Skylar had hatched a plan that (according to him) was mostly hers. It included five simple steps.

Step one: Get enough cash to convince Maddie Leon was better off than he really was.

Step two: Lure her in.

Step three: Abduct her.

Step four: Kill her.

And step five was only slightly more complex. Posting as Maddie, Erin would claim she had escaped captivity. Then she would claim she'd moved to Europe. But even that wouldn't be particularly hard to pull off. All they had to do was snap some pictures of Erin in front of the Eiffel Tower or the Pantheon and—*Voila!*—Maddie was in Europe. Since she kept to herself, they figured nobody would ask too many questions. Not even her sister—not as long as "Maddie" kept posting.

They would then be able to step in and claim everything in her life as theirs. Who would ask questions when Erin showed up with Maddie's ID at the bank or put her house up for sale?

It would finally be Erin's turn to benefit from the life her parents had provided Maddie for so many years.

There was plenty of evidence against Skylar at trial—text messages between her and Leon, the cell phone records that tracked her movements, DNA at Aleshia's house and on the belly button ring found on the beach, her fingerprints on the gun that had been used to kill Sam and his men, ballistic analysis—but Leon's testimony was the star of the show.

Skylar tried to take the stand in her own defense. That only made things worse. It gave the prosecution a chance to ask her about the backup plan Leon had mentioned and how she had ended up working at Southern Trust to begin with.

Skylar tried to cover herself as much as she could by explaining she had been working as a banker for five years. But when pressed by the prosecution, she was forced to admit that until one month ago that entire career had been spent at Fifth-Third Bank. That, according to Leon's testimony, was when she sought out an opening at Southern Trust intending to track Maddie down by the activity on her account.

When all she found was a series of transfers from one bank to another, the backup plan was born, ready in the wings in case Maddie didn't turn up soon.

"How's she doing, anyway?" Connor asked, referring to Maddie. He and Olin were back in their small New York apartment, with the heat on high and Dylan on speakerphone.

"Better," Dylan said, which was kind of what Connor had gathered from Maddie's Facebook feed.

Dylan and Maddie had become friends during the trial—bonding over their loss of Aleshia—and Dylan was slowly trying to help her out of her shell. "There's a whole world out there. She deserves to experience more of it."

Connor knew Dylan could be relentless. If she wanted to get Maddie out of her shell, she would do it eventually. Maddie was lucky to have her.

After Connor got off the phone, he leaned back into his desk chair. He was not looking forward to tomorrow. He would have to fight his way through New York traffic and face a bitter cold that felt like knives slicing into his skin, and all to go to a job he didn't like.

Maybe he shouldn't do it anymore, he thought.

There had been an idea forming in the back of his brain ever since he'd left Atlanta. It had started with something James had said: *Are you like private investigators or something?*

The answer then had been "No." But why couldn't he be? It was a better use of Connor's computer skills than what he was doing now, and it would give him a sense of purpose his current job did not.

However, he did not think he could do it on his own. He would need Olin and Dylan to make it work. He knew Dylan would be on board. She was already trying to figure out how she could do something similar. Olin was the wildcard.

Connor decided he couldn't put it off any longer. He had to ask. He leaned forward in his desk chair and looked at Olin, who was in his usual spot on the sofa.

Best to keep it simple, he told himself.

"I'm thinking about being a private investigator."

Olin's eyebrows went up.

"If I do, I want you and Dylan with me. What do you think?"

He was expecting some resistance.

To his surprise, Olin mulled it over for only a couple of seconds before he said, "You'll need somebody to do your books. I don't need you having problems with the IRS."

"Does that mean you're in?"

Then Olin smiled. "You and Dylan will also need somebody to keep you from going too far."

"Are you serious?"

"Yes." Olin nodded toward the cell phone on Connor's desk. "Call Dylan back."

Connor grabbed the phone off his desk and dialed Dylan's number, afraid that if he didn't move fast enough Olin might change his mind.

He never did, and Dylan greeted the news with all the enthusiasm Connor expected. She had only one question: "Does this mean you're moving to Atlanta?"

Connor had not thought about the logistics of how they would make this work. But Atlanta made sense. After what happened to his parents, New York still had too many bad memories. Although they'd dulled some over the years, they would likely never go away completely.

No doubt Olin felt the same.

Maybe if Connor felt like his mom still needed him here, he would have to stay. But she was doing fine. She was even dating somebody now. What was there for him to stick around for?

Connor looked at Olin, and Olin shrugged. *Why not?*

He returned his attention to the call. "Yes, we're moving to Atlanta."

A NOTE FROM THE AUTHOR

Thanks for reading *A Good Plan*. If you're looking for another great story, I hope you will check out the next book in the Connor Callahan series, *Last Trip to London*.

Already finished it? Keep reading to discover more great books by the author.

GET AN EXCLUSIVE COPY OF *THE LAYOVER*

Connor Callahan is back in this exclusive novella that takes place three years after his parents were abducted. When he sees a man discreetly tag a stranger's suitcase with a black magic marker, he sets out to discover what is going on. It's a decision that will thrust Connor into a conflict far more dangerous than he could have imagined, and when it's over he will know one thing for sure: You're not always safer on the ground.

When you join my readers club, you will immediately get a free and exclusive copy of *The Layover*, not available elsewhere.

I usually e-mail once or twice a month with things I think you'll find interesting, such as behind-the-scenes stories, new releases, and fan discounts. Of course, you can unsubscribe at any time.

Join the readers club by signing up at
read.reagankeeter.com

ALSO BY REAGAN KEETER

Gone

A masked man charges into Connor's house. He knocks out Connor's father, tasers his mother, and then, as quick as he came, he is gone. When the police exhaust their leads, Connor takes it upon himself to find his parents before it is too late. That quest, however, is complicated when he crosses paths with a group of anarchists bent on causing chaos in New York City. And their plan, Connor learns, is not only related to the abductions, it will also upend everything he thought he knew about his family.

The Redwood Con

High-rolling illegal gambler Liam Parker finds his girlfriend dead in her apartment, and it's not long before the police charge him with her murder. Desperate to avoid a lifetime behind bars, Liam's hunt to clear his name uncovers unexplainable secrets about the woman he thought he knew. And with the police revoking his bail and his freedom under threat, he goes on the run in pursuit of two strangers . . . and their deadly answers.

Misery Rock

Sharron Freeman's world gets shattered when she learns her husband, Ben, is a killer. Worse than that, he kills as part of a group. Desperate to keep herself and her daughter safe, Sharon sets out to discover who else is involved and find evidence against them before they meet to kill again. It's a journey that will require her to draw on courage she didn't know she had and come face to face with enemies she didn't know existed. And in the end, it all might prove to be in vain.

ABOUT THE AUTHOR

Reagan Keeter is the author of multiple Amazon bestsellers and a National Indie Excellence Awards finalist. He has worked as a writer and editor at Georgia newspapers. From Georgia State University, he earned his undergraduate degree in Journalism and from Southern Polytechnic State University his master's in Technical and Professional Communication. He lives with his wife and their two dogs in Atlanta, Georgia.

You can connect with him via:

His website: reagankeeter.com

Facebook: https://www.facebook.com/AuthorReaganKeeter/

Twitter: @ReaganKeeter

Email: reagan@reagankeeter.com